GOD, SCIENCE, AND A REALLY DUMB EXPERIMENT

By Sasha DeVore

Red Pendulum
PRESS

God, Science, and a Really Dumb Experiment

Library of Congress Cataloging-in-Publication Data is available.

God, Science, and a Really Dumb Experiment/ Sasha DeVore- 1st ed.

Summary: Alex wants nothing more than to enjoy her summer break, like any other self-respecting middle school teacher. But when a science experiment brings God to Earth – and utter chaos along with her – Alex teams up with a mailman, an engineer, a priest and a scientist to undo the experiment. Add two demons with just the perfect solution and an ever-greater plot unfolds – one which would change humanity forever. Alex must navigate this scientific conundrum, as well as face some demons of her own, in this humorous and irreverent tale.

ISBN 979-8-218-63197-0

[1. Fiction – Science Fiction, General. 2. Fiction – Action and Adventure]

To Junior – Write!
Little by little, day by day.

Chapter One:
Let's Not Call Those Zombies

Scientists have got to be some of the dumbest people on the planet. Seriously. And if you happen to be a scientist, well, I think deep down inside you *know* what I'm talking about.

And I'm sure some of you will argue with me on this. I mean, sure, scientists have accomplished some pretty cool things – like sending rockets to Mars, programming robots to read braille, and cataloging over six states of matter. All of that's totally cool. But even after all of those technological advancements, they still manage to make utterly dumb decisions. And that perfectly illustrates what my daddy used to say: So smart, you're dumb. Somehow that's an actual thing. Good job pointing that out, dad.

I'm speaking strictly from experience, too, of course. I wouldn't make a claim like this unprovoked. Because not only did they ruin my summer break – the holiest time in a public-school teacher's existence, by the way – but they man-aged to screw up the entire planet, too. All at once. In some sort of record-breaking, fantastically stupid experiment.

And I promise I'm not one of those science nay–sayers, either. Ironically, I'm one of the biology teachers at Rockwell Middle School. At least I *was* before the aforementioned experiment took place. As it stands now, I no longer have a job.

I do, however, have a beautiful apartment I can't afford and a cat that hates me. All in all, not terrible for a twenty-five-year-old, I'd say. But none of that really hits right if the world's fallen into utter chaos. You know what I mean?

It began, as these things usually do, at the worst possible time – on the very first Saturday in June. Like, seriously? Could the universe at least let me enjoy a single day of summer break? Which I do believe was well earned, because teaching isn't just teaching anymore, in case you didn't know. Teaching has evolved into Teaching *Plus*. This means on top of the teaching and grading, I get the additional features – like extra-long staff meetings on Tuesdays and mandatory committee memberships. There's also the 'call every single student's parents at least once every two weeks' bonus. Not to mention I get to join in on those campus-wide evening summits once a month where everyone is trapped in the cafeteria for four excruciating hours. I'm still not even sure what those are for.

And had I known about the end of the world ahead of time, I would've definitely rearranged my schedule to be somewhere more suitable. Like my bed. Or maybe a bed in a very far off cabin in the woods. Or on a remote beach. But I'd definitely be well rested – perhaps having napped under an umbrella or something. Either scenario would have offered a softer introduction to the apocalypse. But as they say, hindsight is always 20/20, right?

I was actually out hiking one of my favorite trails when it happened. I had just finished, in fact, and decided to sit for a while in the grass. This particular trail led to Rosewood Park – which offered a beautiful view of downtown Austin – and there were plenty of flat, grassy areas to choose from. I peeled my flannel off and spread it as wide as I could over a soft patch on a knoll near a small playground. Then I plopped on top of it.

I cupped my knees with my arms and noticed my leggings were running thin from chafing at the thigh area. And though my flesh threatened to ooze through the strained fabric, I clacked my boots together, content to pretend I hadn't seen it at all. Since they were my favorite shade of pink and I forgot where I'd gotten them from, I was determined to carry on wearing them for as long as I could. Either I would stumble across another pair or I'd be charged with public indecency. I was prepared for either outcome.

In those last few moments, before chaos descended, I drank in the Texas sun. Young children squealed just behind me, enjoying some made up game on the playscape. A boy near the swing set was training his dog to shake his hand, but was unsuccessful so far, by the sound of it. A mother scolded a child somewhere in the distance, her voice cut through all the others. I was mildly interested but didn't bother looking because, for once in ten months, disciplining a kid wasn't my job and, therefore, none of my business.

I sprawled out, like some of the others on this part of the lawn, but I wasn't really sunbathing like they were. My sable skin didn't need long outside before the sun activated its warm glow, and this had already been achieved for the day. As a matter of fact, I was well into a sweaty bronze. But I didn't mind at all.

In reality, I was just hoping the heat would help melt away some of the fourteen pounds I'd gained from stress-eating during passing periods for an entire school year. But I was only there for about five minutes – long enough to see some snotty kids start a shove-fight over a game of Gaga Ball in the distance – when the wind suddenly picked up.

It was a welcomed breeze – swift and unusually cool. But after a few moments, I realized it was no natural wind. The air thinned as clouds formed in the lower atmosphere. I could tell something bad was about to happen. A tornado? It was possible. I scrambled to my feet. A glance around the park told me that panicked parents had started gathering their children. A toddler raced past me, shrieking in protest, but I wasn't any help. I was frozen to the spot, like many others, watching as tiny little sparks danced through the clouds. And though it started to hurt my eyes to look, I couldn't turn away. The blinding white flashes twinkled in the sky like hopped up fireflies. I'd never seen anything like it before. It was some sort of... unstable lightning. Is lightning even stable to begin with? I should probably know that.

Dogs barked in the surrounding neighborhood. Some howled. Then – without warning – a cloud ignited. Its explosion cascaded through the sky, sending me to the ground with so much force that I could practically hear my rib cage crack. For a moment I lay there, uncertain of what had happened. I rubbed a hand over my chest, expecting pain, but there wasn't any. My skin tingled all over.

After a while I pulled myself to my feet, which wasn't an easy thing to do. My muscles had begun protesting and I couldn't tell if it was from the hike or the blast. I teetered upright. Blood rushed over my lips. It was cold. I spit a mouthful of it into the grass and rubbed my eyes, but everything was a blur. I could hear perfectly well though. People were screaming. There was running. I could sense that something very large was looming over us. Then, when my eyes could focus again, I got a glimpse of it. I clapped my hands to my mouth, holding back a scream that didn't necessarily want to come out. It rolled around in my chest as my brain struggled to make sense of what my eyes were looking at. My stomach lurched. It was an enormous ant – an actual freaking *insect*. Which is a much, *much* creepier alternative to Godzilla, I must say.

As my hand slipped from my face, limp, a quiet 'what the hell?' slipped from my lips. Then, out of habit, my eyes darted to make sure none of my students were near enough to hear me. I was relieved to remember I wasn't in my classroom, but only slightly, given the circumstances. Now that I think about it, it *was* helpful that I could curse freely, because that was the first in a long procession of 'what the hells' from here on out.

I didn't stick around to be the ant's first victim. My feet shuffled unevenly down the knoll. But being as I was already exhausted prior to this new and horrific apocalyptic scenario, my attempt to run was rather pitiful. See how it would have been nice to be well rested?

It only took a few yards for me to realize I was in no condition to carry on running. Whether it was the hike, the blast or the fact that my heart was attempting to beat right out of my chest, I couldn't tell. But I knew I wouldn't be making it much further. I hid under one of the large umbrellas along the walk, gasping to catch my breath. I squeezed my eyes shut, willing myself to collect my wits, to be able to make a plan once I opened them again.

After a frazzled minute I forced myself to keep moving, and when I opened my eyes I found that I was a lot calmer. Well, at the very least, the contents of my stomach had settled back down and I was fairly certain my brain wasn't entirely broken.

I peeked from under my umbrella and was able to get a better look at the hideous thing. It clacked its jagged, hairy mandibles together, lumbering toward the playscape. For the briefest of moments, I couldn't help but admire its sheeny thorax and abdomen. It would've been a perfect opportunity for an anatomy lesson with my students. And fun fact about ants, by the way — some ants farm their own livestock. They form a symbiotic relationship with aphids — protecting them and feeding them in exchange for the opportunity to harvest the sugary honeydew that the aphids secrete.

But I digress. The ant that was currently taking over Rosewood Park tapped along the playground with its antennae, moving toward the edge of the enclosure. It was heading toward a small girl. My feet jerked on their own, but I stopped them. There was nothing I could have done to save her because the ant was already sweeping its antennae over the terrified girl, feeling her hair, her arms, and a large magnifying glass that she grasped in both hands. I desperately hoped she hadn't been using that thing to fry the ant's friends in the sunlight. The little girl, who couldn't have been more than seven or eight years old, held the instrument up to the ant, as if giving an offering. It didn't seem to want it, though. The ant moved on toward the swing set.

I breathed a sigh of relief, then put my eyes on my car in the lot. I determined it would be safer for me to move slowly, so as not to make myself a target – in case it decided to start picking us off one by one. I took a deep breath and strode cautiously past the splash pad. Dark liquid was spilling from its nozzles. It pooled up on the ground before circling the drain. It smelled like... *wine?*

A middle-aged woman was sprawled under it. She allowed the liquid to hit her square in the face, giggling uncontrollably between deep gulps. I thought about dragging her from under the stream, but she was clearly enjoying herself. Further down the path, a swarm of random – and horribly life-like – butterfly kites swooped overhead, forcing me to protect my face with both arms. I ducked under another umbrella, which was enough to cause the kites to lose interest in me. They fluttered lazily toward an open field.

My eyes scanned the park, unable to comprehend what was going on. The Gaga pit was just ahead now. It was ablaze and the kids who were once fighting over it were now beating each other with sticks. Then the older boy, who couldn't have been more than twelve years old, rammed his body into the younger one. His stick turned into a large wooden bat without warning. Again, w*hat the hell?*

But I didn't have time to be stuck in perplexity; my teacher instincts kicked in. "Stop that!" I yelled, running back toward the pit. He could kill the younger one if he got a good enough swing. As I got closer, I could hear their argument.

"You always cheat, Devin," the younger one said. He swung his stick, but Devin dodged it.

"That's why Marissa doesn't even like you," Devin teased.

The younger boy shrugged dramatically. "I don't *like* Marissa, you idiot," he said. His freckled face folded into a scowl.

I didn't know anything about this kid, but his face told me he *did* like Marissa, and that Devin had hit him in the sweet spot. Devin, encouraged by the boy's quivering bottom lip, continued his onslaught. He feigned a swing of his bat, but stopped precisely in front of the boy's face. Then he barked a laugh. "Look y'all," he called over his shoulder. "Anthony's gonna cry!"

Two exhausted-looking boys were just beyond the pit. They had wandered toward the trees and didn't seem to care about the fight.

The younger boy, whose name apparently was Anthony, slapped at the bat, but only hurt his own hand in the process. The flames from the Gaga pit fire whirled, sending smoke into our faces. The boys didn't seem to notice.

"Ha ha, you're so dumb!" Devin taunted.

I smacked my lips. "Boys, stop it now," I demanded, grabbing the end of Devin's baseball bat. He gave me a look I was all too familiar with as a teacher – it read, *fuck off*. He sneered. "Why don't you go shave the rest of your head, you dyke?"

Ordinary people would've probably been offended by this, but ordinary people don't have Shanice Torey for a mother. Stubborn and opinionated, she had already attacked this particular life choice of mine from every possible angle.

But the zig-zag fade above the nape of my neck was what made me feel like me, and I was glad to show it off on hot days like this with a messy bun on the top of my head. Plus, it was an absolute flex among my friend group, so whatever. I didn't miss a beat.

"Someone's gonna get seriously hurt if you guys keep fighting," I pressed. "Do you wanna go to jail?"

I glanced over the chaos, hoping to find a park ranger. I wasn't even sure if they'd be on patrol anymore – *I* wouldn't be patrolling this crap.

"Yeah," Anthony jeered. His ochre eyes flashed a threat at Devin. "*He's* gonna get hurt."

Then the stick he was holding only moments ago turned into a very small pistol. He wasted no time aiming it right at Devin's face. His finger squeezed the trigger. I couldn't react in time.

But someone else did. A man, who had been near and watching the whole thing unfold, intervened just in time to pull Anthony's arm upward. The shot fired into the air with an echoing boom. The bullet hit one of the butterfly kites, but it didn't seem bothered by the sudden hole in its wing. It kept on flapping happily above the field. Anthony, unwilling or, perhaps, unable to put up a fight, slumped into the grass.

"What's happening?" I half yelled at the man.

He held up a finger to his lip to silence me. His face furrowed thoughtfully; his tawny skin, sparkling with sweat, was tinged copper by the sun around his forehead. I could see blood had run from one of his ears and dried up somewhere below the collar of his tee shirt. He checked Anthony's pulse, then took a quick look into each of his eyes. Thick red veins laced the white parts of them. The boy blinked placidly, unaffected by the man waving a huge hand across his face.

I hovered. "Are you a medic or something?" I asked. "Is he gonna be alright?"

The man shook his head. Then he stood up. "No clue," he said. "I'm just a mailman." He rubbed his beard thoughtfully, then glanced around the park. "As far as what's happening…" He guessed. "Could it be mass hysteria? A terrorist attack, maybe?"

"I don't know," I said. My voice cracked. I tried to fight down my jitters, but they had already begun to explode out of me. "That wouldn't explain a three-story ant crawling off into town, now would it?"

"No," he agreed. "No, it wouldn't." He dragged Anthony toward the shade of a tree and laid him on his side. I followed suit, grabbing Devin. It was easy to drag him by his wrist toward the tree and away from the fire. He came without too much of a fuss, his legs shuffling underneath him almost automatically. He even sat down on his own. But seconds later, he was just as limp as his trigger-happy friend.

A glance around the park let us know that everyone else had slowly become incapacitated, just like the boys. Many of them were unceremoniously slumped in the grass. I could tell they had been trying to leave the park. It sounded like those who *did* leave didn't make it very far. In the distance, we could hear tires screeching and people yelling and, briefly, the crunching of metal.

I fumbled through my fanny pack until I found my cell phone. It wouldn't let me dial. I groaned. "No service." I clicked the buttons frantically, like that would make it behave.

It only beeped at me to alert me of a low battery. "My phone's dying. I don't think it's allowing me to call anyone."

"Emergency calls always go through," the man scoffed. He pulled out his own cell phone and dialed 9–1–1, but it rang indefinitely. Then it suddenly cut out. He shook the phone, but to no avail.

I paced the grass. "Yeah, good job getting through," I jeered, but I didn't have much time to relish my own pettiness before a gaggle of geese approached us. The lead goose honked, warning us back. I stepped aside begrudgingly and huffed. "Excuse me, you little turd."

I didn't think twice about the bird until its upper portion transformed into a cobra's head, hooded and ready to strike. The man pulled me by my shirt. I stumbled backward. "Well, that's not normal," he breathed. His eyes bulged as he studied the thing. It shook its feathers threateningly.

"Oh, *hell* to the naw," I said, maybe a little louder than I wanted to. The goose-snake was where I drew my line. "We gotta get outta here." And thankfully this was the kind of guy you didn't have to tell twice. I certainly would've left him at that Gaga pit, but he was right on my heels as I booked it to the parking lot. The gaggle of geese honked sharply behind us.

In my frenzy, I dropped my keys on the pavement. They slid under a car. But the man was already letting himself into a Jeep. "Is this you?" I smacked the hood of the truck as I made my way to the passenger side. But he didn't have to answer. He was already inside and starting the engine.

I gave myself a reassuring nod. "Yeah," I breathed, throwing open the door. "A Jeep's perfect for an end of the world situation." It was better than my Nissan Versa, at least. Maybe we'd have to jump a few curbs and, I don't know, chunk random items through the back window if the geese decided to continue pursuing us. I threw on my seatbelt as an afterthought when he pulled out of the lot.

Despite what I had anticipated of our escape – obviously I would've forgiven him for driving fast and recklessly, like they do in every single apocalypse movie I've ever seen – it was a relatively anticlimactic descent from the park. Not to say that I didn't appreciate the lack of thrill, because my head was still reeling from the incomprehensibleness of the last twelve minutes. Besides, the slow wind away from the city quickly provided us new reasons to be utterly shocked – buildings had begun twisting and melding into one another and vehicles were strewn about.

A large, medieval looking hunting party chased a unicorn down Springdale Avenue. It consisted of mostly men - some of them weirdly jacked. I was surprised their horses could carry them - and what they lacked in teeth, they made up for in hair. A couple of armored women flanked them on either side (also very hairy) wielding lassos with hooks on the ends. The unicorn itself was as fantastical as it should be. The beast was the sharpest black I'd ever seen, with iridescent greens, blues and purples flashing under its coat in a way that was pretty obviously mocking its pursuers. Its mane was a lustrous waterfall of red, orange and yellow sprouting from a golden horn atop its beautiful head.

The party disappeared down an alley, forcing me to find less pleasant sights to behold. "Um, I'm Alex by the way," I said through dry lips. I didn't dare pull my eyes away from a hole that was crumbling open in the street just ahead.

"Conner," said the man. He bit his lip in concentration then veered into the front yard of a small green house, leaving plenty of room between us and the hole. Then we took a sharp right turn onto Airport Boulevard. He navigated the chaos with the expertise that I should expect from a mailman. I wondered if his route took him to this side of town, but I couldn't care enough at the moment to ask. We had more important things to discuss.

I tried to steady my breath. "So, uh, Conner… where are we going? Do you have, like, a plan or –"

Conner shook his head. "Plan?" He came to a halt to allow a group of blank-faced men in business suits to bumble across the street. "I don't even know what this *is*," he said, gesturing toward the men. "This… this," he shrugged, trying to find words. "This is *different*."

"It's different," I nodded. "Yeah, I get it." I tried to force my brain to come up with anything helpful. I checked my phone again; it wouldn't even turn on at this point.

He continued, utterly flabbergasted. "Like, what are these – zombies?" he asked, turning himself all the way in his seat to face me. The wider his eyes got the higher the pitch in his voice. "Are those zombies!"

I threw my arms up. "I don't know man. Don't freak out – you're gonna make me freak out, too." I felt my voice cracking again and a lump was forming in my throat. "Look," I said, taking a deep breath. "You've been doing great – the way you saved that kid's life, and how you've been driving really carefully – all that has been great."

Conner nodded. "Yeah," he agreed. He glanced around and caught sight of someone at the other end of the intersection. The man would've been an ordinary person, except spiders sprouted out of the top of his head in a writhing tangle of hair. Conner slammed his eyes shut; his nose fluttered as he drew in a smooth, even breath.

"Okay," I said. "This is obviously a city–wide crisis. And no – no, let's not call those zombies." I racked my brain for more, but at this point I was pulling at straws. "Okay, so it may be some kind of medical epidemic or, like, an effect of climate change, you know... there are probably scientists out there right now –"

"Yes!" Conner clapped his hands. Then he checked the rearview mirror. "Yes, yes, yes!" he yelled, burning his tires into the road.

A hollow chuckle escaped me. "Alright," I said, clutching the grab handle above my window. "I didn't think that would work."

"No, you made a good point," Conner said. "Scientists are gonna be the first ones to figure it out..." He turned a little faster than necessary onto the highway and was forced to swerve out of the way of a herd of longhorns. "I'm not even gonna ask if those are real," he mumbled to himself in an angry aside. We descended over a median and onto the access road. "My uncle's a particle physicist at the Colorado National Laboratory," he explained. "He'll know what's going on, or at least he'll have an idea, you know?" We continued parallel to the highway, weaving through a myriad of disruptions.

"I don't know if I can go with you to Colorado," I said, desperately hoping I didn't just get kidnapped. "I've got a cat I need to check in on... and a... a…"

I actually didn't have much more than that, I realized. It probably should've made me question my own livelihood, but I'd have to unpack that later. Anyway, Conner was waving away my worries.

"We don't have to leave town," he said. "We just need to get to 130."

"The toll?" I asked.

"Yeah," he said. There's a satellite laboratory out there along the Colorado River – they transferred him out there about two years ago…" Conner studied a flock of giant paper airplanes that swooped down to fly alongside us. They zipped around other airborne obstacles, all the while keeping pace with the car. "Let's see if he's at work today."

Chapter Two:
Talk About Weird Science

After a few quiet minutes, the mess along the highway grew sparse and we found ourselves turning down a narrow, unmarked road. City street gave way to a patchy gravel path with thick, dry greenery dominating either side. The path led to a clearing that housed a two-story cement structure. With its sleek, angular design, it looked terribly out of place among the overgrowth of vines and bushes.

Conner made quick work of interpreting the obscure layout of the place. He scaled the smooth exterior, pulling me in tow. "I don't think we're supposed to be here," I whispered. But Conner ignored me. Instead, he pressed against a square pad that was barely distinguishable from the rest of the building's surface. The face of it folded away to expose a speaker.

"Nope." I shook my head. My voice rasped, though I tried to hide my panic. "This is where they shoot us down 'cause we're not even supposed to know about this place."

Conner responded only by raising an eyebrow at me. I thought about walking away, but I knew well enough there was nowhere else to go.

A voice from the speaker box made me jump. It was firm. "Access code?"

"Yes," Conner started. He sounded surprised, as if he didn't really expect anyone to answer. "Look, uh, Sherman Jackson is my uncle," he explained. "He's on the Exotic Hadron project." Indistinct static fizzled on the other end. Conner continued. "I don't know how to explain this, but there's some crazy stuff going on out here, and I need to talk to him… make sure he's okay."

"Who's with you?" asked the speaker box. I noticed a tiny camera scanning the area between the two of us. I waved stupidly. "A friend," Conner explained. "Look, people are out of it. I had to bring her. We're the only two – I don't know – *intact*, as far as I know." He patted his own chest for some reason. Perhaps ensuring that he was, in fact, still intact. I thought about doing the same, but just then a door folded open from an indistinct part of the building, just as it had with the speaker box, and a tunnel revealed itself. I glanced suspiciously over my shoulder. I don't know what I expected to see – maybe a horde of not-zombies chasing us in – but the woods behind us were placid. I followed Conner into the facility. And just as I suspected, the laboratory was a huge secret underground base that regular people like me weren't even supposed to be aware of.

We crept through a sterile hallway into a vestibule where a mechanical voice told us to wait for authorization. It seemed Conner had done this before, which made me a little more comfortable. He twiddled his hands around in the pockets of his basketball shorts, bouncing impatiently on the balls of his feet. Through the glass walls, I could see that this floor in the lab was partitioned into sections – mainly offices and what could have been storage rooms. At the end of a long hall was a set of stairs leading downward. Seconds later a grizzly man hasted into the room.

"You shouldn't know where or how to access our entry port," he breathed, inspecting Conner and me. His was the voice from the speaker box. It was much deeper in person. And with his long white beard, he looked very sure and wise, and frankly, very wizardly. I smirked, thinking this was what happened to Saruman after he was defeated. He was forced to get a day job.

He went on. "It appears your uncle has given you access to classified information."

I gave Conner a look that he, hopefully, interpreted as, *this man is gonna have to kill us now, and it's all your fault.*

Conner straightened himself up as best he could. "My uncle didn't tell me about this place," he said. "I found out about it myself. By accident." He drew in a sharp breath and paused. Then, when he continued, I could tell he was embarrassed. "My auntie had me follow him a few times," he said. "She wanted to know where he was going at all hours of the night. She didn't believe he was working on anything confidential, but he was telling the truth. He always ended up here." Then he bobbed his head, possibly considering how much he wanted to incriminate himself. "Eventually Uncle Sherman caught on, and started letting me in to help him with his work."

If it was a lie, it was a good one. The man offered a little laugh. "Lucky for your aunt it was only his love for science that kept him away."

Conner smirked. "No, I think Uncle Sherman was the lucky one. Auntie Jade has a favorite crowbar and three gang members that owe her a favor."

At this, the man's eyes became perfectly round. I laughed, finding that my hands had drawn up to my face in utter surprise. Conner shrugged at me apologetically.

But maybe it was enough to exonerate his uncle. At least, the man seemed to relax a bit. He inspected us again, perhaps deciding if he'd carry on with us. Then after a few quiet seconds, he nodded. "I'm Valencio," he said, gripping Conner's hand. "I'm the Director here."

Conner introduced himself, then glanced at me. "I'm Alex." I smiled awkwardly. Valencio smiled briskly in return before shaking my hand, then turned back to Conner.

"I don't know what to report, except your uncle was in the lab today when…" he gestured just outside the door, "*this* happened. I initially thought it was the result of a leaked biohazard or a latent reaction to one of our recent experiments." He gestured for us to follow, moving quickly for a man his age down the hall. He continued. "I've been able to make contact with the World Health Alliance, and I was informed that this is, in fact, a global phenomenon." He punched a code into a pad along the back wall and another door appeared, allowing us into some sort of medical chamber. Rows of beds in cylindrical pods lined the room. Then he said, "Your uncle is one of the affected, but they all seem to be stable for now."

Conner rushed ahead, searching the rows. He stopped at a pod at the far end, which housed a man barely in his fifties.

His thick black hair grew in puffs along the top of his head, in his nose and even from his ears. He was awake, but unaware, just like the others at the park.

"Can he hear us?" Conner asked. He cupped one of the man's hands in his own.

"Unsure," said Valencio. He drew in a steadying breath. "Your uncle, along with most of the staff here, appears to be suffering from reduced perfusion in the dorsolateral prefrontal cortex." I was impressed that he was able to figure out what was going on so quickly, but also because he didn't mince his words when describing it. He continued smartly. "I've also detected a pervasive delta brainwave pattern – I've been unable to interrupt it."

My brief awe turned to confusion. I shook my head. "Come again?"

The fact that I was a science teacher and still couldn't comprehend half of what he was actually saying, wasn't lost on me. But I decided it was only fair since he was the director of a military grade laboratory, and I was still fighting down my vomit when dissecting frogs with my class. I focused on the words I did know, like prefrontal cortex and delta brainwave. As far as I could extrapolate, their brains were on the wrong channel.

Conner didn't appear to be too privy either. He caressed his uncle's hand, but Mr. Jackson only blinked leisurely at the ceiling. "So, perfusion means like a tear or something?" he asked.

Valencio was more than happy to paraphrase. "Not at all," he said. "There's simply a reduction of blood flow to certain parts of his brain. And the brainwave pattern indicates he is asleep, but clearly, he is not." He monitored a small glass pad near the pod. At the whim of his finger, holographic charts and numbers popped in and out of view. Conner and I gawked at the technology, having never seen anything like it before, but Valencio barely noticed. He went on. "Nobody is showing signs of discomfort, but I have no idea what is causing this condition or what the long-term effects will be."

"But you'll find a way," Conner said. The rims of his eyes were red, threatening tears. It wasn't clear if he was asking Valencio or telling him. "That's what you all do – you solve these kinds of problems."

Valencio's deep-set eyes twinkled with determination. "We do, and we will," he said.

The hum of the medical chamber's door made me jump. A husky man clamored in. He looked to be about my age, and he was wearing a fawn-colored jumpsuit. He rifled through files on a glass pad of his own. "Oh yeah, V," he said. "We're screwed alright," his voice broke. He gave a short, mirthless chuckle. "They screwed us real bad –" He paused in his tracks, realizing Valencio wasn't alone. "Um, sorry," he said. His round face wore a mixture of embarrassment and urgency. "I gotta brief you, like, now. Should I –"

"You may as well, here and now," Valencio said. "I don't believe we must keep confidentiality when a threat of this magnitude is present."

"Right on," said the man. His voice jittered. "My name's Theo, by the way." He pointed to a small badge that seemed to be stitched into his jumper. "Engineer." Conner nodded his acknowledgement but didn't introduce himself.

"The report?" said Valencio.

"Oh, yes. Um... well," Theo gave another nervous laugh, then he took a short breath. "As it turns out, God can be summoned." He pinched his lips together briefly, eyeing Valencio. "And the good folks at CERN decided to do so."

For a moment, the three of us simply looked at Theo, who continued to nod at us. I shook my head as if it would help me understand better. Valencio also shook his head, but slowly, a deep sorrow arrested his wrinkled face. Conner's eyes bulged, his face twisted up in firm disbelief.

"Summon? Like, from the… the other side?" I wasn't sure if I understood what he meant, because what he said sounded less like science and more like voodoo. So many questions flooded my brain, which really didn't do well for me because it was my summer break, and I wasn't even supposed to be thinking at all. Then a gasp escaped me so sharply I almost choked on my own spit. "You mean that 'God particle' stuff was real?"

"Wait," Conner sputtered. "What the hell is CERN?" His eyes blinked several times in his tightly scrunched face.

"It's a giant laboratory out in Switzerland," I explained. "Or is it France?"

Theo helped. "It's an intergovernmental organization with the largest particle physics laboratory in the world." His breath rattled. "They discovered the Higgs Boson a little over a decade ago. They call it the God Particle. But on that note – " he nodded at me, "it wasn't the Higgs Boson they were manipulating. This experiment was light-years ahead of all of that."

Conner nodded, but it was unclear if he understood. I didn't bother checking, though. I had more questions. "So you mean they did, like, some sort of scientific ritual? And God's on Earth right now?"

"Yeah!" Theo exclaimed. He clasped a hand to his forehead, pulling brown curls up into his hairline. He chortled, then double checked the log on his glass pad, roving through the text with a finger. "Apparently, they summoned God and the moment she arrived, she left the laboratory – completely uncooperative."

"*She?*" said Conner.

Theo shrugged. "That's what the report says."

For a moment we were quiet, attempting to drink in all of this new information without choking. No doubt the others had the extra challenge of making peace with God being a woman. My first response was to celebrate; to rub it in their faces. But something gave me pause. Would God being a woman make it easier for me? Would she be more understanding of all my sins and all that? Or would it be somehow worse? Now, I do know my mother could draw out an argument for three whole episodes of Everybody Hates Chris because I didn't clean the toilet right. Surely, God would have all kinds of quarrels with me. My gut churned just a bit.

After several moments of self-inflicted confoundment, I decided it would be best to look on the bright side. There was nothing to fear, I told myself. I was a schoolteacher after all. I was practically a modern-day saint.

I clapped my hands together loudly, causing everyone to jump. "All things considered, I guess that's cool," I said.

"Kinda always knew God was a woman." I held a hand up for Conner to high-five, but he left me hanging.

"So what – is she, like, mad at us or something?" He jutted his chin, gesturing beyond the chamber door. "All of that out there… all of this –" He waved a hand at the pods in the room. "Is this a punishment?"

"No," said Valencio thoughtfully. He drew in a long, deep breath, then paused. I shifted my weight, unsure of what he was waiting for. And when I was starting to think that's all he would say, he continued. "The fabric of our reality, if you will, cannot sustain the quantum hyperexcitation that results from being exposed to such a field as God's presence." He rubbed his beard with an agitated hand. "I never would have predicted this particular result, but given the nature of the experiment, I would say that this is an inadvertent effect."

I rubbed my hands together to keep from fiddling with the smooth patch of hair at my left temple – something I often did when organizing my emotions, which is why it's so smooth in the first place. Years of preening had trained those particular curls limp. I squinted at Valencio. "Is that a fact, or are you hypothesizing?" I asked. "How could you possibly know?"

Valencio raised his eyebrows. He leaned against one of the unoccupied pods and folded his arms. "And as it turns out, I have personal experience in this matter," he said.

"You've tried to bring God to Earth, too?" asked Conner. He was thoroughly scandalized.

Valencio went on pointedly. "I was an applied physicist for ion beam development nineteen years ago at CERN when our director dispatched a team to assist with that very project.

It was proposed by a very small, and little-known, research group." He sniffed, smoothing out the front pocket of his lab coat. "Their initial findings were theoretically sound, and our director was impressed."

"Why would anyone want to bring God to Earth?" Theo interrupted sharply. "Who just sits around and thinks this stuff up?" He strode briskly toward the door, and we assumed he'd heard enough, but then he suddenly turned back up the aisle. "Why bring God to Earth?" he demanded.

Valencio drew in a long, contrived breath. "Peace," he said. "Answers to life's greatest questions… an end to the constant human squabbling..." He shook his head in a poor attempt to battle down the guilt creeping across his face. "Science can sometimes make you believe that even God can be commanded."

"I don't get it," I shrugged. "So you guys started this project nineteen years ago, but God's just now showing up?"

"The project was shut down before it could begin in earnest." Valencio shook his head again. "The closer we got to success, the further away we moved from our ethics." Valencio rubbed his chin thoughtfully. "We decided the price that was to be paid was too great, and our director agreed."

Conner, who had been ruminating in a far reach of the room, spoke quietly. "So, everyone's in some sort of trance," he said. His eyes focused on the floor as he worked through his own puzzlement. "What does that have to do with the world going…"

"Nuts," I helped. "Melting and burning…" I said, unable to stop the words as they came out of my mouth. "… and that spider-haired dude we saw on the way here –"

"Yeah," Conner agreed. "Nuts."

"I, uh, actually might have an answer to that," Theo said, his simmering vexation replaced by reluctant excitement. He waved a hand over his glass pad and fingered through a series of data sets. "We've just experienced some sort of 'Little Bang' that generated a type of neurogenic field in the lower atmosphere. I detected it moments before the blast – and the blast itself, by the way, produced a *huge* spike in free floating exotic matter –" he nodded at Conner's uncle, "– including a number of tetraquarks and some funky pentaquarks that Sherman would've been particularly interested in."

His words spilled into one another as he spoke, making it difficult to keep up. I nodded nonetheless as if I understood, relinquishing to the fact that whatever Theo would say from here on out was above my pay grade, which capped off exactly at eighth grade biology. "Anyway," he continued. "This neurogenic field is consistent with the data Valencio collected from our tranced–out friends, and I actually think *they're* causing it." At that moment he breathed in a particularly nerdy way that made me grin, but I think he mistook my laughing at him for laughing with him. Encouraged, he continued. "And this is pure theory, but I believe with the combination of the new field with the unknown hadrons in the atmosphere, that what we're experiencing is physical reality being acted upon and changed, according to what's inside the subconscious *minds* of these people."

"So, reality is changing because of them?" Conner asked dubiously.

"Like manifestation," I said faster than I meant to, but I was excited. I felt goosebumps prickle up on my arms. "What you focus on you can create," I added. But it was clear the others weren't as excited as I was.

Valencio nodded. "It is to be considered that God's presence has stimulated a reorganization of the laws of physics," he said. "These... *manifestations*... should certainly be studied. Perhaps we can find clues that would help us reverse our current condition."

"Wait," I laughed, throwing a hand on my hip. "Have you even been outside?" I asked. "The only materializations we've seen out there are shoddy and nonsensical ones. You're telling me we can create what we want, and *nobody* thought about world peace? Or at least free health care?"

Theo scratched his head. "I think when it comes to the subconscious mind –"

Unfortunately, I was already on to the next question. "Does it only work for the people in the trance?" I asked. Everyone froze simultaneously, each of us attempting to make something appear. A few fleeting moments promised excitement, but nothing changed as far as I could tell. I relaxed my shoulders, subtly disappointed. It was all for the better though, I suppose, since my mind kept wandering off to dumb stuff like roller coasters that fling you into space and spider–haired dude. "I could see how dumb stuff ended up materializing now," I admitted to Theo.

"So why aren't *we* in the trance?" Conner asked. "What makes us different from everyone else?"

We all studied one another. "It can't be random," said Theo. "Maybe we have a trait that makes us immune," he theorized.

"It would probably be best to find that out as well," said Valencio. He ruminated for a few moments.

Conner cleared his throat. "Okay, so while we're figuring all of this stuff out, here's another question: where's God, and how do we send her back?"

"Yep," said Theo. "That's the real question."

Valencio massaged the bridge of his long leathery nose, then committed to the task ahead with a sigh. "I believe we have our work cut out for us now, don't we?"

Chapter Three: This Is Definitely Not a Seance. Maybe.

The weeks following our visit to the lab were eerily peaceful. Before we left, Valencio was kind enough to allow me to use his landline to contact my family. It was funny that the laboratory housed technology the rest of the world didn't know about – DNA secured data, self–sterilizing walls and toilets capable of sphincter recognition (I don't know about that last one; it's a hunch I formed after a strange visit to the bathroom) – but the old man preferred to keep a landline phone that should've been buried in the nineteen–nineties.

And it proved a prudent move, because when everyone else's cell service failed, he still enjoyed uninterrupted calls – only to other landlines, of course. I wasn't able to contact my parents directly, but I was able to get hold of my great aunt Geralyn, who reported that they were unconscious but safely tucked into their bed at home. I was uneasy about how I felt about this news. I was glad they were effectively cared for, but it was the relief that they were unconscious that had my gut twisted up with guilt. But I couldn't lie to myself – the apocalypse would be that much easier to navigate without my mom sticking her nose in all of my business.

Conner was kind enough to take me back to the park so that I could collect my car. Then we parted ways with a plan to reconvene as soon as Valencio was able to determine a way we could help undo the damage that CERN had caused. I didn't really expect to hear from anyone, since I had no vested interest in the lab itself, but I kept the small walkie talkie I was gifted on my hip, just in case.

I spent my time checking in on just about everyone I could think of, moving their bodies as needed to safe and comfortable locations. By doing this, I learned that touching them seemed to interrupt whatever it is that they were in the process of dreaming up.

Someone more observant would've probably picked up on it right away, but it took me nine days to make the connection that every time I moved my upstairs neighbor, Mrs. Saddler, her cats would disappear. In my defense she has actual, real cats – and plenty of them. Maybe I was stereotyping to think she had twenty, which was about how many that were roaming her apartment when I first checked in. She was a quiet old recluse, and it was no secret that she collected them, which is why the other neighbors and I were weary of eating the loquat pies she would deliver on Sunday mornings. They were delicious, but also unavoidably laden with cat fur.

But anyway, I'd moved Mrs. Saddler from her porch to her couch, to her bed and, finally, to a comfortable place on the bedroom floor since she kept rolling off the bed anyway. And every time I did, I assumed the cats were scattering to the far corners of the apartment. I finally cared enough one day to turn and assure a particularly large tabby that I was only helping Mrs. Saddler - in case it decided to bite me - when it suddenly disappeared before my eyes. I felt very silly for not noticing sooner, but also very clever for finding out at all. I knew this information might be handy, but I didn't know how or why.

I also decided that I wouldn't let my summer break be halted by the experiment. So, while waiting for news from the lab, I continued with my summer bucket list, which mostly consisted of activities at Lady Bird Lake. My days had become a ping pong game of checking in on my own cat and exhausting myself in the water. I left my apartment every morning with the same ritual.

"Bye now, Milus," I sang to my cat. He grunted at me fatly before escaping my clutches. I sighed, watching him race down the three steps that lead from my apartment porch to the courtyard in a fawn-colored blur. He found a sunny strip along a garden wall and hoisted himself up, then glanced back at me disdainfully. Tail erect and flickering, he gave me a haughty meow.

"Keep that same energy at lunchtime," I mumbled under my breath, popping the door closed with my hip.

I try not to let my mood be soured by Milus' bad attitude. As a matter of fact, I take our coexistence as a challenge for me to keep a positive attitude, regardless of what outward circumstances may appear to be. But now that I say it like that, I'm certain this is an unhealthy relationship.

Regardless, I wasted no time gathering my tools for the day – sunglasses, a paddle, picnic blanket, a cooler. I checked my reflection in the mirror and found my curls had become quite limp. I slicked the locks up into a ponytail, inspecting the nape of my neck. I had been in charge of edging up my signature zig zag fade, and had become pretty damn good at it as of late. When I determined I was satisfied, I ambled out the front door of my apartment. I knew there was very little reason to lock up, but I did so anyway. Though my mother was two states away, her voice still rang in my ears, warning me against thieves and vagabonds. I knew that if I didn't, she'd somehow detect it. I could just imagine, despite being comatose, her disappointed scowl, her judging eyes, lips pursed so tight they could squeeze change from a dollar bill. I shuddered the thought away.

I pulled my car out of the parking lot, careful to punch the gas hard enough to allow my tires to spin, just because. I ignored the halted vehicles in the road, grim and faithful reminders of the failed rapture, and wound my way down the road toward the lake. There, I quickly unpacked.

The landscape was quite different as of late – the crystal-clear waters that once reflected the architectural wonders of the city, now hosted several types of creature; the colorful cognitions of the lake enthusiasts who were now bound to its shores. There were mermaids and a giant lion-turtle, and a more elusive creature that I'm sure was supposed to be a Loch Ness monster. I have a fun fact about lakes, by the way – these types of creatures obviously aren't real, but it is possible for sea lampreys, which are even weirder, to migrate into certain lakes. When they're young, these eel-like organisms latch on to host fish with a suction cup mouth and razor-sharp teeth, and proceed to suck their victim dry.

But I digress. I took in the beauty and strangeness of it all with a sigh. And with a pang of guilt, almost small enough to ignore, I admitted to myself just how grateful I was for slow days on the water with no prospect of school letting back in any time soon.

Of course, I *do* love my students. I've grown to care about them more than I could imagine, actually. It was the rest of teaching that had frayed me to within an inch of my existence. But I couldn't dare quit. What else could I do with a degree in education? My little piece of paper wouldn't even be enough to keep me warm at night as I tucked myself into the full-sized mattress in my old room at my mother's house. That's exactly where I'd end up, by the way.

And I absolutely couldn't go back there. Not after slamming her front door right in her face two years ago and vowing I'd never come back. She and I argued for the last time that day about how nothing I did was good enough for her. Wearing flannel wasn't girly enough. The music I listened to wasn't classy enough. My career choice wasn't smart enough. I didn't have enough money. Not enough friends. Not enough grit. Not enough.

I daresay that I *am* smart enough to remember two things – one, I'm never too old for an ass whoopin.' She won't easily forget me slamming her screen door; it nearly flew off the hinges. And two, her whoopins accrue interest over time. So I'd been very careful to be as polite as I could at our Sunday night FaceTime calls and during holiday visits, so as not to stir her memory.

And because of all this, I much preferred the apocalypse to having to run back home with my tail tucked between my legs. I shook off the invading sense of suffocation, which regularly accompanied my thoughts about my mom-work-life trifecta of doom. Then I hiked smoothly down the bank toward the shore. My eyes panned the lake. I learned to come and go undetected, for the most part, coexisting with these nonsensical things. The age-old rule of not sticking your nose in other people's business applied here in a way that nothing messed with me unless I messed with it first.

I settled in my usual spot under a young oak tree, where I had been leaving my kayak in the evenings. The sun kissed my skin, welcoming me back. I dragged the kayak out to the water, swallowing up the smell of cool, damp algae. It would've been lonesome if I hadn't still been recovering from the school year behind me. Being a schoolteacher is always like being on a rollercoaster – you're excited at the beginning, but the twists and turns keep hitting you and there's literally no way to stop until the ride is over at the end of May. And speaking of May – in teacher years, that month is actually eight hundred days long. So, having survived another year, the relative quiet – and even the outlandishness in the backdrop – was a much-needed respite from my own reality.

Hours later I dragged myself ashore again, cold and heavy and satisfied. Then I took my ritual walk, checking up on the entranced people along the shore. In my mind I assigned them names and personalities.

"Marla, you can't keep losing your shoes," I nagged at a short and stout woman. She washed ashore on her own only a few days ago, but her shoes kept finding their way back into the water. I don't know if this was by her design or not, but I always put them back on her feet.

I tucked her bangs behind her ear and wiped a smudge of mascara from her cheek, just in case Jorge from two trees over decided to make a pass at her. Then I folded her legs at the knee and into the shade to avoid them being subject to the harsh sunlight all day. "Concentrate on some shoes with straps," I said in her ear. Then I paused. A seedling of a thought sprouted in my mind. I bent over Marla's limp body and spoke as slowly and clearly as I could. "World peace," I said. My mind reeled with all of the possibilities I may have unlocked. "Rolls–Royce Phantom. Student loan forgiveness. Climate stability." I whispered my list in her ear over and over again like a mantra, until I was certain it seeped into her subconscious mind. I'm pretty sure that's how that works.

I rooted myself to the spot, listening for the slightest change. A cicada started up its song in a neighboring tree. I lowered my head again, this time clasping my hands in a prayer position. "I beg of you Marla," I said. "Give me a Rolls–Royce Phantom. Black. I don't care what year." I squeezed my eyes shut, hoping my brainwaves would carry the message. "Please grant me this one blessing, Marla. Amen." Then I gasped. I stared at Marla for a moment. She gazed placidly at the water, unaware of the breakthrough we just shared. I raced to my oak tree without another word. Hands shaking, I fumbled through my bag, spilling its contents until I found my walkie-talkie.

I slammed it to my lips. "Alex to Conner." I scooped random junk back into my bag. A bottle of sunscreen slipped down the bank. I chased it unsteadily, glad nobody was around to watch me act like a loon. Then I checked the channel and tried again. "Hello – Conner, Theo?"

A voice fizzled in. "Theo here, what's up?"

"Hey, so we're trying to get God to leave so everything goes back to normal, right?"

"That's the plan, yes."

"Have you gotten any ideas yet?"

There was silence for a length of time. Then the radio fizzled again. "Not particularly, no," Theo said. "We're still trying to locate the mechanism used to bring her here in the first place."

My thumb smoothed over the button on the walkie-talkie, but I didn't press it right away. It was a stupid idea. Not grounded in any sort of data. Not scientific at all. And I would be presenting it to an engineer and the director of a military grade laboratory. And, well, there was Conner. But I guess even a mailman would know how ridiculous it was. I was increasingly deflated. But there was a reason I had the idea, I supposed. I pressed the button. The walkie-talkie chirped. "Grab Conner and meet me on the corner of Tenth Street and Brazos in half an hour. I think I have something."

I left my kayak where it was and hiked up the sloping trail toward my car in the parking lot, keeping an eye out for any Rolls–Royce Phantoms that may have recently appeared.

I was only five minutes away from the cathedral that sat on Tenth and Brazos, but I needed time to collect some materials. I pulled right up to the curb of a large grocery store and threw my car in park. "Don't mind me," I said, stepping over a security guard who lay sweating on the sidewalk. Then

I backtracked, throwing a baseball cap from a display just inside the doors onto the woman's head. It perfectly shielded her eyes from the sun's blare. "You're welcome." I smiled. And with no time to lose, I found what I was looking for – seven white candles and frankincense.

I arrived at the cathedral well before everyone else, and was apprehensive to find that half of the building had changed shape entirely. The whole east wing melted dramatically into itself like a scoop of ice cream in the sun, only to reform – bricks completely smooth and solid again – and then begin the process of melting once more. A soft, glowing rainbow arched happily overhead. I gathered my supplies and, for extra measure, grabbed the amethysts that I kept in my glove box. One of my teacher friends gave them to me and said it was for 'connecting to higher realms.' She seemed super Zen, too, so I'm sure she knew what she was talking about. I decided the crystals would definitely help my mission. Then I had a sudden chill, realizing maybe she knew I'd need them one day. Was this divine timing? She talked about that a lot, too.

With a good feeling, I entered through the double doors along the west end. The passage was dark and quiet, except for the steady smacking of water dripping into a puddle that formed along the tiled floor somewhere up ahead. I followed a faint glow to the nave. The building appeared to be abandoned now, but had been previously well kept. It smelled of lavender and wood. I searched the walls for a light switch but found a window first. I drew the heavy curtains, spilling sunlight into the beautiful room. Rows of elaborately carved wooden pews faced a single dais, behind which a marbled

Jesus loomed – his face set in a hard to read expression. It looked a little judgy, but that wasn't my call to make. I took a moment to appreciate the wilting flowers along the altar, then I set myself to work. I arranged my candles and crystals in a circular fashion and lit the incense in one of the copper bowls along the altar. Soon after, I could hear hesitant footsteps down the passageway.

"Conner?" I called. "Theo?"

It was Theo. "So, we're having church?" he asked.

"Yes," I said. "Well, no. Where's Conner?"

Theo pulled out his walkie-talkie and held it to his face. "Conner, come in."

Conner's muffled voice came in on the other end. "Is it the church?"

"Yeah, we're at the church," he said. "Come through the side that isn't in the blender." Theo straightened the neckline on his jumper and clipped his radio to his waistband. "Didn't know you were religious," he said to me. He strode over to the altar to inspect my work, picking up an amethyst.

"I'm not," I started to explain but my voice was drowned out by a cacophony of discordant tones. We clasped our hands to our ears in an almost futile effort to muffle the sound. The ringing reverberated off the walls in a cascade of misery and finally rolled to a stop.

Theo peered into the passageway that led to the dilapidated east wing. "Church bell," he said. "I guess it makes sense the ringing would be warped, too."

Just then, Conner clamored into the room, accidentally kicking over a small box of hyssop branches. "If the bell rang like that when I was growin' up, I would've stayed awake at Sunday service," he said, rubbing his temples.

Me and Theo laughed. "Yep," I nodded. "Freaky church bell would've done the trick."

Conner moved toward the altar. "What's this?" he said, eyeing the candles.

The question slapped my attention back to the task at hand. I clasped my hands under my chin, grinning. "We're going to *appeal* to God," I said in what I thought was a pretty good holy voice. I raised my eyebrows expectantly, but they weren't as excited as I was.

"What?" said Conner.

"We're going to pray to God and ask her to leave," I explained. "She *may* go willingly. Ask and you shall receive, right?"

"No," said Theo.

Conner agreed with him. "Plus – *crystals?*" he said. He grabbed the stone from Theo's hand and inspected it. "This looks like witchcraft. You know God's gonna see this and send us straight to hell, right?"

I scoffed. "Crystals *are* religious," I defended. Then I faltered, but only for a second. I could hear my mother's gasp in my ear, plain as day. Lord Jesus, if crystals really were witchcraft then she'd have something else to moan about. So since I wasn't entirely sure, I grabbed them up and tossed them under a pew. "There, now we're already here, so let's pray."

"I don't know," Conner said with uncertainty.

I grabbed his hand and locked it into Theo's, then I pursed my lips together threateningly and held out my own hands so that they could close the circle. "Bow your heads!"

Theo chuckled under his breath. Conner sighed. Then when they lowered their heads to a satisfactory degree, I closed my eyes and began to say what I assumed was a respectable prayer. "God, Almighty Woman of Grace, please hear our cries and answer your faithful children. God, I implore you to make your presence seen here so that we may know your heavenly countenance and commune with you." Theo's shoulders shook violently. I opened my eyes, thinking perhaps he was being filled with the holy ghost, but to my dismay he was laughing. I yanked his arm. He tried to hide his giggles behind a cough, but quickly quieted after realizing I was glaring at him. I continued. "God, we have prepared a space for you. Please join us here in your holy house. In your name we pray —" Conner interjected in an urgent tone, both eyebrows raised. "And I'm gonna add, God, that I didn't participate in this unholy séance willingly, therefore I shouldn't be punished when you get here." I pursed my lips threateningly again, but it didn't matter. They were already saying *'amen.'*

We stood there for a few awkward moments, waiting for something to happen. Then it became too long. My mind had the opportunity to drum up a slew of stupid questions. *Could* the amethysts be witchcraft? Probably not, right? Would God arrive in a cool way, like riding on a flaming chariot? When I gaze upon her, would I find love in her eyes or condemnation? Love, right?

But what if God actually did show up and deem us unworthy of her presence? Would she send us to hell? After all, I hadn't been to church for my entire adult life. My hands started to sweat, but it only made me grip Conner and Theo's hands tighter.

Then there was a dull echo of soft footsteps behind me. My heart began to race. I knew I was about to come face to face with God. A voice called into the room. It was actually a rather unexpected voice – deep and gravelly, but also euphonic. Its sureness quelled my anxiety in an instant. It asked a simple question. "Have you come here seeking refuge, children?" I wouldn't have guessed God's voice would be so handsome, but I didn't question it. I smiled in amazement at Theo and Conner, neither of whom dared look up yet from our bubble of prayer. It felt as though someone shot electricity up my back, and my stomach began to churn. I gave them a reassuring nod and turned, preparing my eyes to behold God. It wasn't at all what I expected.

I was the first to speak. "Wait, you're *not* God, right?"

Standing at the back of the room was a gangly and freckle-faced man in his thirties, wearing thick black robes and carrying a bible. He donned a silver cross pendant on the left side of his white collar.

"What, no – obviously I'm a priest," he said, striding up the aisle to meet us. "Do you need help or not?" But we ignored him, continuing to search the room distractedly. I blew out my candles and dropped myself into a pew. "What's with you people?" he pressed, clearly annoyed now.

"Sorry dude," Theo said to him. "We were expecting someone to show up, and we got you instead."

"Well, she could still be on her way," I said hopefully. I craned my neck to look down the passageway.

"Yeah," Conner feigned excitement. He turned to the priest. "You showed up just in time for her to smite you, too."

"Nobody's getting smitten." I glowered at Conner. "Or is it smited?"

He shrugged.

"You're waiting on a friend, then?" asked the priest. I scratched the side of my head, deciding if I would lie or not. I decided to tell the truth.

"Uh, actually, we were waiting on God," I said. The priest narrowed his eyes with confusion. I explained further. "Okay, so there were some idiot scientists who did this experiment where they pulled God to Earth, and now her presence has made the entire planet –" I gestured toward the ceiling in big sweeping motions with my hands.

"I don't understand," said the priest. The place between his eyes bunched tightly as he tilted his head. "First, God is *not* a woman," he laughed. "And second –" But we wouldn't hear his second argument because just then the giant stone Jesus behind the altar started morphing in a rather frightening way. "Holy crap!" I yelled, grabbing my chest in order to keep my heart from jumping right out.

Then there was a crack like booming thunder, and another voice. "Does it make you feel uncomfortable that I'm a woman?" It was strong and velvety, and just a little saucy. And it was certainly a woman's voice this time.

My eyes wouldn't cooperate as I tried to focus them on the dais. A woman had, in fact, appeared there, leaning against the pulpit with an amused grin on her face. She wore a simple pleated white dress and black combat boots, and she would've been otherwise unremarkable had she not had the subtlest ethereal glow to her skin.

She walked toward the priest, her boots thudding against the tiled floor. Each step she took sent little flickers of light falling from her thick hair into the ground. "What do I call *you*?" she asked.

The priest drew a nervous breath but stood firmly in his spot. "You... you, of course... you can call me anything you wish, but my name is Matthew," he tried to smile. "You can call me Matt, if you're comfortable with that. Or... or also Matthew is just fine."

God smiled and nodded. "Well, Matthew," she said in a sweet voice. "I'm so sorry I didn't meet the expectations you've set for me. Find it in your heart to forgive me, will you?" She patted him firmly on the back. The priest didn't know what to say. A mixture of awe and fear was painted on his face. He nodded slowly.

"Excuse me," I interjected. I stood up as tall as I could and smiled. "Hey there," I waved. "I'm Alex and I just wanted to say that I always knew you were a woman."

God nodded her approval. "Girl power, am I right?" She held up a hand, which I high fived way harder than I meant to. She didn't seem to care though.

I laughed way too loudly, even though I was about to barf all over her cute little boots. Then I tried to look as serious as

I could, but I couldn't stop my hands from tugging at the bottom of my tee shirt. "Yeah, so God, listen," I said. "I'm just going to get right to it – and don't take this the wrong way, but um... you were never supposed to be here." I looked to Theo and Conner for support, but they only stared dumbly; petrified to the spot. This only made me more nervous. "I mean, you can technically do what you want, but as a planet, we just weren't ready for you and – I don't know if you know this – but now we're suffering for the mistake of only a handful of people."

"Mistake?" God shook her head at me. "Everything has a divine purpose, my dear. Everything. It's no mistake that I'm here."

I didn't know what to say to that. Conner recovered from his stupor, possibly sensing that I needed help. "So, God," he gave a small and weird bow. "I'm just gonna bring it to your attention that some scientists forced you to come here, without telling the rest of us. People did that. People make mistakes all the time." Then he quickly added, "respectfully."

"Right," I said. "What he means is it's clearly not the natural order of things, because people – all our loved ones – are zonked out. We need things to go back to how they were."

God looked thoroughly offended at this point. She put a hand on her hip. "Back to how they were?" she scoffed. "You mean you enjoyed working ten hours a day and paying taxes and fighting with politicians who don't have the good sense to end homelessness?"

"Well, no," I admitted. I groped for words. "But... but people are still suffering. All this crazy stuff is happening now."

God walked toward the window, arms outstretched. She drew a satisfied breath and said, "This is the beauty of creation." Then she turned on her heels so quickly we all jumped. "You four seem to be the only ones upset by this."

I was bewildered. "Beauty of creation?" I breathed. "I passed a guy who was on *fire* on the way up here. I'm sure you'll find that he's downright pissed!"

She bit her lip pensively for a brief moment, then snapped her fingers. In a flash the man appeared, sitting cross–legged on the floor. Flames licked at his robes and body with a roar. Everyone screamed. The smell of burning flesh filled the cathedral, but the man's face remained expressionless. God raised her voice slightly over the crackling of the flames. "Thich Quang Duc," she called to the monk. "Are you pissed?"

The monk looked up at God, a sliver of a smile threatening at the corner of his lips. "I bear no anger within my body," he said simply. And he continued burning peacefully.

God snapped her finger again and he was gone, leaving a smoking soot stain on the floor. "There," she said in a satisfied way. "He's not pissed at all." For a while after that nobody said anything. My lips had gone incredibly dry, and I couldn't even remember what I was arguing about. This gave God the opportunity to continue. "Humanity is simply experiencing a new form of expression," she explained. "You are me, experiencing everything there is to experience – creating *new* realities." Then she smiled contentedly. "You'll get used to it."

I could tell it was the end of the conversation for her, but I forced the issue. I knew I was risking being smitten. Smited. Or maybe smote. Or turned into a pillar of salt. Or whatever it is. But I had to try. I inhaled sharply through my nose. "God, we called you here to ask you to leave," I said. "I'm sure you can go... *anywhere* in creation. Can't you just hear our prayers and go?"

God smiled warmly at me. Then she dropped her shoulders and said a very firm, "No."

"Well, what's the point in praying if you don't listen?" I asked.

"You guys made that up." God crossed her arms. She smirked, and for the first time, I noticed freckles sprinkled over the bridge of her nose like pepper. "It's totally a made–up thing," she said.

"So we're supposed to just... be okay with planes full of people crashing and... and..." I swept a warm tear from my cheek.

"Oh, don't be a Debbie Downer," God said, throwing her hands up. Then she raised an eyebrow. "I ran into Debbie Downer the other day, actually... sent her ass straight to hell."

Matt suddenly spoke up. "Blasphemy!" he yelled forcefully. His hands trembled as they fumbled around in a storage compartment behind the dais. A moment later he held up a heavy–looking silver cross. "This is not God," he said, holding an arm out to shield us from her. Theo, who had been quietly observing all of this, bunched up his face at me in confusion. I shrugged uncertainly.

Conner took a step back from the priest as if he were about to be struck by lightning. "Dude, what do you mean?" he asked.

Matt took a step forward, the cross still in his outstretched hand. He began to recite a bible verse in a weird and robotic voice. "The Lord is gracious and righteous; our God is full of compassion –"

"Psalms, Matt?" said God. "For real?"

"Unbridled tongue!" he continued, waving the cross violently.

God rolled her eyes. Then at the flick of her fingers, Matt burst into flames. "What have you done?" he yelled. But he didn't run, or roll around, or curse. *We* cursed. Matt simply stood there staring at his hands. The flames licked at them violently, charring his skin, just as they had done with the monk.

God spoke in a high-pitched voice as if she were talking to a beloved pet. "If I weren't full of compassion, this would really hurt right now, right?" she said.

Then she put two fingers to her forehead in a salute and said, "Alrighty, y'all, I'm out," before turning promptly on her heels.

Theo, who had been trying to fan Matt's flames with a hyssop branch, stopped her. "No!" he yelled. "You have to put him out first!"

She paused for a moment, debating whether she would help or not. Then she put her hands up, but she had waited too long. Matt fell to the floor in a pile of ash.

The nave was deathly quiet as we stared at the horrific, chalky gray mound.

"Oopsie," God said. She shrugged apologetically. Then batted the air dismissively. "Just throw some water on him. He'll grow back." She smiled, but her shoulders were drawn up in a way that made me think she didn't really believe it would work. And I certainly didn't blame her, because it was a stupid idea. I was both mortified and curious if witnessing this would be a kind of trauma that turns me into a serial killer or something. I shook my head, hoping that last thought would fall out of it and never return.

"What?" I couldn't produce any real or useful language from my mouth.

Theo was having the same problem. "What?" he asked separately.

"*Hell* no," said Conner. "I'm out of here." Then he stormed pointedly toward the passageway.

God started to walk off, too. I decided to let her. I turned my attention to finding the puddle of water I'd heard when I first came in. I found it at the entrance to the passage that led to the east wing. But before I could get to it, the infernal church bell started to ring again. We all clapped our hands to our ears. Then I heard God's muffled voice indignantly say, "What's this?" She turned in a half circle, holding the skirt of her dress out in front of her. It seemed her body was being pulled in all different directions. She flickered and waved, like static on an old television set. It got worse with every strike of the bell, until her entire being was a cloud of dust. The cloud hovered briefly, rippling and waving, then escaped through the crack under the doors on the far side of the nave.

"Interesting," said Theo. He rubbed his baby-smooth chin, nodding. "That was pretty damn interesting."

I nodded, too, staring at the crack God disappeared through. Then I remembered the pile of ash. I sprinted toward the puddle and dipped both hands in. As I waddled back toward it with my hands cupped, Conner realized what I was doing and, begrudgingly, ran to help. Theo rolled his eyes and rummaged through the storage compartment along the dais. He found a large and ornate goblet of some sort and filled it with water from the sink. He tossed the water on the ashes, making them pool up and start to run. We stood over the pile of wet ash, encircling it.

And just when we decided that nothing more could be done, Matt sprang back up – robes and all – still looking at his hands. The sun from the window bathed his bright green eyes as they bulged. Then he patted himself down, laughing timidly. "I'm alive," he whispered.

We laughed with him. And for a while that's all we did. Our laughter filled the church until we were all laughed out. Then we were wordless. I sat down on a pew, unable to process what we'd just experienced. Matt sat down next to me. Then Theo sat. Then Conner.

Matt was the first to speak. "So that was God," he said. We nodded. He sighed. Then he continued pensively. "You guys are telling me I've been lied to my whole life? That God's a woman... and she curses?"

"Well," said Conner. He rubbed his hands along his legs, giving them a little squeeze. "Apparently so."

Matt's face twisted up and I could tell there was an internal battle raging as his whole reality was reorganizing itself in his mind. "So everything I learned in seminary…" His voice trembled. I looked away to give him a moment of privacy. Then, when he spoke again, it was steady. "Nobody really knew what they were talking about," he said. "For all we know, it was *all* a lie." He turned suddenly, and I could tell he wanted reassurance. I reluctantly locked eyes with him, offering a small smile and hoping my face was displaying sympathy or hope or whatever you're supposed to feel in this kind of situation. I patted him gently on the back. And it must've been encouraging enough, because Matt's face relaxed considerably. Then he asked, "So this basically means we can do what we want, right?"

I looked at Conner. Then Conner looked at Theo. And after careful consideration, Theo nodded, his lips turned downward on each side. "Yeah, man. Why not?"

Matt popped up from the bench. He put a hand to his forehead and paced toward the dais. "Alright," he said. He nodded his head enthusiastically. "We can do what we want."

"Yeah," I said, encouraging him along. "You can do what you want!"

Matt looked cautiously up and down the aisle, then over his shoulders. Then he whispered, "*Hell* yeah!"

Then we were silent again, unable to move forward from the strange encounter with God. It was Theo's turn to speak. "So, um… she's not gonna go down without a fight, is she?"

"Not at all," I said. "She seems to be enjoying herself."

Theo nodded. "But she's definitely gotta go."

"Yeah," said Matt smoothly. "Bitch gotta go."

The three of us stared at the priest.

"What?" he said, throwing his hands up to his collar. He loosened it with a hooked finger. "We can do what we want now."

Chapter Four:
Is That Magic Falling Out of Your Hair?

Matt stuck with us, having no real reason for staying bound to the church anymore and having very little else to do. Even he had a somewhat useful role – filling in the gaps about God for Valencio where science had failed Of course, it was all speculative, since he had been wrong about so much already. But Valencio found value in the conjecture.

I hadn't really figured out what to do with myself, having exhausted my one good idea. Of course, the lake never got old to me, but the two neurons I had left in May had begun to bump up against each other and repopulate my skull – a phenomenon that occurs annually for schoolteachers, by the way, usually in the middle of July. So I was ready to be intellectually useful again. The best I could do, though, was check in at the lab every once in a while. And it was always well worth the drive when I did, because it was a little bit like coming home to family.

"You really need to stop eating those," Valencio said over his shoulder.

"Why?" I tossed a wrapped chocolate bar onto Theo's desk.

He ripped it open with his teeth and shoved half of it in his mouth. "Cause we'll get cavities," he said.

"No." Valencio pushed his glasses up the bridge of his nose and eyed me. "Because you don't know what effect it's having on your body."

Theo looked up from his microscope. "We'll be fat," he said. "That's what chocolate does."

Valencio faked a gasp; a wide smile crossing his face. "What does chocolate manifested from the subconscious mind do to the human body, I wonder," he said with mock curiosity.

"First," I said. "My neighbor loves me. I think Ms. Marino's been making all this candy appear to thank me for checking in on her." And it was a fair deal, if you ask me. I always bought the most chocolate from her daughter whenever she came knocking on my apartment door with her wagon full of candy. The Anderson High band certainly knew how to fund raise. They did it often and aggressively, picking off weaklings like myself. Contributing to the addiction that I formed as a result was the least she could do to support me in these times of apocalyptic uncertainty. I unwrapped my second bar and nibbled off the brittle toffee that was wedged on top. "And second, I think it would've hurt us by now," I said. "But why don't you do a study on it – *you're* a scientist."

Valencio sighed. "I have better things to do.

"Like wait for the phone to ring?" I said. "Come on, it would be interesting! You would be the first scientist to discover what dream food does to the human body."

"When the phone rings, it will hopefully bring us all very good news," said Valencio. He pressed his hands down the front of his lab coat. Then he repositioned the large clunky phone at the far left of his desk.

"Oh yeah," I said. "What good news?"

"An update on the template," he said. "A couple members of the World Health Alliance were able to travel to CERN in order to recover it."

"An update on *what?*" I licked the melted chocolate from my hands, making Valencio cringe. He drew up two tissues from a box behind the phone and threw them at me.

Theo finished whatever he was doing with his microscope and turned it off. Then he plopped himself into a chair next to me. "The template," he said, rummaging through my bag. I unzipped my secret compartment and produced one more candy bar for him. Theo sighed. "Where do I begin?"

Valencio leaned back in his chair.

"Start at the template," I said. "What is it?"

"It's a machine, essentially," said Theo.

Valencio interrupted testily. "It's a *human.*"

Theo smacked his lips. "Okay, it's a human that CERN *altered* to make very machine-like."

I shuddered. "Alright. I'm following."

"The template was used like a gateway," Theo continued. "They altered the field of the human — down to the quantum level — so that it essentially attracted and pulled God's essence through, like a gate."

"Wait," I scoffed. "Let me get this straight — they turned a person into a portal of some sort?"

Theo nodded his head and said, "The word I was thinking was *rat trap*."

"Right," sighed Valencio. "But what has been most disturbing is that the template has been *unattended* since the day of the experiment."

I screwed up my face. "What does *unattended* mean?"

"There were several people in the building at the time of the experiment who were unaffected," Valencio said. "I attempted to guide them – have them secure the template and provide me any information they could about its condition. It has been difficult since they weren't directly involved with the experiment." Valencio paused for the briefest of moments. "They are unsure where to look, and therefore cannot find the template."

My eyes pinched. How could actual scientists not figure out where to look? Even if they weren't involved, there's got to be some way to track that kind of information. "You mean it's lost?"

Valencio tried his best to preserve his denial. He pursed his lips together, making the bottom one stick out stubbornly. Then he conceded. "It appears so," he said.

Theo sat up excitedly in his seat and started talking fast, like he usually does when he's nerding out. "According to Valencio, God would need an 'adjustment period' where she assimilates fully into form – the form she's in now," he explained. He bit the chocolate bar. Then he continued with his mouth full. "She would depend on the template until she was fully integrated into Earth's field. So, I was thinking she probably stole it and put it somewhere safe until the process could be completed."

"What do you mean, she would *depend* on the template?" I asked.

"She was initially able to enter Earth's field only as a complex manifestation from the mind of the template," Valencio said. He gestured toward my purse. "Much like your chocolate bars are a manifestation from the mind of your gracious neighbor."

"Easy," I said. I clapped my hands together triumphantly and grinned. "When we find the template, we can just give it a good jostle, then God will disappear!" I was proud of myself for being able to contribute my hard-earned information, but was quickly disappointed.

Valencio waved an impatient hand. "These manifestations all around us, serve the will of their dreamer, and can easily be disrupted. But God has a will of her own – is an *entity* of her own – so she will not simply disappear."

"Oh," I said. I leaned back in my chair.

"And what's more," Valencio added. "The progression of the experiment is causing her to convert the template's essence into a structural field that she can occupy. The longer she's on Earth, the more she will draw from the template. And the more she draws from the template the more potent, if you will, God will be."

"So, God is going to become more God-like?" I asked. "What we saw at the church was, like, *diet* God?"

"Yep," said Theo. "Omnipotent, omniscient... all that God stuff..." He sighed loudly. "And the three scientists on the original project that knew how to safely shut down the template ended up dead. So once we actually get it back, Valencio's gonna have to carry out a series of shut down protocols that I don't even understand. If he doesn't do it right, –" he gestured toward Valencio. "Would that be like a big bang scenario?" he asked him. "Or the opposite of the big bang, maybe? What's the opposite of the big bang?"

I wrapped my chocolate bar tidily back in its paper. "Alright," I said. "Find the maybe stolen template. Fast. Then figure it out from there."

"Now you see why I am waiting by the phone?" asked Valencio.

I conceded with a nod.

"Well, that's the crappy part," said Theo. Then he smiled widely. "The good news is, I made a weapon!"

"What?"

Just then the doors hummed, letting in Conner and Matt. "What's up, buttercup?" said Matt. He pulled me out of my seat and wrapped an arm around me. Then he squeezed a warm cheek against mine. The smell of whiskey spilled from his clothes. "You're looking like a billion mucks," he slurred.

I checked my watch. "It's ten in the morning, Matt. Why are you drunk?"

Conner squeezed the bridge of his nose. "He found my auntie's liquor cabinet, y'all. I tried to stop him."

"Oh, don't act so innocent," Matt said indignantly. "You had a drink, too."

"One," said Conner. "One drink. You had *twelve*." At that, Valencio jumped up and grabbed a glass from the far end of the room, near the sink. He filled it with fresh water from the tap. Matt raised his hand for a high five from Theo, who gave it a hearty slap.

"Right on!" said Theo.

Valencio pushed the glass into Matt's other hand and gave him a very firm command to drink. Matt thanked him and put both lips right inside the rim, slurping the water up like a toddler might. Then he plopped down in the chair of an unoccupied desk and rested his head on one of his hands, smiling contentedly.

Conner clapped his hands together. "Alright, what did we miss?" he asked.

"You didn't miss anything," said Theo happily. "I was just about to pull out the Hertzinator." He gently placed an aluminum case on Valencio's desk and opened it, revealing a contraption that looked much like a small boom box, with two funnels spiraling outwards on either side. "Or the Save Wave," he added as an afterthought. "I'm still working on a name."

"Cool," I said, even though I wasn't sure what it was, or if cool was an appropriate assessment of it. "So, you said it was a weapon..."

Theo pulled it out of its case and displayed it for us to appreciate, kind of like how they display the prizes on game shows. "Remember that day in the church when God turned into... whatever that was?" We nodded. "She seemed to have an adverse reaction to the combination of frequencies that were being emitted from the warped church bell. I was able to isolate those frequencies and recreate them here."

"To use against God," Conner said plainly, though his raised eyebrows told us he was very much alarmed.

"Just as a last resort kind of deal," Theo defended. "If we ever need to escape a… *bad* situation."

"Will it work after she becomes all powerful?" I asked.

Conner bit his bottom lip. "I hope we never die, cause y'all know we're going to hell, right?"

Matt stood up suddenly, making everyone jump. Then, with a small hiccup, he said, "I've been to hell… It's nothin'."

I scoffed. "You were not in hell," I said. "You burned for like three minutes."

Matt held up a finger in an attempt to drive home whatever point he was trying to make. He blinked hard. "And I turned to ash…" he whispered. "And I rose…" Then he raised both hands triumphantly and yelled, "Like a phoenix!"

Theo whooped. "Like a phoenix!" he repeated. Matt slapped him another high five. Conner cracked a grin, and I giggled harder than I had in a few days. Valencio even laughed – something I've never seen him do.

"Seriously, though," said Theo. He placed the clunky contraption back in its box. Then he clapped his hands. "The Save Wave is up and running."

"No," I said. Theo turned around. "I vote Hertzinator."

Theo was about to ask everyone else what their vote was when Valencio's phone rang. Matt stumbled around the desk to answer it, but thankfully Valencio got to it first. We held our breath while he uttered, *mmm… mmhmmm… yes…* to whoever was at the other end. Then he hung up, his face dejected and long.

I swallowed hard. "They have no clue where the template is," I guessed. Valencio shook his head, but his eyes were darting – something he did when he was thinking hard. "They accessed every single security camera at the facility. Nothing to be seen. The template simply… disappeared."

"Well," I sat down gingerly in my chair, thinking. "This *is* God we're talking about," I said. "If she's hiding the template, she wouldn't make it easy."

Theo smoothed his hand over the front of his jumper. "But everything – every organism, event, – leaves evidence… leaves a trail…" he said. "Telltale signs, like residual photons or energy distortions. We can probably find it ourselves. We just have to know where to start."

Matt took a deep breath and exhaled, filling his immediate area with the smell of stale whiskey. Then he recited a bible verse in his weird robot voice, "And I saw the dead, small and great, stand before God; and the books were opened: and another book was opened –"

We all groaned.

"Not now," I said.

But he raised a finger to silence me. "– which is the book of life: and the dead were judged out of those things which were written in the books according to their works."

And when he was finished, he stared at us as if we were supposed to know what he was talking about. He was able to understand the blank looks on our faces, though. He clarified. "The Book of Life leaves no deed unrecorded," he said. "We may be able to find the whereabouts of the template if we can access the Book of Life."

"Oh yeah," I said. "We'll just take a quick look at the Book of Life." But he didn't seem to get that I was mocking him. He let out a weird hiccup burp, then nodded surely.

"Where would we even begin to look for it?" asked Theo.

"You can summon God, apparently," said Matt. "Why not the Book of Life?"

I wanted to smack him in the back of the head. But the more I thought about it, the more I considered that it wasn't a terrible idea. After all, I didn't have anything better to present.

For a while nobody said anything. Valencio's eyes darted, and I could almost hear the neurons in his brain firing off. And speaking of neurons, by the way – I do know it's actually impossible for them to dwindle down to just two. Your brain actually consists of over one hundred billion neurons that can live as long as you do. And you can't actually hear them firing off, but scientists have recently developed a way to see the process through new, noninvasive measures by observing the subtle change in their shape as they fire off the electrical signal.

But I digress. Matt eventually got distracted by the tools on the desk and eventually moved to twirling in his rolling chair. Conner stubbornly crossed his arms, probably wondering why he still hung out with us.

Theo cleared his throat as if he were about to speak, but I shot up first. "Can you hypnotize people in their sleep?"

¤ ¤ ¤ ¤ ¤ ¤ ¤

The following day, the five of us met back at the lab. This gave Valencio the time he needed in order to construct a meaningful hypnosis protocol. We gathered in the medical chamber toward the back around Mr. Jackson, Conner's uncle. The lighting in the room was brighter than it usually was, and we could see that the hair along his face had grown out into an impressive beard. It was well trimmed and moisturized evenly - evidence of Conner's meticulous care.

"You actually can't hypnotize people in their sleep," explained Valencio. "They must be able to hear your words in order to participate. But it's a good thing our friends here aren't asleep." He positioned a chair right next to Mr. Jackson's face and sat. We all looked at one another apprehensively. Conner gave the nod for him to begin. Valencio breathed deeply, his chest rising and falling; matching pace with Mr. Jackson's, then he lightly rubbed the man's hand. "Sherman," he said. "This is Valencio. Your nephew, Conner, is here, too. He has given me permission to interact with you in this way today." At this, Conner touched his uncle's hand. Valencio gave Conner a small smile and firmly grasped Mr. Sherman's forearm. "I am touching your arm gently, and you are moving further and further into a state of deep relaxation." His voice was very low, a few octaves lower than usual. I screwed my face up in confusion. Conner shrugged. Valencio continued. "You are relaxing further and further into your bed… until you can relax no further," he said. Then he paused for a moment. Mr. Jackson sighed and blinked leisurely. "Now, you have a strong desire to locate the biblical Book of Life. You can see it clearly in the annals of heaven." Theo suddenly giggled, then apologized. Valencio blinked several times at Theo, then continued. "You can touch it. It is in the room with you now. Show us the Book of Life."

Before we had a chance to look around, Matt shrieked. His left foot was being sucked into some sort of distortion in the room. He pulled it out relatively easily.

Theo put his arm up, sweeping us all backward. The distortion grew, quickly revealing a room on the other side. White and pink marbled pillars lined either side of a long pathway and toward the end, a beautiful archway. Golden ribbons danced lazily from the high ceiling as a soft breeze emanated from the place.

It took a few moments for my eyes to drink in the ethereal sight. When I finally peeled them from the room, I realized everyone was looking at me. "*What?*" I asked. I was just as bewildered as they were.

"Someone's gonna have to go in," said Conner.

"Absolutely not," I sputtered. "None of us even knows what that is!"

"Come on," said Conner. His hands splayed toward the distortion. "Science is your jam, right?"

"Biology, yes," I argued. I blinked at the thing. "This is some sort of interdimensional… bullshit." It wasn't the most appropriate assessment of it, but I was running out of descriptive words for what I was witnessing. Plus, everyone was looking at me with eyes that agreed with Conner. I wasn't having it. "And what do I look like, going in there – Ms. Frizzle from the hood? This is not a field trip."

Theo threw his hands up, attempting to dismiss my angst. "It'll be fine," he said. "Besides, it was your idea. You should have the honor."

I seethed at him. But before I could retort, Matt cut in. "I think I actually know what it is," he said. He leaned in closer to inspect the room from a safe distance, then he nodded surely. "It's the Hall of Records. You'll find the Book of Life in there for sure."

I smiled at Matt. "You know way more about this kind of stuff than me," I said, crossing my arms. "I think *you* should go."

Matt was indignant. "Never," his voice pitched. "You know how God feels about me. I won't be caught dead in that place!"

I smacked my lips, looking to the others for support.

"She did sit there and let him burn," said Conner.

Theo elbowed me. "Plus, y'all have that *'girl power'* thing going on," he added. "She probably won't attack you if she finds you in there."

Valencio gave me a look that said he wouldn't be dragged into it. I sighed. "Fine, whatever," I said. "I'll go, but if I don't come back in five minutes, somebody better come in and save me."

Matt nodded vigorously, though we all knew he wouldn't be coming after me even if my life did depend on it. I rolled my eyes.

"Before you do," said Valencio, "You may need to put on something more accommodating." He eyed my sundress and thin sandals. "You don't know what you may find in there."

I glanced around the room, which had a shortage of extra clothes lying around. "Like what - a lab coat?" I asked.

Valencio blinked at me. Then he said, "That wouldn't offer you additional protection at all."

I shouldn't have been surprised to find out that Valencio was, once again, light years ahead of me in the sciencey stuff. He beckoned me toward the hall and down three flights of steps. I could barely keep pace with him as he strode down the crisp, quiet corridors. There, at the end of the hall on the sixth floor, was a whole division of the laboratory dedicated to protective gear and field equipment – impenetrable vests, flame retardant suits, goggles, hard-hats, gloves, boots, utility belts and garters, scuba gear, weapons. I found what I needed rather quickly – a simple brown jumpsuit with a utility belt and a pair of boots – but I continued looking out of sheer curiosity. The inventory was expansive. I could only guess what kind of expeditions these scientists would be going on to have a need for mechanical robot gloves.

I returned to the medical chamber at my own pace, but nobody minded since they were each conducting their own observations of the distortion. Theo was running a scanning tool along the edge of it. The machine clicked subtly as it recorded data that only he could possibly understand. Matt had his bible opened and was refreshing himself on everything he knew about the Hall of Records and Valencio was operating a glass pad, which was scanning the distortion in short spurts of blue–white light. Conner sat quietly at his uncle's side.

"Let's get us a Book of Life," I said, clapping my hands. "So, what's the verdict? Is it safe?"

"Quite so," said Valencio distractedly. "So long as nothing happens to Sherman, of course."

I looked at Conner. He gave me a reassuring nod. "Okay," I said. I could feel jitters starting up in my hands, and I was uncomfortably aware of my heart rate picking up. I let out a hollow laugh. "I'm just gonna jump right in," I announced.

"Not just yet," Valencio grabbed a small walkie talkie from his desk and turned it to channel two before handing it to me. I clipped it onto my belt. "I don't know if the signal will carry," he said. "Doesn't hurt to try, though."

Theo held out a hand. I used it to steady myself as I lowered into the hall. My boots hit the floor with a crisp thud. The air in the room was cold and thick, as if I had stepped into water. I took a cautious breath and found that all my angst had disappeared. I felt at ease; lighter than I had in years. I glanced over my shoulder. Their faces were rippled by the distortion.

I turned back toward the hall and adjusted the collar of my jumpsuit. It slicked against my skin in this new environment, clinging as if it were wet, but thankfully the material was forgiving. I started walking forward along the line of pillars. The ribbons seemed to sense my presence, reaching out to touch me as I walked by. They chased me dreamily — the further I moved into the hall the closer they seemed to get — but I wasn't afraid. I walked until I reached the archway. Then I glanced back and saw that the ribbons had made a golden wall behind me. If I had to, could I cut through them to get back? I pressed a hand to the knife on my utility belt. Hopefully I wouldn't have to use it.

The archway seemed to create its own distortion. On the outside of it, there was just a room — beautiful and marbled, with pillars connected by low buttresses — but inside was something entirely different. There was no floor. No ground at all. Just air. Or perhaps water. And floating inside of it were rows and rows of granite bookshelves. The rows twisted and turned, like a maze. "Oh great," I moaned. There were bajillions of books. How could I tell which one was the Book of Life?

I put a foot through the archway, careful not to go all the way in until it found something solid. Surprisingly, I was able to stand. But not on anything I could see. My foot just met some sort of resistance in the air. I leaned into the archway, bringing my other foot down. The air was suddenly thinner, and I felt a thrill, as if my stomach was dropping. I crept to one of the bookshelves and looked up. Small books were stacked tidily along the full length of it, each labeled with a different name. I pulled out the walkie talkie and whispered, "Alex to Valencio…"

For a while there was just a staticky buzz. I took it as a good sign; at least some sort of signal was getting through. Then a muzzled voice, but it wavered and broke in some places. I was pretty sure he said, "Copy that."

"I think I'm in the annals," I whispered.

Then there was garbled laughter on the other end of the line. I could make out Theo's voice. "How does it feel to be in the anal," he wheezed.

"*Annals*," I snapped.

Valencio and Theo wrestled over the walkie–talkie. Then I heard Theo's voice again. "You're in God's anal. Got it."

I pinched my lips together, only slightly irritated. I fought down the laughter that was boiling up inside of me. Then I briefly wondered if I was even an adult. I pressed the button again. "Totally not the time for butt jokes." I sighed.

I shifted my weight, then stopped short. The placement of the bookshelves created a pathway that led straight to a marbled pedestal. I followed the path and found a rather thin book on top. It was subtly ornate, with geometric patterns crawling over russet leather binding. Besides these delicate etchings, it was otherwise plain. I rifled through its pages. They were empty. I picked up the book and hid between two shelves. Then I put the walkie–talkie back up to my face. "Theo, ask Matt what the book looks like."

"Oh my," said a velvety voice from behind me. "How did you find your way here, I wonder."

I whipped around, sliding the book behind my back. God was removing a pair of gloves from her hands. Her windswept hair embraced a pair of thick goggles, which were perched atop her head. "God," I smiled. I clicked the button rapidly on my walkie–talkie, hoping the others would take it as an SOS. I raised my voice, hoping she wouldn't hear it chirping. "What a pleasant surprise. Have you been out riding a… motorcycle, or something?"

"Unicorn," she said briskly. Her eyes were narrowed. She took a calculated step toward me. "What have you got there?"

"Well, funny you should ask." I tried to keep my smile, but I'm sure my mouth wasn't doing what I was telling it to do. I tittered nervously. "I was just exploring… looking for some light reading," I said. My hands fumbled around behind me as I tried to hide the book on one of the shelves. "Is this your place?" I asked. "I didn't realize you'd be needing it."

God continued to glower at me. "You're looking for some light reading?" she asked dubiously.

I grabbed a random book from the shelf I was fumbling with and revealed it. "Yes, I was just reading up on –" I read the name on the front cover. "– Emma Jean Smithers. She was a good person, bless her soul."

"Emma Jean is still alive," said God offhandedly. "And I'm not sure if I'm gonna bless her soul yet."

"Yes," I said. "I would know that if you'd let me get to the end of the book, but since you just told me, I'll just put it back where I found it." I turned completely around and hoped desperately that God didn't notice me trying to shove the unmarked book into the front of my jumpsuit. Of course, she did.

"Okay, clearly you're trying to steal," she said. I could hear the thudding of her boots coming closer. I zipped the book snugly into place and pressed the button on the radio frantically. "What could you possibly need from here?" she asked. I felt her hand on my shoulder. Knowing I had run out of time, I allowed her to turn me around. We could both see the outline of the book down my front, but the sound of Conner cursing loudly gave me a much-needed distraction. I tore away from God, running to help him off the floor. The ribbons on the other side of the archway had wrapped themselves around his legs, causing him to fall face forward into the Hall of Records.

"Theo's right behind me," he groaned, tearing at the ribbons. I pulled out my pocketknife, but God was already pulling me to my feet by the back of my collar.

"I'm not done with you, little thief," she said. "There are only a few things in here. Which of them are you stealing?"

Conner had cut himself free and was wresting with the rest of the ribbons, which had become quite violent. I could see Theo's torso and right arm. In his hand, a corner of the Hertzinator's case. I just needed to buy us a few more seconds. I blurted the first thing I could think of. "Where are you hiding the template?" I asked. God loosened her grip, letting me stumble free. I slapped my hand to my mouth. I knew that I'd tipped our hand. Her brow furrowed. "Template for what?" she asked.

Theo stumbled into the hall and scrambled to free the Hertzinator from its case. Conner clapped his hands into a praying position. "God, I'm going to ask your forgiveness in advance," he said, but God and I were still exchanging some pretty intense eye contact. He went on, nonetheless. "I'm really not here to attack you personally –"

"Wait," said God. She shook her head. "There's too much going on. Back up."

And when she said, 'back up', she meant it. In a fraction of a second, I was standing between the bookshelves again with the walkie talkie in my hand. I glanced toward the archway. It was empty. It took a few seconds to realize what happened. But when I did, I moved quickly. I clicked the button on my walkie–talkie frantically. Then I zipped the unmarked book in the front of my jumper and threw my knife into the archway. I could hear it slide to a halt just on the other side with a faint scraping sound.

God materialized right behind me, just as I suspected she would. But she wasted no time as she did previously. She crossed her arms and frowned at me. "What is it you're asking me about a template?" she said.

I wasn't expecting her to get right to the point, so I blurted without thinking again. "Aren't you, like, omnipotent or something, you tell me."

"You know I really would have wiped you from the face of the planet, but I'm trying to be nice." She put a hand on her hip. "Why are you so uncooperative?"

I took a deep breath before answering this time, having recalled Matt's smiting. I still needed to buy myself time, so I started asking less inflammatory questions. "So, um, I was wondering... do you always wear that outfit? Don't get me wrong – it's beautiful," I said. "But do you, like, shower? Or do you even sweat? Or pee and poop? Like, how functional is that body? And what's that stuff falling out of your hair, magic?" These were all questions that I genuinely wanted answers to. And the more questions I asked, the more they cropped up in my mind. But God wouldn't indulge me. She knew what I was doing.

"Being weird and sneaky won't work out for you," she threatened. "I'm just going to say now that it didn't really work out for Lucif –"

Theo was able to catch her off guard. He burst through the archway, Hertzinator in hand. She turned just as he mashed a small black button along the side of the machine. It emitted six discordant tones – two inaudible and four very audible. We clapped our hands to our ears. God's eyes narrowed at me. She raised a quickly disintegrating finger. "Oh, you tricky little –"

Then I was suddenly being sucked backward through a very dark and tight tunnel. The air had become extremely dry and thin, making it impossible to breathe. I squeezed my eyes shut and pressed my hands tighter against my ears. Maybe this was some sort of side effect of the Hertzinator, I thought.

I fell out of the tunnel and hit the ground so hard it knocked a puff of air from my lungs. I scrambled upright. My head ached terribly and a sudden coughing fit only made it worse. I unzipped my jumper and pulled out the unmarked book. That, at least, allowed me to breathe more easily.

After a minute or two, I was able to make sense of my surroundings. I blinked and blinked, but I wasn't sure if my eyes were working correctly. Gloom hugged everything there was to see, giving the world a dull appearance. There was grass under my feet, but it was the blandest green you could imagine. I was in a park, perhaps abandoned. There was a dilapidated playscape surrounded by wooden benches that were broken and splintered. Garbage floated by on a mucky, hot breeze. I could see the city looming overhead, but the skyscrapers didn't reflect the sunlight as they usually did. I squinted my eyes, searching overhead, but I couldn't actually locate the sun. It had to have been somewhere. I didn't know why, but at that moment it was important I find it. I searched, walking here and there, thinking maybe it was hidden behind a tree. I walked in a small circle, then a larger one. But it was nowhere to be found.

Finally, I gave up. I unstuck a burger wrapper from the good end of a bench and sat down, still nursing my chest. Then I took a deep breath, forcing myself to reflect on what just happened. I was in the Hall of Records. Theo and Conner showed up. We used the Hertzinator.

Then I shot straight out of my seat.

"Oh my God, she sent me to hell."

Chapter Five:
I'll Take a Black Coffee. Lukewarm.

My eyes darted, finding confirmation in all the dreadful and sickly sights. It was all coming into perspective now. I cursed loudly at the sky. But I knew I was only being melodramatic. Of course she would send me to hell, especially with the 'thou shall not steal' thing. That one was laid out pretty clearly in the ten commandments.

With as much indignation as I could muster, I tucked the stupid book back into my jumpsuit. Then I searched the park, hopelessly unsure of what I was looking for. I guess something to distract me from the panic pressing in on my chest. My heart raced at the thought of what could possibly be awaiting me in this sad, ghostly world. I clenched my fists, determined that I wouldn't be staying if I could help it. After all, God sent me here. I was fairly certain she could bring me back.

And with little to no idea of how I could get her to do such a thing, I raced up the sidewalk toward town. It didn't take long to find a familiar path once I crossed Eleventh street. There, I could walk a bit slower and blend in. But I wasn't sure if I would be able to blend in enough. The world looked just like mine, but there was no *life* in it. There were people. I could see them in the distance, crossing the street and driving their cars along the overpass. But they were all so *lifeless*. A woman jogged slowly past me wearing headphones. I gave her a small nod, then had to jump out of her way. She never even pulled her gaunt eyes from the pavement to notice me. Further down the street, people were carrying on about their business, but it was in the dullest way possible. And they were rude, but that wasn't even vigorous. A man wearing a blazer and slacks spit along the sidewalk right where a much older man in a fedora was about to walk. The man in the fedora barely paused to mumble, "You jackass…" The man in the blazer kept walking as well. He threw up his hands lazily. "Well, whadduyu do?" he asked half–heartedly. Then they continued shuffling up the street.

I didn't know where I was going, but nonetheless my feet moved. I turned right on Durgen Street. There was a coffee shop there, I remembered. I could at least sit undisturbed while I racked my brain for what to do next.

The further I walked, the more certain I was that this was hell. I passed Joe's Alterations but at a second glance realized it had become Joe's Disfigurations. Further down, The Wine Barrel became the Vinegar Barrel, with a sidewalk easel that advertised sixty–two unique vinegar blends. The smell emanating through the front doors made my stomach lurch. Then, at last, I found the coffee shop and was surprised to see that very little had changed – until I glanced at the menu to find that they only served one thing: black coffee, lukewarm.

I wound my way through the stale crowd to find a seat in the corner of the little boutique. My chair made a scraping sound against the wooden floor, but nobody cared enough to look up, not even indignantly. I took a deep breath, then pulled out my walkie-talkie. I clicked the button, and even though it didn't chirp, I spoke into it. "Alex to Theo," I said. I knew nobody could hear me. But I tried again. "Alex to Valencio." I waited a minute. "Alex to *anybody*."

It didn't surprise me that the walkie-talkie didn't work, so I wasn't too disheartened. Of course, nobody's invented walkie-talkies that can span from Earth to Hell. That would be an amazing feat, I thought.

I took my time thinking of other plans, which mostly centered on praying to God again. I couldn't imagine how I might appeal to her after what we'd just done, though. Maybe if I confessed myself a sinner and asked for forgiveness, she would have mercy on me. That's probably how that works.

I mulled through my very limited arsenal of ideas as slowly as I could. If I exhausted them all too soon I knew I would start to panic, and my chest was still very tight - separately from the fall. I glanced leisurely around the coffee shop, but I was far from calm. My hand had already gone to work, twiddling with the lock of hair at my temple. I considered if hell coffee was safe to drink. Then I noticed someone watching me.

Across the boutique, sitting at a small table was a woman, with deep chocolate eyes and wavy brown hair. We locked gazes for a microsecond before I looked away. But I could tell she *saw* me. I pretended to be interested in my utility belt, then looked at the menu until it didn't make sense for me to do so any longer. There was only one thing written on the entire pamphlet. Why even have one?

After a painfully awkward minute I tried to sneak another look at her. She was still watching me. I pretended to look past her, at some passers-by on the sidewalk just outside the door. My eyes couldn't help but gravitate back to her, though. There was something very different about her. I realized it after another look. Her sandy beige skin was vivid. I looked down at my own arms. They were a healthy sun-kissed bronze – clearly different from the almost grayish hues of everyone else in this world. Hers wasn't exactly like mine though. It was luminescent. I could almost see it through her plain maroon button–up. Could she have been God in disguise, following me to watch my suffering? I didn't think so.

I figured I'd have to start thinking hard now. I was in hell, with no allies, and a Peeping Tom was staring me down right in public. I thought about approaching her. Maybe she was just hitting on me? But that didn't explain her luminous skin, and why she was so… alert… watchful? A thought struck me – maybe that was the Debbie Downer that God mentioned, and she recognized that I was also sent here by God – but I quickly dismissed that. Someone named Debbie Downer would never have such an alluring demeanor.

I didn't have enough time to think before she stood up, scraping her chair softly along the floor. I prepared to fight, clenching my fists, just in case that's what she wanted to do. But then she grabbed her coffee and walked right out of the door. I leaned back in my chair, exhaling slowly. "Thank you, Jesus," I breathed. Then I added. "Not you, God. You really, really suck right now."

Hours later, after I'd assessed my situation from every possible angle, I left the shop with three conclusions. One, I was in possession of – hopefully – the Book of Life, and still needed to get it back to Valencio and Matt. Two, this world mirrored mine, and there had to be some undiscovered advantages to that. And three, I wasn't going to achieve anything by sitting at a coffee shop all day.

So I set out to my apartment, with the assumption that it would still be mine, and that if there was a hell-me, she would be helpful in some way.

I wasn't even able to get as far as Doge Street, though, before the woman returned. This time she had a friend – a man, tall and fit. His raven–black hair fell over his contoured face in short sloping waves and his skin luminesced, just as hers did. As I crossed over Doge to get to Herring Street, they were just up ahead, at the intersection. I had an eerie feeling that they knew where I was going.

The two of them watched me as I doubled back. I walked quickly down the row of duplexes on Doge and cut through an alley, moving east through a series of bushes and the train track. After that I crossed over, further down Herring Street, but kept to the bushes. But when I came out on Briar Avenue they were there again, calmly waiting at the bus stop. I couldn't believe it. I dove back into the thicket that I'd crawled out of, panting. I watched them as they watched me. The woman gazed down the street, and though I was sure that all of me was well hidden, I knew that she could still see me. The man had both hands leisurely in his pockets. He looked as though he was simply waiting for the bus to arrive. But I knew they wouldn't be going anywhere.

Fighting down my fully matured panic, I watched them until kneeling in the bushes became uncomfortable. I shifted on my haunches, and when I looked up again, the man was checking his watch. Then he said something to the woman and disappeared. Right into thin air. I only had time to gasp before he appeared right behind me.

"Okay, stop wasting everyone's time," he said. I stumbled backward onto the street but was able to catch myself before falling to the ground. Then I was frozen to the spot. The woman appeared next to me with a sucking sound, and I shrieked. "This is why you can't just pop up on people," she argued with him. "It freaks them out." I took this opportunity to run.

I dashed down Briar Avenue but sure enough, just ahead was the man and woman again. I skidded to a halt. "You'll only exhaust yourself like this," he said lazily.

"Look," said the woman. "We weren't trying to scare you." She rang her hands together. "We just didn't want you to –" Then she stopped suddenly and smacked her lips. "Put your hands down," she snapped. She slapped down my outstretched arms and I realized I had been in a defensive position the whole time. "Stop looking like that!"

I exhaled, wondering if I had been holding my breath the entire time, too. I relaxed my shoulders. "Okay," I said slowly. "I'm listening."

The woman flung her hair over her shoulder and began again. She spoke slowly. "This is Shax. I'm Danel," she said. "We want to help you. It's just that the last person we approached was all freaked out and ran off the edge of a cliff, so we were trying to be careful."

"You ran someone off the edge of a cliff?" I yelled.

"Not my fault," said Danel. "She was all depressed and weird."

"Wait," I said. "Was her name Debbie, by chance?"

Danel stopped short, putting a hand on her hip. "Actually, it was. How did you know that?"

"The point is," Shax interrupted, his voice low and sultry and very creepy, in my opinion. He also had an accent I couldn't place. Not because he was so mysterious, but because I was not well traveled at all. He took a gentle step closer, his piercing eyes watching mine. "We can help you, and you can help us." He winked at me.

I barked a laugh. "You can save whatever all of *that* was."

He crossed his arms. "All of what?" he asked defensively.

I simply raised my eyebrows, because I knew that he knew what I was talking about. Then I shook my head. "So, who exactly are you and what is it you want from me?" I asked.

"We live here," said Danel. "And we want what you want."

"You live here?" I eyed them doubtfully.

Danel nodded softly. "Yes."

"You don't look like you live here."

"We absolutely live here," Danel said. "But that has nothing to do with –"

"Wait," I said. "So if this is hell and you live here, does that make you…" My eyes grew wide. But I didn't bother strumming up another panic. How could I be surprised by anything anymore? Besides, I knew I couldn't outrun them.

Shax threw his hands up. "Demons, yes," he said in a fluster. He curled his fingers into claws and feigned a growl. "We're demons, aaarghhh!"

"Stop that." Danel grabbed his hands and forced them to his sides. "You're giving us a bad name."

"A bad name?" I scoffed.

She smacked her lips. "A *stupid* name."

"Okay, for real," said Shax. "We're demons, you're human. God has taken over your realm, and everyone wants her gone, including us."

"How do you know that?" I asked. "And what does that have to do with you?"

Danel crossed her arms. "Because it's affecting us, too. God's essence is seeping down here," she said. She gestured toward a nearby store with a nod. "Just look at it."

I followed her gaze. She was looking at a taxidermy shop. It was vaguely familiar – or at least, I had passed it a few times on my way out from my apartment. The display window in the front typically housed beavers and racoons, dressed in tacky little suits and dresses. This world's taxidermy shop housed what I prayed was a mannequin, wearing a red and blue oversized onesie and a colorful wig. His face was painted white with highlighter-yellow eyebrows smacked across the forehead, and he clutched a small vinyl balloon on a string.

"That's horrific," I said.

"I disagree," said Danel. "He looks way too happy."

Shax shook his head slowly. His jaw, strong and stubbly with a hint of a beard, jutted indignantly. He sighed. "There goes the neighborhood."

"So, you're saying hell isn't as gloomy anymore since God's on Earth."

"Yes," said Shax. He rubbed his chin. "It truly lacks the… How do I say it?"

"Quality of evil you're accustomed to?" I helped.

"Yes," he agreed. "But it's more than that." He put his hands back in his pocket, peering over the sad trees now. "The natural order of things has been completely uprooted… Everything we're used to…" Then he glared longingly at me. "Demons haven't been able to *eat* since God arrived on Earth." He strode over to me. "We're starving down here. It has become hell for *us* now."

I took a step back, and though I suspected the answer, I had to ask. "And what exactly is it that you eat?"

"Humans, of course," Danel said pointedly. "Don't be so naive."

"But we literally can't eat you," Shax assured me. He grabbed my arm and gave it a deep sniff. "I'm literally trying as hard as I can right now."

I yanked it away sharply. "Stop that," I said. "That's just… *weird.*"

"Seriously though," said Danel. "Your ass would be grass under normal circumstances."

"None of this makes sense," I scoffed. I scanned Briar Avenue. "I saw plenty of butchers and –" I gestured toward what was ordinarily Zuri's Daycare. The sign on the front of it read, '*Zuri's Daymare.*' "– and… and…"

"Oh, we can still do a little torturing and maiming here and there," said Shax.

"General discombobulation," added Danel. "Spook you. Cause mental and emotional damage."

"Ruin your credit score," Shax added. "Stuff like that."

Danel sighed. "But even all that fun can't distract us from the fact that we've been starving to death," she said softly. "And death doesn't come for demons."

I crossed my arms, resting my chin on a closed fist. I had to think. A hot breeze blew between the trees, making my hair poke me right in the eyes. I fought the loose strands out of my face. Then I spoke slowly. "So you want to help me get rid of God, so that you can go back to eating humans?"

Shax stretched his arms out. "It's only the natural order of things."

"But you guys are demons," I said. "God's pretty pissed with me already. I don't know if I can go as far as working with you."

The woman scoffed. "What's she going to do, send you to hell?"

"True," I said bitterly. I sighed. "What do you have in mind then?"

Danel nodded at Shax, who smiled.

Though there was no sun to set, the city had begun to darken. "We'll come and find you in the morning," he said. Then there came a sucking sound and for an instant I could only see a glimmer of their silhouettes – their eyes gleaming for a lingering moment – and they were gone.

I turned on the spot, but they had sure enough left. A man in a pair of shorts and a muscle shirt pushed past me blandly.

A woman drinking a chunky smoothie strolled along the other side of the street. Nobody seemed to notice what happened.

I took a determined breath and walked briskly up the sidewalk toward my apartment. I passed the burrito shop that lives on the edge of my neighborhood – unfortunately named Burritorria in the world of the living; its name remained unchanged in this world – then I doubled back. My stomach grumbled. I would have to take a chance on a hell carne asada.

The establishment was packed, but not busy. Nobody moved too quickly and there wasn't the usual buzz that fresh fajitas usually inspired in my neighborhood. I went through the line quickly, building the simplest burrito possible, then got nervous as I reached the cash register. "Um, I think I left my wallet at home," I said to the pale cashier. I was ready to negotiate, but I wouldn't have to. She simply held out the wrapped burrito, her face expressionless. Uncertain, I took it from her hands. "I guess I'll just go then…" I said. I gave a little nod. The cashier mumbled feebly. "Have a … great…"

I strode further into the neighborhood, burrito in hand. Then I rounded the entrance to my apartment complex. It was eerily identical to the real thing. Except the cannas dotting the garden wall were terribly droopy, making the place look miserable against the already dark and gloomy sky.

My stomach suddenly churned. I knew it wasn't entirely from hunger. I was getting nervous. The thought of seeing a hell version of me, tepid and dry like the rest of this place, made me feel weird. Even though I failed psychology in college twice, I was fairly certain that I would be traumatized by the encounter. I plopped myself up onto the garden wall.

Hell-me would have to wait until I've eaten, I decided. No sense in being emotionally scarred on an empty stomach.

I unwrapped the burrito and shoveled a huge bite into my mouth. Then, I couldn't spit it out fast enough. I gagged. The entire thing turned into ash – crumbling and dry. So dry that it wicked the moisture from my tongue. I scraped as much of it as I could with my finger, but that seemed to only make it worse. A taste of burnt plastic lingered in my mouth.

I threw the burrito over the garden wall and cursed. Someone on the far side of the courtyard looked up, but wasn't interested enough to investigate. I dusted the ashy crumbs from the front of my jumpsuit and proceeded grumpily to my apartment.

When I got to the door I paused. My stomach churned again, but I was too annoyed to nurse it. I pressed my ear to the cold wood. It was silent. My hand reached for the knob. I gave it a quick turn, and the door unlatched. Of course hell-me would leave it unlocked. I swung the door open and, to my relief, no one was home.

The apartment was identical to my real one, down to the pile of laundry that lived in the hall right outside the utility room. I inspected the place, touching my jewelry box, my favorite lamp, my game console – each of them possessing the subtle dreariness of the world I was in. As I examined the ghost of my apartment, a seedling of a thought forced its way into my mind. I tried to ignore it; to not let it bloom. But there was no way I could look away from common sense, at least not forever. I wouldn't have to worry about the hell version of me showing up because *I* was the hell version of me. I instinctively looked at my own hands. Had they already lost a bit of their sheen? Would I wake up in this place one day just as dull and thoughtless as everyone else, bound to my own self-imposed regiment of torture? Oh my god, would I be expected to show up to work?

My heart squeezed. It was so tight that it got heavy and weighed down into my stomach. I was angry with God for sending me to this mindless place. But not a fiery, piercing kind of angry. This anger was flat and simmering. And I wasn't just angry for what had become of me in particular, because even if she hadn't sent me to hell, she ruined life on Earth anyway.

I thought about Jorge and Marla from the lake. What would they accomplish if they were left to live a normal life? Would they have a chance at love? I mean, sure Marla could be married already and Jorge could be too focused on his career to get involved, but the point is – regular people won't have a chance to live out their lives. They won't be able to make their mistakes, or create beautiful art, or grow into old people that complain about their grandchildren's trashy music. The world won't have a chance to create new technologies or solve any of its social problems; to culminate into what it might ultimately become. It was all so wasteful.

I unzipped the unmarked book from my top and rifled through its pages. There wasn't a single mark in it – helpful or otherwise. I threw it on the nightstand then curled up on my couch, pulling a throw blanket right up to my chin. The wool scratched at my neck, but I didn't care. I squeezed my eyes tight to keep tears from spilling out. There was screaming in the distance and somewhere in the neighborhood a fire truck's siren was wailing half–heartedly.

My anger didn't require much wrestling with. I was too hungry and tired to do so anyway. It turned to desperation all on its own, and quickly, too. "God," I whispered. My voice cracked. I cleared my throat. "If you can hear me, I'm sorry. If you send me back home, I'll give you your book back." My eyes darted around the room. They landed on the book. If she wanted it she could probably come and take it at any time. It was a stupid deal. But there was no sense in *not* trying.

Eventually I fell asleep, but it was a restless kind of sleep one can only expect from being in hell. My dreams were painted in the same dreariness. I was at my job, at the school. The hallways were dark and unsurprisingly creepy and, for some reason, there was a burrito in the middle of my path. I reached for it, then recoiled as it turned to ash. I turned. My mother was there, wearing a badge and holding a small megaphone. It was my principal's megaphone. She put it to her mouth. "You're not trained enough." Her voice blared into the hall. I slapped my hands to my ears, but I could still hear her words. "Not resourceful enough. Not organized enough. Not enough. Not enough!"

My eyelids slammed open. Sweat sealed the blanket to my face, but I was afraid if I peeled it off me right away, if I moved too quickly, I'd lose what few marbles I had left.

Of course, I knew I wouldn't escape hell without some form of psychological scarring. It was *hell* after all. And it had done an excellent job of curating the perfect ratio of both childhood and adulthood traumas in its recipe of despair.

I'd have to unpack all that later, though, because someone was in the room with me. I could hear quiet shuffling. My body suddenly felt like jelly. I peeled the blanket back slowly, and my dread was slightly relieved. The gloomy sunless daytime was back, and so were the demons.

"I'll never understand how humans can eat this crap," said Danel. She rummaged through the fridge for a moment before pulling out a jar of mayonnaise. "Look at this," she said. "Absolutely gross."

Shax, who was busy smelling handfuls of dirty laundry, barely looked over his shoulder before saying, "They're the worst." Then he dropped the clothes, having realized I was awake. "Good morning," he said in his sultry voice. He sauntered toward my couch and sat, leaning in close to me.

I pulled my blanket tighter around my chest. "You know that does nothing for me, right?" I said.

Shax sighed. "Yesterday you were tired… frightened. I thought maybe we could have a fresh start."

"Words of a predator," I sneered. Shax sat back, crossing his arms indignantly. His bristly eyebrows and perfectly sculpted cheekbones worked together as he pouted. I blurted without thinking. "And why *are* you guys so… good looking?" I shifted in my seat to find Danel, who had been scooping coffee grounds from a can into her mouth. "Is that some sort of trick to lure people to you or something?"

Danel rolled the coffee grounds around in her mouth before spitting them out into the sink. Then she licked her lips. "Well," she said thoughtfully before sitting on the countertop. "If you look at it that way, yes. We represent either everything you want or everything you want to be."

Shax added, "That's why we're so tempting."

I scoffed. "*You're* not tempting," I said.

Danel suddenly cackled. She clapped her hands. "I'll tell you who else isn't tempting," she said to Shax. "Angels." She turned to me enthusiastically. "Have you ever seen an angel before?"

I shook my head.

"I ran into Azrael a few weeks ago," Danel said. She chuckled. "I don't know what God was thinking. I mean… Azrael does *not* get laid. I just know it."

The demons spent a few moments laughing, probably harder than necessary. I waited for an explanation. Shax sniffled, wiping a tear from his eye. "He's got probably a billion eyes," he explained. His laughter faded. Then he sighed before adding, "and some of them are not well placed."

"Wow," I said. But I wouldn't allow myself to be surprised. Angels and demons were basically mortal enemies, after all. "Okay, moving right along," I said. I got up and folded my blanket over the back of the couch. "You said you could help me yesterday. Help me how?"

Shax stood up too, placing himself right next to Danel in the kitchen. "We can take you back to Earth," he said. "That would actually be very easy."

My stomach seemed to float into my chest. "Okay," I said happily. A grin crawled across my face. But it quickly faded. I wasn't very religious, but I knew a demon wouldn't give you exactly what you wanted unless you were willing to pay a steep price. "But what will I have to do for you?" I asked.

"Well, that's the cool part," said Danel. She pulled an old wooden box from thin air. It was no bigger than a shoe box, with a delicate inlay of golden leaves snaked along the sides and top of it. There was a small golden bowl at the center of the lid, which looked like it could've served as a handle. "All you need to do is open the box," she said.

"And what will that do?" I asked. Danel slunk off the countertop and placed the box in my hands. It was heavy and surprisingly warm. And I wasn't sure if it was my own pulse I was feeling in my hands, or if the box had a life of its own.

"It'll send God back," Shax said simply.

"And the world will go back to how it was?" I asked.

"Ours, yes," Danel smiled, the corners of her beautiful eyes pinched. "And so will yours."

I rubbed my hands across the golden inlays. "But *how* will it send her back," I asked. "I mean, it's not gonna hurt her or anything, right?"

"Not at all," said Shax. "Frankly I don't think God can be hurt."

I wasn't satisfied, though. The demons weren't dodging my questions, but they weren't exactly answering them. I tried again. "Okay, so what's in the box?" I asked. "And how will it send her back?" Is it a repellent of some sort, or is it a portal?"

Shax nodded his understanding. "The experiment that brought God to Earth biologically modified all of humanity," he said. He spoke briskly, but his eyes were kind. "Most of the planet is overloaded with an imbalance of God's essence. There is an inoculation in the box which will spread around the globe, correcting humanity's ability to interface with God."

My mouth had gone dry. "It'll spread around the globe?"

Danel smiled again. "Everyone is affected," she said. "The entire planet needs to be corrected."

"So, what do you mean by *correcting*?" I asked.

"It'll dial back the amount of God essence each individual can hold in their physical bodies, like before she arrived on Earth," she said. "That'll make it more difficult for her. She wouldn't be able to stick around in that kind of environment."

"So, she'll leave," I said.

"Exactly." Danel clapped her hands. "So, once we take you back, you'll need to open the box immediately."

"Why immediately?" I asked.

"Well," said Danel. But Shax jumped in.

"The longer you wait," he said. "The stronger God will get."

Danel agreed. "Right," she said. "And the stronger she gets, the harder it is for the inoculation to work."

I nodded. "Okay," I said. "And how is this going to help you?"

"Your world and our world are connected," said Shax. "Once yours is fixed, ours will be too."

"How do I open the box?" I asked.

"You'll just pour some of your blood into the chalice," said Danel.

"What?"

Danel pointed at the small bowl. "It must be *your* blood," she said. Then she extended a hand. "Do we have a deal?"

I stared at her hand for a moment. I wasn't an idiot. Demons cropping up with solutions to both my problems at once sent the alarms in my head blaring. But my stomach started gurgling in a way that I had never heard before. I fanned myself with the hand she was expecting me to shake with. I was suddenly dizzy, and I might have been making it up, but my brain was a bit fuzzy, too. Could it be low blood sugar? I should know that, being a biology teacher and all. It was probably low blood sugar. Whatever the case, there was real danger that I would starve to death on my own. I wondered if they waited until I was this desperate on purpose.

Shax watched me have my mini panic. His face was soft and patient. It made me feel weird that he didn't offer a more soothing gesture. I probably preferred he didn't anyway, but he definitely should have tried. I looked around the sad apartment and, with very little choice left, I hiked the box under my arm and took Danel's hand. "Deal."

"Alright," said Shax brightly. He extended an arm for me to grasp. "Let's get you home."

"Wait," I said suddenly. I ran to the end table and grabbed the unmarked book. I shoved it back in its place along the front of my jumpsuit and shifted the box back under my arm. "Okay," I said, linking my arm around Shax's. His eyes fell down my front, and I couldn't tell if he was trying to hit on me again or if he was curious about the book. "Let's go," I urged.

And with a now familiar sucking sound, we were gone.

Chapter Six:
Supernatural Loan Sharks & Other Hauntings

I experienced the sensation of going through a very dark tunnel again, but this time I was traveling forward. It didn't feel as natural as falling back. My stomach was uneasy, but I didn't have to worry about barfing because there was nothing in it to barf up. My legs wobbled and my ears popped as we came to a sudden stop on solid ground.

"Mind your step," said Shax. I grasped his arm tighter than I wanted to keep from falling to the floor. We surveyed the place – desks, chairs, cabinets filled with glass contraptions, computers, all gleaming violently against my eyeballs. I almost had to squint in order to see properly. I ran my hand over a nearby desk. It was cold and smooth and vibrantly metallic. I smiled. We were in one of the storage rooms in the laboratory.

Shax's gagging interrupted my moment of triumph. "Oh," he cried. "I can barely breathe up here anymore." He grabbed his chest, making an exaggerated choking sound. "It's disgusting," he complained loudly. "Just dreadful!"

A moment later the door opened with a soft hum. We both jumped, then I was grateful to see Valencio striding up the walkway, a look of perplexity on his face.

"Alex." He grabbed me by the shoulders, turning me this way and that to examine me. "We thought you were dead." Valencio shook his head, his face pinched at the bridge of his nose. He noticed Shax. "And who have you brought with you?" he asked, stooping to get a good look, but the demon was doubled over now.

I was about to explain that it was Shax who actually brought me back, but he raised a finger, distress on his face, and said, "I was just leaving." He gestured toward the box under my arm and said, "You *must* remember your end." And before I could make any introductions at all or half-heartedly confirm that I would be following through with opening the thing, he was gone.

Once we were back in Valencio's office, where the crew had gathered in my absence, I had a chance to explain everything that had happened to me – including my deal with the demons.

Conner, who was sitting at an empty desk, held the ancient box up to a nearby lamp. The fluorescent light hit the box sharply, and the golden inlays gleamed seductively under the harshness of it. "So, let me get this straight – you're gonna do a demonic blood ritual to get rid of God," said Conner.

"I don't know," I said. I locked my fingers together. "It would make sense, right?"

"That Evil would drive out Good?" asked Matt. He held a hand out for Conner, who gave the box up promptly. "How can you trust a demon at his word, though?"

"They said that they just wanted their world to go back to normal, too," I explained to Matt. It sounded naive coming out of my mouth. I didn't know if I was trying to convince him or myself. "And you've never heard about this kind of box in the bible?"

"The only box that comes to mind is the Ark of the Covenant," he said. He hiked himself up on the desk Conner was occupying. "But this definitely isn't it."

Valencio took a turn with the box, rolling it over in his hands. But he wasn't thinking about the box at all. "Was that the first encounter you've had with this demon… *Shax*," he asked. Deep concern was twisted into his face as he looked at me.

"I've never seen him before yesterday," I assured him. "And the way he reacted to being here, hopefully we won't ever have to see him again."

"Oh," said Valencio. He paced the room slowly, patting the box with his palm. "He seemed dreadfully familiar to me."

For a while we were quiet, each of us thinking about what had transpired so far. Then I jumped in my seat. "I almost forgot," I said. "Did anyone else notice how God acted when I asked her where the template was?"

"Yeah," said Conner. He nodded slowly. "It seemed like she didn't even know what you were talking about."

I nodded. "She seemed genuinely confused," I said.

"But that could've been to throw us off," Conner suggested. "She is God, after all. Wouldn't she be smart enough not to tip her own hand?"

"At any rate," said Valencio. "We must continue our search in earnest. We'll weigh the risk of opening the box, but the template should continue to be our top priority."

Theo, who had been quiet the whole time, stood up and took the box from Valencio. "Great," he said. "I'll analyze the contents of it before anyone does any kind of… *ritual.*" He put it to his ear, then smelled it. A smile crept across his face. "We'll start with an atomic absorption spectroscopy," he said. Then he bounded out of the room.

"And the Book of Life," said Matt. He picked it up from Valencio's desk and flipped through the pages once more. There was still nothing to be read. He commanded it to open in his weird robot voice, using as many priestly phrases as he could — like, 'servant of the most high' and 'we prostrate ourselves to you' — but the book remained uncooperative and wordless. He begrudgingly dropped it into my hands.

I rubbed the top of it, allowing my fingers to dance across the thin grooves in the leather. "I wonder if only God can read it."

Conner sighed. "We have a book we can't read and a box we don't trust," he said. Then he sat up suddenly; his hands squeezing the armrests on either side of him. For a second, I thought he was about to throw up, which was unfortunate because it had turned my attention back to the fact that I was literally starving to death. I grabbed my stomach as it gurgled angrily at me. How did I not remember to eat something? I actually do have a fun fact here — humans can live for about three weeks without food. Of course, there are all sorts of variables that make it more or less, like the person's health and environmental stressors. And, of course, it's only approximate because scientists can't ethically starve people to death in a controlled experiment. So, anyway, I knew I wouldn't actually die, being well-within three weeks, so I decided to put it off a little while longer. But I digress.

Conner had begun raising himself out of his seat so slowly I thought maybe he was having some sort of a heart attack. Or he was being possessed. Hell, anything was possible, apparently. I watched on intently as he narrowed his eyes, and then it became apparent that he was birthing an idea. He stood, neurons firing off. "We needed the book to find the template, right?"

I nodded. So did Matt.

Conner raised an eyebrow. "Maybe we don't need to find where the template is right *now*," he suggested. "Maybe it doesn't matter that we can't read the book."

To my relief, nobody else seemed to be following Conner's train of thought either. Matt gestured with his hands for more, encouraging Conner to go on. Conner continued. "Remember when God turned back time?"

"Yeah," I said. "There was too much going on at once."

Conner nodded slowly. "She moved us backward, but we remembered everything. We knew what would come next because it already happened." We took turns eyeing Conner and then each other. He gestured at Valencio. "We know exactly where the template was the day of the experiment, right?"

I blinked dumbly, trying to follow. "It was at CERN the day of the experiment," I said. "But how is that helpful?"

Conner's forehead furrowed. He snapped his fingers in an attempt to jumpstart his brain again. Valencio appeared to know what he was thinking, but he didn't help. Which was okay, because Conner finally remembered the words he was searching for. "Tachyonic displacement," he said simply. "We could stop the experiment from happening altogether, if we do it right."

This prompted Valencio to walk wordlessly across the room and sit at his desk. He took a contrived breath, his eyes darting. Then when he spoke, it was as if he was calculating each word. "Our access is almost as limited as my level of confidence in operating the technology," he said. "That would be a very last resort." He crossed his arms. "I'd like to focus on the book for now."

"Wait," I said.

Matt screwed his face up. "Tachyonic displacement?"

Conner shifted his weight. "It's time travel," he said.

"Woah," I laughed. "You weren't gonna tell us about the time machine?" I turned in a circle, then quickly realized there were no windows in the room since we were underground. "Is it parked around back? I gotta see it —"

Valencio interjected. "It's just as dangerous as the experiment we're trying to correct," he said. "And not to mention, there are rigid regulations in place regarding the manufacture and use of temporal vehicles."

"But this facility was authorized to build one," said Conner.

Valencio reached into the front pocket of his lab coat and pulled out a thin pair of glasses, which he unfolded and placed on his face. Then he unlocked his computer. "It would seem your uncle has told you too much," he said nonchalantly. He typed a few commands into a program and then turned to us. "It would behoove us all to keep that information private indefinitely."

Matt nodded. So did I. Valencio gazed calmly at Conner. "With our lack of experience, a potential consequence of temporal travel is total gravitational collapse of the planet and surrounding region of space," he said. "I'd feel more comfortable performing a heart transplant than calculating the quantum perturbations necessary to arrive at our desired destination."

Conner nodded. "Okay," he said. "Dangerous, but it's an option, right?"

Valencio gave the slightest nod. Matt and I looked at each other. Matt's eyes said, 'Not it.'

"On the note of the book," said Valencio. He projected an image into the room from his computer. It looked similar to an incubator you'd see at a hospital nursery, holes along the side and all. He gestured toward me. "If your theory is correct —" he said "— that only God can read it, I believe we can trick the book into thinking we're God." He typed fervently for a while as the three of us looked on. Then he continued. "The 'Little Bang' we experienced at her arrival gave us all of the materials we need to disguise ourselves."

He used his fingers to toggle a series of switches on the display, which animated the simulation. As a gaseous compound entered the chamber, a couple strings of complex calculations that I didn't bother to try and understand appeared alongside the image. One of them glowed green, the other glowed red. "Of course, I'll have to work on the exact mixture of exotic matter in order to create an exact match," said Valencio. "But I think that under the right environmental conditions, the book may allow us to command it."

I wasn't sure if I understood how it would work, but at least I could hold off on opening the box until we'd exhausted the idea. And I was confident Valencio would give it a good run, too, being as he just created all of those complex calculations in five minutes. I could only imagine what he could do with a cup of coffee and an afternoon. I nodded at Valencio. "Okay," I said confidently.

And with that, Valencio took the book and excused himself. Matt, Conner, and I spent the afternoon together, catching up on the minor details of hell, until there was nothing left to talk about. Then we all went our separate ways for the evening. And just like that, I was left to take myself back home.

I don't remember the drive, or even what I ate for dinner. I do know I ate *something*. It was actually a mish-mash of all the somethings I could find in the refrigerator. I had eaten enough of it to be satisfied, then I dropped myself into my bed.

But sleep didn't come easy. Maybe it was because I didn't shower before crawling into the sheets. My mama always said an unwashed tail don't make for good sleep. I wasn't about to get back out of bed, though – not even to wash up. I pulled the sheets stubbornly right up to my chin, then I punched the pillow a bit. There was a dull ache threatening its way into my stomach. I ignored it. I rolled to my side, my eyes wandering the room. They moved from my chest of drawers to the abstract watercolor above it. The piece featured hues of blues and greens. I bought it from one of my student's parents at the winter bazaar at the school last Christmas. I noticed a stain on my lampshade at the table beside my bed. I didn't have enough energy to be upset about it. Especially since I bought the thing for thirteen dollars at the thrift store. Plus, why would I buy anything white? I'm not sophisticated enough for that kind of responsibility. My eyes found my bookshelf next, taking in all the vibrantly colored spines that lined it. I smiled. I was home. But my smile quickly faded.

The ache that was slowly boring into my stomach had settled in and started to open it up; to make a pit. My hand found my emotional support lock at my left temple. I squeezed my eyes shut, but it made it worse. I could see the hallway at Rockwell middle school, dark and dreary. I could see my mother's face. I could hear her voice through the megaphone. My heart beat against my eardrums. I wiped my sweaty palms along the underside of my pillow and drew my legs up into a fetal position.

Then I remembered something else: my fourteen-year-old self, lying in bed in this exact same position. There was an empty pit in my stomach that night as well. I had a sleepover, but Tara, my best friend, didn't stay long enough to fall asleep. Tara and I had been friends for so long. We were comfortable with each other. We *understood* each other.

We had been huddled in my bed, watching YouTube videos on her phone. We laughed so hard at one with a fat cat, laying on its back and eating sardines from its owner's hand. The voiceover was on point, making it seem as though the cat were a king and his owner was the servant. After that video was over, I did something I'd never done before.

It happened automatically. And maybe it was because her laughter was ringing in my ears. It rolled around inside me, creating a heavy, magnetic current that threatened to spill from my chest. I lifted my head from her shoulder and, without even thinking, I kissed her. She kissed me back. Then there was electricity on my lips. It made my head buzz; made my brain go fuzzy. I wanted to stay there forever.

But it only lasted seconds. I didn't see my mom come in with two bowls of ice cream. I didn't hear her drop them to the floor in front of her. I only realized what was going on when she whipped me around; her eyes arresting me to the spot.

People say I have my mama's eyes. Brown, almond-shaped, and exactly twelve eyebrow hairs plastered on top. She arched hers to give them the appearance of being shapely, or at the very least more obedient than they actually were. I left mine wild, sparse as they were. Other than that, they were exact. But I didn't see myself in her eyes that day. I saw disgust and anger and hate.

I cringed, pulling my pillow right over my head, hoping to squeeze the memory out. I forced myself to think about anything else. Unfortunately, the first thing that came to mind was that hell burrito. That didn't inspire any uplifting feelings at all. I looked at my hands and appreciated their brownness.

It was only hours ago that I was fading, sinking into my place in hell. Bland. Not dead. *Unalive.* I started to worry. Had hell broken me? Found a way to follow me here?

I rolled to the other side of my bed, as if that would prevent the thoughts from finding me. But they were inside of me, floating up from the pit in my stomach. I shooed away all of the questions I didn't want to ask myself; that I didn't want answers to.

¤ ¤ ¤ ¤ ¤ ¤ ¤

I spent the next few days trying to follow my usual routine – visiting the lake, taking care of my neighbors and checking in at the lab – but I couldn't shake this new sense of unease; I was, in fact, growing more anxious by the day. I even called my great aunt from Valencio's phone every once in a while to check in on my parents, but it was clearly redundant. I knew there'd be nothing to report until we finally got rid of God.

And just when I thought my angst couldn't get any worse, I had an unexpected visit. It happened while I was on my kayak. I had just finished navigating through an illusory set of rapids, and was floating peacefully under a bridge when a voice made me nearly flip over. It said, "You haven't fulfilled your end of the bargain."

"Damn it, Shax!" I yelled, bracing the sides of the kayak to stop it wobbling. He sat on the other end, looking very out of place with his silk button up and black slacks. He adjusted a cuff link in a very grossly cliché kind of way, unconcerned about falling into the water.

"We've been very patient," said Shax. He smiled coolly, but I could tell he wasn't happy. I wasn't sure if it was because of me or because of the environment, though. His skin was noticeably less luminous, and his face looked just a bit chalky. "What are you waiting for?"

I wasn't sure how to answer. Clearly, I'd lie. But what could be convincing enough? My brain flipped through the encyclopedia of lies told to me by students trying to get out of Friday assessments. Diarrhea. Head injury. My cousin's dog is having a quinceañera. Bobby Terrance gave me a wedgie in the hall now I'm too embarrassed to stay here. Okay none of these would apply in this situation. I opened my mouth and hoped for the best. "I'm… having lady issues," I said. He grimaced. Good. I continued. "You know, hell really did a number my constitution. My blood pressure's been out of whack and I'm hardly able to eat nowadays. I'm just trying to get back on my feet before drawing any blood, you know?" I tried to keep a serious face, even though my soul wanted to squirm out of my skin and fall straight into the lake. "But I *am* going to open it," I assured him. And I felt like he could sense my fibulation so I added, "… I'm just about healed up, so any day now."

Shax studied me for a few uncomfortable moments, his jaw clenched so hard the muscles in his face bulged. "Be sure you do." He smiled faintly. "Soon. Remember, yours isn't the only world hanging in the balance." He raised an eyebrow. "We had a deal."

I nodded. "Soon," I agreed. And without another word, he was gone. The kayak rocked at his departure, forcing me to steady it again. And though I knew he was gone, I still glanced over the water. The rapids roared in the distance, but it was otherwise peaceful. I grabbed my paddle and made my way to shore as fast as I could.

▢ ▢ ▢ ▢ ▢ ▢ ▢

The weeks after my initial visit with Shax were downright straining. He or Danel would pop in about every six days, by my count, for short visits – urging me to open the box. And with each appearance, they were visibly more agitated in their own way. Danel's lips had become permanently pressed into a tight circle as she nosed through my things. Clearly, she was looking for the box, but for some reason wouldn't outright ask for it. I assumed she was still deciding if she wanted to take it back or not. Shax, on the other hand, was a bit more bearable since he stopped with all the flirty-flirty stuff. I was actually appreciative of that. But he did adopt a habit of sneering at me right before disappearing into thin air. I've never owed money to a loan shark, but I'm certain this was a very similar experience. I was literally being haunted by supernatural loan sharks.

I continued to stay diplomatic during these visits, assuring them that we were close to fixing everything, but it was becoming harder to justify such a long wait to starving demons. I wasn't sure what they would do to me once they grew tired of waiting, and I certainly didn't want to know, so I checked in at the lab more frequently than usual. It was nice to be involved in Matt's antics, or see how much we could stress out Conner, but I soon learned that hovering wouldn't make science happen any faster.

After several days of fruitless worrying, I decided to change my routine. A new hobby sounded like a promising way to pass the time, or at least make waiting less difficult. And with cooler weather coming in, I figured gardening would be a sensible activity to adopt. After all, you couldn't really mess up putting seeds in dirt. The hardest part would be remembering to water them, but being as I had literally nothing else to do, that didn't seem like a problem I'd encounter. Fun fact about gardening, by the way – dirt germs are good for you. Well, some are. Mycobacterium vaccae is a certain microbe in the soil that absorbs through human skin and promotes the release of serotonin in the body, which means gardening can literally fight depression.

But I digress. One windy afternoon I found a patch of soil in the courtyard that hadn't been occupied and dumped my materials along the walk. I sprawled them out, making sure I had everything I'd needed – seed packets, fertilizer, mulch, a hand shovel, a watering can, and strangely, just one glove. I put it on, then fumbled through the tote bag that I got from the supply store for the other one. It wasn't there. I stood up but didn't have to go very far because the glove was right behind me, underneath a fat and lazy cat. "Milus, you naughty thing," I teased, pulling the glove from underneath his butt. "Now get out of here!" I shooed him with my hands, but he didn't leave. Instead, he glared at me pompously. This wouldn't have been out of the ordinary except he opened his mouth and began to talk.

"I guess it's *not* personal," he said.

I bolted up, blinking at Milus. "Did you… Did you just…"

The cat scrunched up his fuzzy little snoot. "You think you can get rid of anyone who inconveniences you." His voice was familiar. I recognized it, but how the actual heck?

I stepped toward the cat. "*God?*"

Just then, Milus transformed in a most disturbing way. His face stretched out and his limbs elongated until he was no longer Milus. God stood in front of me, chuckling. I was mortified. "What did you do to my cat?" I yelled. I looked around her boots, hoping for a sign of him. I felt my lip quiver. "You killed Milus!"

"Oh, buck up!" She gave me a good pat on the back as if we were old buddies. "The dumb cat's alive," she said, pointing to the other side of the garden wall. "He's over there being an asshole, as usual." I looked to where she was pointing and – sure enough – my cat was laying atop a flattened row of lilies, batting at a large grasshopper that he'd cornered. I let out a whimper.

God stared at him for a moment, eyes narrowed. "You do know he's an asshole, right?" she glanced at me over her shoulder. "Even for cat standards… Look at him." Just then he tore off one of the grasshopper's legs, then allowed the insect to limp off. She raised her voice, as if the cat would care what she was saying. "You could at least eat it," she said to him. He whipped his tail contentedly; unashamed. "And he doesn't show you *any* affection at all," she added. "Why do you put up with him?"

I closed my eyes and pinched the bridge of my nose. "Because he's *mine*," I said. "And I've grown to love him, that's why."

"Wow, that's an interesting thought," God said, putting a finger to her chin. She smiled wryly. "The cat acts differently than one would expect, yet over time you still grow to *love* him…"

"I know what you're doing," I said. "The cat's not the same as you." I rolled my eyes. Then I stopped short as a, perhaps unreasonable, amount of anger suddenly welled in me. "And what's with you people, anyway?" I said. "You know you don't have to just suddenly pop up and scare the crap out of me, right? You can just knock on the front door, like normal people." I groped for words. "This is harassment," I said. "This is supernatural harassment. Stop haunting me!"

She held her hands up, surrendering to my childishness. "Wow," she said. "Are you finished?"

I didn't immediately answer. I drew in a grumpy breath, then glanced over the garden again. A bird flapped clumsily from underneath a bush and barely escaped Milus' claws.

I considered apologizing, but figured there was no need. If it wasn't for her I wouldn't be dodging demons and having my nerves frayed in the first place. She could have brought me back from hell when I asked nicely, or better yet – she didn't have to send me there at all. I settled on giving her a small nod. Then I committed to being as nice as I could for the rest of the visit, because as far as God went, I had a lot to answer to – particularly about why I stole her book – and I couldn't risk being sent to hell again. Not before sending her back to… *heaven*, I assume. Does God just sit in heaven, looking down on everyone all day long? I would have to ask her another time.

For now, I wouldn't miss an opportunity to try and convince her to leave on her own. I peeled the glove from my hand and hiked up my jeans. Then with a sad voice I said, "Do you realize if you stay here, I'll never have another Christmas at home with my family?"

She waved a dismissive hand. "Oh, spare me," she said. "You barely even like your family. Your mom wants you to get a boyfriend and your dad's a drunk." She adjusted a small golden ring on her pointer finger, then picked at one of her teeth. "I think I greatly improved it," she said offhandedly. "You haven't had to have one of those weird conversations about you being a lesbian in months."

I wanted to be angry with her. After all, she just said a whole bunch of fightin' words. But for some reason I couldn't. The fury that initially churned in my gut grew more flaccid by the second. "Yes, but that's still *my* family," I mustered. "It's my right to hate it if I want to."

God side-eyed me, saying nothing for a while. Then when she spoke again, her voice was soft. "What's the point in having a family if you're gonna hate it?" she asked.

I sucked in air, ready to argue with her. Then I realized she wasn't looking to fight. Her eyebrows squeezed gently, making wrinkles in her forehead. "Well," I sputtered. "Family makes you who you are…" I wasn't sure where I was going with this, but I figured if I kept talking, I would eventually come to a profound conclusion for why I actually wanted my family back. I thought about what I might say next, but she was too impatient.

"Well, you're a whole entire hot mess right now," she snipped. "Maybe they should stay asleep a while longer so you can get yourself figured out. I mean come on – you're playing in the dirt for crying out loud." She put a hand on her hip. "You mean to tell me you've got all this freedom, and gardening is the best you can come up with?"

I stomped my foot into the dirt, kicking up a little bit of it. The dirt glittered down on her boot. "How could you say that?" I slapped both hands the sides of my jeans dramatically. "Besides," I added. "Gardening is therapeutic. Why are you so *rude?*"

"Oh, you're so testy," she said, throwing her shoulders down. She shook her boot, letting the dirt settle back to the ground. "Is it because you haven't been sleeping well? Do you need a nap?"

The blood surged up my neck in a way that hadn't happened since I was a kid. My face was suddenly hot. Had she known about my nightmares? About Tara? Mom? Would God look at me the same way she had? I wasn't ready to have that conversation. Thankfully, God wasn't either. She went on.

"Is it 'cause I sent you to hell?" she asked.

I swallowed hard. I wasn't sure if this was the better topic. "Are you here to send me back?"

"Nah." God picked up my hand shovel and inspected it. She rubbed a finger across the sharp yellow paisley pattern on the handle. "You got yourself back fair and square."

An inkling of alarm started up in me. Did she know about my deal with the demons? Was that fair? *Or* square? I didn't understand the rules in this wild, wild west of hers.

God trudged out of the dirt and sat on a nearby bench. Then she let out a quiet, "*Ah*," as she straightened out the wrinkles in her dress.

I shifted my weight from one foot to the other. I wasn't sure if she wanted me to follow her or not. I took a step closer. "Did you come for your book, then?"

God patted the empty part of the bench with a gentle hand. I sat obediently.

"I can take my book back whenever I want," she said. "I won't be needing it for a while, though." She raised a brow at me. "I'm curious as to why *you* want it, but I know you won't tell me."

I was uncertain if she wanted an explanation or not. I dared not look at her. But she continued leisurely. "I didn't really come for anything," she explained. "I just came to *be*." And with that, she took a deep and satisfied breath. We sat in silence for a while, until the uncomfortable squirming in my stomach had given up and my shoulders relaxed. I watched as the small flickers of light floated from her hair and disappeared near the ground. Then I had a thought.

"Why don't you just wake everyone up?" I asked. God glanced at me, then continued watching the hydrangeas dance in the breeze. I continued. "You know – that way everyone gets what they want."

God nodded. "That's a thought," she said. "But has it ever occurred to you that they don't want to wake up?" I clenched my hands, ready to yell at her for her stupidity. But I realized it wouldn't help. Whether she sensed my anger or not, I don't know. She went on. "From your perspective you couldn't possibly understand," she said. "Everyone that you think is asleep is, at this very moment, experiencing the joy of being in oneness – peace, love, bliss. Everyone needs a good rest every once in a while." God took a deep breath and closed her eyes. I assumed she was taking her own advice, so I said nothing for a long time. My eyes wandered to just outside the garden wall. A squirrel skittered up a nearby tree to escape a roving swarm of mechanical bumble bees. It chittered indignantly from its branch, but the bees were uninterrupted. They continued surveying the outer edge of the lawn in angular motions. God's voice made me jump. "You may not have envisioned this in your life's plan," she said. "But that doesn't mean it wasn't part of the plan all along."

With my anger mostly resigned, I settled on a soft scoff. "So you're saying those scientists were meant to botch up that experiment?"

"Nothing is ever accidental," said God. She crossed one leg over the other and glanced at me before I could change my expression. She didn't seem to mind that I was sneering, though. She leaned in closer to me. "You know, the dead don't mourn death. Only the living do."

"What?" I failed to see what she meant.

God sighed. "Okay, so nobody's dead, but they've transitioned in a way, right?"

"Right," I said.

"But the only ones who aren't happy about it are you and your little friends." I crossed my arms, but I allowed her to continue. "Everyone else is in exaltation; the happiest they've ever been on Earth – even your mom."

It didn't make me feel any better. "How do you know that?" How *could* you know that?"

She turned to me, a smile reached her twinkling chestnut eyes. "I'm God," she said. "And everything is a part of me, including your mother. Including you. Including that rock over there." She gestured over her shoulder with a small nod. "And even including that asshole cat."

My eyes roamed past the row of broken lilies to find Milus, who was now stretched along the garden wall. He noticed me watching him and rolled over promptly to face the other direction. "So if everything goes according to some divine plan," I said to God. "Why are my friends and I still awake?"

She gave me a wry smile. "How you manage to ask and answer the same question in one breath is very amusing."

I rolled my eyes. Then I rubbed my forehead firmly with my fingertips, thinking of a different way to ask the question. But when I looked up, God had gone, and I was alone again.

There was no point in being annoyed, I told myself. But I still managed to have a tantrum right there on the bench. As I sat there, kicking and punching the air like an overgrown toddler, something stopped me in my tracks. A thought. Fleeting. Both ridiculous and wonderful. What if we didn't send God back? After all, she said it herself – everyone who's asleep is having the time of their lives. Who am I to interrupt that? And I wouldn't have to worry about being a constant disappointment to my mom. I wouldn't have to go to work ever again. I wouldn't have to do *anything* I didn't want to do!

I would do exactly as God said – I'd take the time to work on myself. After all, it was in my life's plan.

But how would I convince Theo and Valencio to stop their efforts? I wouldn't be able to. Was I bold enough to sabotage their attempts, then? That was the logical choice. Yes. I'd have to sabotage them. But how? I let the questions roll around in my mind without really finding any good answers. I'd have to give my new plan more than an afternoon's thought.

Then, with a resolute nod, I put my gloves on, scooped up my hand shovel, and found a soft place in the dirt to dig. I wouldn't let a good day for gardening be wasted.

Chapter Seven: This Is, In Fact, An Unholy Exorcism

One crisp afternoon, when I was ready to burst at the seam from thinking myself in circles, a call came over my walkie talkie. I was in my bedroom, ignoring all of the laundry that actually needed folding in order to reorganize my large collection of decorative blankets. I unfolded stacks of them only to shake them out and refold, then stack them into columns that were both fancier and easier to navigate. When the walkie talkie chirped, I knocked over the column I was working on in order to reach it, then cursed as I realized what I'd done. "Come in Valencio," I breathed. I could barely contain my angst. How do you pretend to be excited for something you're actually trying to prevent? It doesn't feel good to be a scumbag, just in case you were wondering. "Did you find… what did you find?"

After a moment it chirped again. "I believe you'll want to come in," he said. "We have many things to report."

I attempted to upright the spilled column, moving slowly and deliberately to restack the blankets, but I was unsuccessful. They just sprawled all over themselves again in an outrageous act of disobedience.

But I didn't care. I knew I was just biding my time until my nerves calmed. When I got to the lab, could I find a way to sabotage them? Would I even have an opportunity? I abandoned the blankets and, with shaking hands, put on my Go Time outfit. This was a special outfit, consisting of my most supportive (yet stretchy) jeans, a practical top that tucked well, and lightweight tennis shoes. In my anticipation – or possibly desperation – for action, I set these items aside so as to be prepared for such an occasion. But I wasn't nearly as excited as I thought I'd be when I originally laid the outfit on top of my nightstand.

I quickly followed my leaving-home protocol. I fed Milus and kicked him out with a halfhearted apology, then locked the door and was off. Within minutes I was navigating down the now familiar road to the lab, no longer astonished by the anomalies along the way. I actually started to expect them, and was delighted when I saw a new illusion crop up.

Today there was a cave that had grown over the highway. I was pretty certain I would come out on the other side and continue down the road, but I slowed down nonetheless, just in case it was full of spiders or something that I could crash into. My delight was only briefly overshadowed by terror, when the obstacle I would encounter turned out to be a dragon's nest. I realized too late that I would have to scrape by three enormous eggs – glossy and wet with a protective bloom. Fun fact about eggs, by the way – some animals lay trophic eggs, like poison dart frogs and some worker bees. These are unfertilized eggs that are actually meant to be eaten by the offspring. Super weird. But I digress.

Whether these particular eggs were fertilized or not, I wouldn't know. But what I did know was that a magnificent serpent with oversized wings happened to be guarding them. She placed a scaly leg in the road between me and the clutch, warning me with a low guttural groan. Too late to turn around, I hunkered in my seat as low as I could – like that would help – and allowed my car to coast right out on the other side.

A few miles down the road I was still struggling to recover from the ridiculous encounter. It helped when I turned onto the dirt path. I could see Conner's Jeep just ahead, kicking up dust as he turned into the clearing.

When we arrived at the building, a very festive-looking Matt greeted us in the vestibule. "What's up, Brojitos?" He smiled dazedly at Conner, then pulled the sombrero he was wearing off his head and did a weird dance with his shoulders. He waved the hat around and then plonked it on my head.

Conner fanned the smell of alcohol from the air. "You're still a priest, right?"

Matt slapped his hands clumsily in a praying position. "Absolutely," he said. "But you can be a priest, and enjoy the more… fleshy… fleshy… " He chuckled. "Sins of the flesh!" He pulled out a poorly rolled cigarette and patted his robes for a lighter. Then he started pulling the robes up and we realized he was stark naked underneath.

"No!" Conner yelled, slapping down the thin fabric. "You're not even supposed to smoke in here."

"Don't worry," said Matt, shoving the cigarette in Conner's face. "It's not even tobacco, see?"

I grabbed Matt by the robes, pulling him with us down the long hall toward the stairs. He raised his hands and said, *weeeeeee!* all the way down.

"Is that Alex?" Theo called from a storage room. There was a loud bang and a rumble as several metal containers fell to the floor.

"We're here," I called.

Matt continued dancing to a tune that only he could hear.

Valencio appeared from nowhere and swept us into a large room that I'd never been in before. There was an array of bulky machines – some that looked plain, like plastic boxes and others were complex, with intricate wires coiling in on themselves and little puffs of smoke emitting into long vents that came from the ceiling. He brought us to a long table and operated a glass pad to pull up a series of data points on a holographic board. It cast a calm blue haze in the area immediately in front of it.

"Alright," he said in a no–nonsense way. "We have much to cover today." He swatted at Matt, who was playing with a dial that made the data zoom in and out. Then, as if dealing with an inquisitive toddler, he held up a Rubik's–like contraption and allowed Matt to wrestle it from him. Then, satisfied, Valencio turned back to the hologram. "On the point of the Book of Life," he said. "I have been able to administer simple inquiries successfully," he said. Conner and I clapped our hands. Matt whooped loudly, and I'm certain he had no idea what we were celebrating. Valencio shushed us with his hands. "I've been able to ask, 'where is heaven?' and 'where is hell?'" He laughed in a bemused way. "The answers to which are already changing my scientific understanding of the world."

Theo stumbled in, having found whatever he was looking for. He held a small canister in his hand, and his jumper was unusually dirty. He nodded for Valencio to continue.

"But when I asked the question, 'where is God?' or 'where is God's Earthly template?'" He clicked a link that played a recording of the book. Words and pictures flashed nonsensically across its pages in short, random spurts. "It fails to find a meaningful answer to the inquiry."

I shook my head. "I don't understand," I said. "Does the book not know where the template is?" I allowed myself to be distressed briefly, then realized this, in fact, would be a good thing. Maybe I wouldn't have to sabotage anything at all. We were naturally failing already.

"The book not knows," said Matt from the corner of the room. "It knows not nada."

"Thank you," Valencio said sharply to Matt. Then he nodded at Theo. "That in isolation is something to be noted, but let's hear what Theo has to say about the box."

Theo pointed our attention to another set of data on the board. "I used several different processes to get an understanding of what exactly is in the box," he started. He inhaled a sharp breath. Then he expanded a picture of what looked like something I'd seen plenty of times in my middle school's textbooks.

"Is it a virus?" I asked.

"At first, I thought it *was* a virus," said Theo. "But after further analysis, I was able to determine that it's actually some sort of hyper advanced nanotechnology." He paused briefly, zooming further into the picture. Several of its parts were labeled. "There are trillions of them," he said. "Nanoid robots that are self-guiding – completely autonomous – powered by a packet of interesting components that I didn't understand until today." He zoomed in on a very small chip, a single wire connecting it to the main structure. "The chip at the center of each is made of an unknown alloy and houses an artificial intelligence – designed to specifically target the epithalamus in the human brain, and the spine at certain vertebrae."

I nodded. "The demons said it was an inoculation."

"Right," said Theo. "So we were curious about the specific vertebrae that are being targeted. What makes them so special? To answer that, Valencio conducted a structural and cerebrospinal fluid analysis on some of our friends down in the medical chamber." He scrolled on the holographic board until he found an x-ray image of a spine. Six of the vertebrae were visibly brighter. Which would mean they were denser than the rest, right? I think I should know that. Anyway, I nodded my head, assuming that I understood enough to get where he was going. Theo continued. "The vertebrae of our friends are inundated with activity from this exotic matter - the stuff that God brought to earth when she came."

"Okay," I said, puzzling together the bigger picture in my mind. "So God somehow influenced those vertebrae -"

"Possibly intersects with humanity through them?" Conner guessed.

"Right," said Theo. "There's some sort of God connection there for sure." He played a simulation of one of the bots entering a human's body. I didn't pay as much attention as I should have at the beginning, though, because I was wondering how they were able to simulate such a thing without having ever opened the box. But the end result was very clear: the once vibrant parts of the spine dimmed until they were nearly invisible. "The nanotech appears to be programmed to restrict functionality of the vertebrae significantly," he said. "Not balance it."

I understood. "It would completely separate us from God," I said.

"I think so," said Theo. He gestured toward a zoomed in image of a nanobot on the board. "I think those demons actually want to wipe God from our plane of existence."

Conner looked at me through piercing eyes. "We wanted to know what kind of box it was," he said. "We have our answer now. It's a Pandora's Box."

I scoffed. "So, they're taking advantage of the situation. They never wanted everything to go back to normal."

"Right," said Theo. "A power play to take over Earth."

"Why the blood, though?" asked Conner. Theo screwed his face up in confusion. He explained further. "They told Alex to fill the cup with her blood," said Conner. "Why the blood ritual, if we're dealing with technology?"

"Oh," that's a good question," said Theo. "Matt was able to tell us how demons deal in symbolism to strengthen their powers, but I think there was a more practical reason." He flashed his hands across a section of the board, which expanded to another set of data. Then he played a simulation, which showed one of the nanobots entering a blood cell. "It would make sense that the nanotech would disguise itself as a blood cell in order to avoid an immune response," he said. He gestured at me. "In order for this disguise to be successful, your blood type would have to be O negative," he said. "Am I right?"

"Wow," I said. "I am."

"Me, too," said Conner. "The universal donor."

"And so am I," said Theo. Then he went quiet for a moment. "I'm willing to bet everyone who's awake is O negative," he said quietly. He opened a separate log on the board and typed in a few notes. We watched quietly as he muttered, "This is amazing…" and, "how intriguing..." After a while, he closed the log and turned to us. "There's more," said Theo. He waved the canister. "The chip in the nanotech contained compositions of matter that seemed familiar to me, and for a while I couldn't figure out where I'd seen them before." He strode over to another table, beckoning for us to follow. There, he opened a door on a small oven–like machine and placed the canister inside. Then he pressed a small button, which made the machine hiss loudly. "This should only take a few minutes," he explained. "But I wanted to confirm with a metallurgical analysis."

There was a loud bang toward the back of the room where Matt was, which prompted Valencio to moan, "Why do I put up with this?" before sprinting off toward the source of the sound.

"Anyway," said Theo. "What I realized was that the composition of matter from the nanotech was oddly similar to that of the stray exotic matter that was sent flying off into the atmosphere the day of the 'Little Bang.' Remember the funky pentaquarks?" I nodded, glancing at Conner nervously. It seemed Theo was about to go to a level of nerdiness that I wouldn't be able to understand, and I secretly hoped Conner would be just as lost. Theo continued. "I looked at those again and realized they weren't pentaquarks at all," said Theo. "What I thought was a packet of four quarks and an antiquark, was really four quarks *masking* an artificial component made of what?" Theo threw a hand out triumphantly, prompting me to answer.

"An unknown alloy?" I guessed.

"Yes!" Theo clapped his hands. "And I'm willing to bet it's the same *exact* alloy as the one in the nanotech," he said. "And I'm starting to suspect that the artificial component hidden in these subatomic particles is programmed to generate the neurogenic field that has everyone in whatever kind of coma this is."

"Okay," said Conner. He squeezed his eyes shut and scratched his beard impatiently. "So, the particles released when God arrived aren't natural," he said slowly. "And possibly have an AI component."

"Right," said Theo.

Conner nodded. "And the demons gave us a solution, the technology of which is eerily similar to the problem."

"Right." Theo nodded.

Then I finally reached the conclusion that everyone else had. It fell out of my mouth in a whisper. "The demons started the problem in the first place."

"It would seem so," said Valencio, making everyone jump. He shuffled from the back of the room, straightening the shirt collar underneath his lab coat. He adjusted the glasses on his face. "I have also given thought to your friend," he said, gesturing at me with his eyebrows. "The demon, Shax."

"You said he looked familiar."

"He did his best to not let me see his face," said Valencio. "The day he brought you back."

"He couldn't stand up straight," I remembered.

"Well," sighed Valencio. "It's been almost twenty years, but I feel quite certain now he was one of the scientists who initially presented the project to my director at CERN." He pursed his lips briefly before continuing. "I don't think any of this was a mistake," he said. "I think they intended for this experiment to happen exactly as it did."

I crossed my arms and leaned against a nearby desk. I couldn't help but laugh at my own shortsightedness. "I guess it's cool to hang out with nerds in a lab after all," I said. "I probably would've opened the box by now if I were on my own."

"It was a really good plan," Conner said. "Almost anyone on Earth would've been fooled."

Theo swiped a hand through his curls. "I guess they didn't count on us working together."

"That was their mistake," I said. "But why would they risk keeping us awake when they could've just poked our sleeping bodies?"

There was a sudden clatter behind Valencio. We turned, thinking Matt had gotten into something else, but it wasn't him. Conner cursed. Danel and Shax had arrived, and they weren't bothering to be careful around the lab's delicate equipment.

"It's human *will*," said Danel, stepping over a shattered burette. She sauntered into the soft light of the holographic board. It cast a blue hue across her face as she turned to me. Dark rings had begun to form under her eyes, but she was still quite beautiful. "*You* have to reject God for it to work," she explained. I shook my head. She smiled coolly, then smacked her lips. "Looks like we're found out," she said to Shax, who was still lurking in the shadow of the room. "I guess we can just kill them and take our box back."

Valencio swept an arm out to make a barrier between Danel and us. Theo looked over his shoulder for Matt.

"Agreed," said Shax. His voice was matter of fact. "We'll try again with another human."

"You lied to me," I said. I shifted the weight of my feet as I searched corners of the room for Shax.

Danel stretched her arms out. "We're demons," she said. "Are you *really* surprised?"

I wasn't surprised. But I was going to waste as much time as possible. If there was one thing I learned from all of their unpleasant pop-ins, it's that they could never stay for more than three or four minutes at a time. I stomped my foot dramatically and pouted, prepared to stonewall as long as possible. Theo screwed his face up, confused by my behavior, and Valencio squinted his eyes as if trying to communicate something to me. I wouldn't be able to explain myself, though. I shook my head slightly, hoping he got the message. I could only hope I was right. "It isn't fair," I whined at Danel.

She shrugged in an offhanded way. "Well, nothing in life is fair," she said, holding out her hand. "Now give me the box, and I'll consider sparing your life."

"It's not in here," I said. "We would have to go upstairs for it." I stepped past Valencio, pushing him backward into Conner. Behind my back, I waved for them to move away from the demons. I couldn't tell if they understood. "I'll have to get the key as well," I said. "It's locked away."

Danel put a hand on her hip. "Do what you need to do," she said. "Just hurry it up!"

I walked as slowly as I could toward a drawer, but my mind was racing. I fumbled with the delicate instruments inside. "I'll just grab the key and we'll go get the box," I said, eyeing Valencio. We both knew I was fibbing by then. He nodded slightly.

Just then, Matt stumbled in carrying the paper shredder. He held the slender metal bin away from his body, a look of embarrassment on his face. "I peed in this," he slurred. "Thought it was a toilet."

Shax appeared behind him. "Put that down and get over there with the rest of them," he said. He tried to snatch the bin away, but Matt pulled it out of his reach. Liquid sloshed against its sides, threatening to spill over. "Mind your manners," he said insolently. Then he squinted, his freckles drawing together at the center of his face. "Who are *you*?"

I slapped a hand to my face. "It's a demon, Matt."

"Demon!" Matt screamed. He reared the bin back. "In the name of our savior, Jesus Christ," he said wildly. "I rebuke you!" Then he swung the bin, splashing its contents straight in Shax's face.

Shax roared, disgusted. He choked on gulping breaths, clawing wet shreds of paper from his eyes and throwing them to the slippery floor. Danel shrieked.

"Go!" yelled Theo. He dove under a desk, pulling out a familiar box. He opened it and pulled out the Hertzinator. I grabbed Matt by the collar and pulled him behind a separate desk where Valencio and Conner were already crouched. We clapped our hands to our ears just in time to hear the discordant tones through our fingers.

I peeked over the desk. Danel and Shax, unaffected by the noise, were grimacing at us from across the room. Theo turned off the Hertzinator as Shax swiped it out of his hand. It crashed to the floor, sending small pieces of metal across the room. Then, in a flash, Danel was at our desk. "Hurry up and give me my box," she hissed, pulling me to my feet by my hair. I clawed at her hand, but she only tightened her grip. "*Now.*"

My eyes darted the room. I couldn't think of a way out. Well, perhaps Matt could continue whatever unholy exorcism he had started, I thought. Shax seemed to be pretty affected by his piss paper method. I grasped for the shredder, hoping its contents would deter Danel from me, but I couldn't reach it.

By then, Shax began ripping drawers from cabinets along the far wall, swiping bulky objects to the floor. "Forget about them," he roared. "It'll be easier to tear it all apart."

"No," said Danel. "It would be easier if one of you just handed it over." She held me at arm's length. "If you don't want to see your friend die, tell me where it is."

Conner rose from under his desk first, hands raised in surrender. Valencio and Matt followed.

"Don't," I said. I swallowed hard. "Don't tell them anything. They can't finish their plan if they don't have the box."

Danel slammed my face into a nearby desk. Flashes of light danced behind my eyes. "Or you can all die, one at a time," she said, "and Shax and I will tear the place apart and find it anyway. Either way, we're getting the box."

I tried twisting from her grip, but only managed to pull some of my hair out. "You can't kill me," I said desperately. "You said so yourself."

"We never said we couldn't *kill* you," Danel sneered. "We said we couldn't *eat* you." Then, without giving me a chance to even think about it, she drove her hand directly into the center of my chest. Her grip loosened from my hair, but I only stood there gawking at her. My body went cold. I clutched the place where she'd pierced me, hoping to hold it closed as if it were merely a flesh wound. But the others' horrified expressions told me that it wouldn't help. Then I was falling through the tunnel again.

Chapter Eight: You People and Your Benches

Having remembered what came next, I squeezed myself into a ball, hoping to roll on impact. But I never hit the ground. In fact, I didn't even realize I was squatting on a solid surface until a very soft voice came into my head. It said, "Be without fear."

My arms were still flailing out in front of me when I opened my eyes. I expected the dull, sunless park and hot breeze, but was surprised to find none of it. Instead, I was in the air. Clouds floated lazily below my feet, which were again being held up by some invisible force. I recognized this place. This had to be the Hall of Records. But I didn't see the maze of bookshelves, or the archway, or the pedestal that once held the Book of Life. There was only me and the clouds. *Whose voice did I hear then?* As soon as the question crossed my mind, silvery footprints appeared in front of me, illuminating a path. I touched the nearest one with the tip of my shoe. It flickered faintly, then disappeared. I decided to follow them.

I walked for several minutes through the crisp air, which gave me time to think. I clutched my chest where the wound should have been. It was completely healed, but I was no fool;

I begrudgingly accepted that I had died. Danel killed me, and she had probably killed everyone else, too. My stomach knotted up at the thought of it. But I couldn't dwell on that. All the worrying in the world couldn't make the situation any better. I continued following the path, one step at a time. I was relieved to find that at least I wasn't back in hell. It had to be heaven, which is slightly better. I mean, not dying at all is preferable. But I guess if this was the end, I'm glad I ended up here.

There was a man in the distance now. He rocked gently back and forth in an ancient–looking wooden chair, wearing a plain white robe and reading a book. I walked quickly to meet him. He looked up at me expectantly, crow's feet etched into the corners of his eyes from a lifetime of laughter. His sandy skin was leathered, telling his age. I didn't recognize him, but he felt very familiar to me. As I approached, he closed the book and set it in his lap. I glanced at the title. It read, 'Alexandria Torey.'

"Was that you?" I asked, gesturing behind me. "Did you… say something to me back there?"

The man smiled. "Yes," he said. He stood and straightened out his robes. "And it would seem you've finally listened."

"Oh." I smiled. Then I wasn't sure what to say next. I looked around at the endless clouds. The man watched patiently as I turned and then turned again. "So, what is this place?" I finally asked.

He smiled, then looked around as well. "It's the after and the before," he said.

"What does that even mean?" I asked. "I know it's not hell, but heaven would have, like, pearly gates, and a staircase and… and… those little babies in diapers with wings." Then I shook my head, "No, that's Cupid. He wouldn't be in heaven." I turned to the man. "Is this heaven or not?"

"Oh, is that what heaven looks like?" he asked. He smiled affectionately.

"Yes," I said with uncertainty. "Or something different than this, at least."

The man snapped his fingers, and the space was suddenly filled. There was a golden river running below us and towering arches framing a dazzling gate in the distance. I stood at the top of a massive silver staircase. It wound steeply into the depths below and disappeared underneath a thick cloud. He rubbed his chin thoughtfully. "I believe the word you were looking for is, '*cherub*,' maybe?" he said. "And those are welcome here, too, if you wish." He waved a hand, and a gaggle of creatures appeared from thin air and began zooming around playfully. They were an uglier version of what I imagined, but they met all the criteria: Babies. Diapers. Wings. One of them swooped down suddenly and tickled my neck mischievously. I swatted it away. It turned around, wearing the ugliest haircut I'd ever seen, and stuck its tongue out at me.

"Okay, those things are just weird," I told the man, swiping my hair from my face. "We don't really need those."

The man chuckled. "Well, they're already here…" he said. Then he took a satisfied breath. "Now that we're nice and comfortable." He pulled the book that read my name from somewhere in his robes. "Let's review your life."

I was alarmed. "Like, my *whole* life?" I asked. I shook my head frantically. "Cause from sixteen to twenty I was a whole train wreck. I'd rather we not –"

"You people are always so scared of being judged," he interjected. He leaned in closer to me. "The only person judging you here is you."

I scoffed. "I'm the only one judging me? Wait 'til my mother comes through here."

"Right," said the man.

"And my boss," I added. "My boss sucks, too. He thinks I'm not committed enough." And though he didn't ask for any of it, I went on. "I think I'm a pretty good person," I said. "I teach hundreds of students every year, and I actually *like* them. Not everyone likes their students." And since the man was content to listen, I found other things to ramble on about. "I don't commit any crimes, either. Not even small ones." I gave a resolute nod. "Other people steal the condiments from the tables at Hoover's, but I don't."

I was unsure of why I felt the need to drive that particular point home, and why that was the best example to use in order to do it. Actually, let me stop lying to myself. I know it was because my mother, of all people, had the nerve to stick the hot sauce in her purse after we paid the bill every single time we visited that place. It's amazing how she could still manage to judge me all the way from her kleptocratic seat on high.

"I'm glad you can make such a positive assessment of yourself," the man said. He smiled, then said nothing more for a while.

This gave me an opportunity to notice a queasy feeling bubbling up from the pit of my stomach. There was no point in dancing around it any longer. I decided I would have to face it. I opened my mouth and almost didn't recognize my own voice. It was small and cracked. "Isn't the point of all of this to be judged?"

"The point of what?" he asked. I couldn't tell if he was playing stupid or not. He would make me say it.

"Reviewing my life," I said. I winced, thinking about Tara. The sleepover. Mom. And for some reason, a burrito that now lives in my head rent-free. "My choices. Things I've done." I licked my lips, which had dried out at record speed.

The man watched me squirm. I would've been angry with him if it weren't for his eyes being so soft and warm. And the heavy, roiling pit in my stomach that was swallowing up all of my other emotions in real time. I took a deep breath to steady myself. Then I forced the words out. "Isn't the point of all of this to decide that I really belong in hell?"

The man chuckled softly. "You people," he said. He shook his head slowly, studying me. Then he sucked in a breath. "You notice how you tighten your gut?"

"What?"

For a moment, I couldn't comprehend what he said. Then I didn't understand why it mattered. Nonetheless, I brought my attention to my stomach. It was firmly squeezed against the growing pit, holding it in place, preventing it from consuming the rest of my body.

He gestured toward me with a nod. "Loosen that thing up," he said. Then he repeated. "Nobody here is judging you but you."

I tried to let my gut relax – slowly, so as not to lose control of the pit. And when I had extended my belly to a reasonable degree, I did feel a lot better.

"Oh," I said. "So then, what are we going to review?"

"Whatever you want."

I thought about my friends. Then my stomach knotted up all over again. "The demons," I started. The words spilled out of my mouth faster than I could think. "They were going to kill everyone and, apparently, they killed me but I didn't see anyone else here and –"

The man raised a hand, stopping me in my tracks. "Everyone else is safe," he said calmly. He smiled. "You were able to buy enough time to save everyone."

I breathed a sigh of relief, but the feeling was short-lived. I laughed bitterly. "Everyone except myself," I said.

The man gave a slight nod and said, "The weakness of flesh matters not when the strength of the spirit is great." He put a reassuring hand on my shoulder. "You were a brave friend." Then he extended an arm, and a golden bench materialized out of nowhere. Two ugly cherubs dropped a glittery ribbon along the back of it and fluttered off. "Have a seat," he said.

I dropped myself sadly onto the bench. The man sat next to me. Then I thought about the last time I was on a bench. It was with God. I turned to the man, studying his patient face. "Who are you, anyway?"

"Oh," he said with a start. "How kind of you to ask." He smiled brightly. "I figured it would be obvious, though. I'm an angel."

"An *angel?*"

He stretched his legs with a small groan. "Absolutely," he said.

I shook my head. "But you look human," I said. "I heard you guys were, like, hideous or something."

The man gasped. He sat up straight, outraged. "I'll have you know I'm one of the most beautiful of *all* the angels," he said.

"I didn't mean to offend you," I said. I struggled for words. "I mean, you actually remind me of my uncle Robert," I smiled. "I feel totally comfortable with you."

He was already crossing his arms, though. "That's the point," he said. "You're supposed to feel comfortable with me, but now I feel obligated to show you my true beauty."

I laughed nervously. "You don't have to," I said. "I trust you."

"Too late," he said stubbornly. He stood up and cleared his throat. "You may want to back up."

Before I could take a proper step, the space shifted. The pearly gate seemed to be a mile away now, and the cherubs scattered like a flock of frazzled birds. And it didn't take me long to figure out why. The angel had transformed into something I couldn't even bring my brain to recognize. Countless eyes – roving, blinking, shrinking and growing – covered a shapeless mass of what would be considered flesh.

It segmented itself into two pieces that orbited one another in a terrifying dance.

Six otherworldly appendages that, I guess would've been wings, flapped to keep it airborne, then it merged back in on itself. Some of the eyes separated from the body and appeared to hover around it like a watchful cloud. They blinked dramatically, making my stomach twist up. I didn't want to see any more, but I couldn't look away. I watched this go on for a while, and then a thought struck me. I put my hand on my hip. "Hey!" I shouted. "Are you… are you showing off?"

In an instant, the angel transformed back into his human form. "I don't know," he said slyly. "Were you impressed?"

"Of course," I said, rubbing my forehead. I was unsure of how to actually feel about what I just saw, but I wouldn't hurt his feelings. "It's hard to put into words," I said. "You were… were… *heavenly.*"

He smiled smugly. "I knew you'd agree."

I hoped my face was smiling appropriately. "You've got to be Azrael, right?"

"How'd you know?" he asked.

I decided to keep my answer simple. "Oh, your beauty has been spoken of," I said.

Azrael took his place back on the bench. I joined him. And, since it seemed to be the thing to do when visiting with these people, I prepared to sit in silence for a while.

And it was a painfully long while. At first, it was okay. I had a chance to think things all the way through — about my plans of sabotaging my friends in order to keep God on Earth. I was slightly relieved to realize I would no longer have to carry the burden of committing scumbaggery against them.

Then I was partially entertained by the cherubs, who had organized a sort of dance race, but even that couldn't distract me for too long. "Okay," I finally said. "I'm dead, and the demons are after my friends." Then I hesitated. "Wait – do you know *everything* that's going on, or do I have to fill you in?"

Azrael drummed his fingers on his knees contentedly. "Fill me in, why don't you," he said.

I took a deep breath, ready to give him an earful. "Well, first of all," I said. "There are these demons who tricked us into trapping God on Earth. Did you know she was on Earth? Also, did you know she was a woman?" I didn't give him time to answer, though. I went on. "Of course, you must know – don't angels, like, report directly to God?"

Azrael chuckled.

I crossed my arms. "What's so funny?" I asked.

"Oh, nothing," he said. "Do go on."

"No," I said stubbornly. "What's funny?"

Azrael peered at me for a moment. Then he spoke. "I am only amused that you would be satisfied that God is a woman." He put a finger up to silence my protest. But I ignored him.

"Are you saying something's wrong with her being a woman?" I asked.

"No, but yes." He shook his head. "It's hard to explain." He rubbed his chin, pursing his lips together thoughtfully. "The individual on Earth right now is not The All."

"What do you mean?" I asked. "She's not all of *what?*"

"*All,*" the angel said simply.

I thought I understood. "Well, she *will* be all of God soon," I said. "If she stays on Earth long enough, she'll be all powerful."

"*She* will still not be The *All*," said Azrael.

I scowled at him. "You're frustrating, you know that?"

Azrael adjusted himself on the bench and drew a quick, thoughtful breath. "To condense God into a single human form would be like fitting all of Earth's oceans into a sippy cup," he said. "And to divide God up into meaningless definitions – male or female, young or old – would limit your very understanding of who and what God is."

"I literally saw God the other day," I said shortly. "She's a woman for sure."

"Why is that so important?" he asked.

"Well," I said. "If you'd been paying attention to the history of our planet, you'd see that women have always been horribly mistreated."

"Ah," said Azrael. "So, if God were a woman, that would change the history of the planet?"

My nose crinkled. "I guess not," I said. "But it'll make all those misogynistic jerks understand how wrong they are." I narrowed my eyes. "You can't take this one from me."

Azrael looked at me from the sides of his eyes. "Then I won't," he said simply. "But when you only see God in the one, you will never truly know God at all.

I glared at Azrael for a few moments, attempting to make sense of his philosophical blather. But the longer I thought about it, the stupider it sounded. I almost preferred to talk to the demons at this point. I opened my mouth several times before actually speaking. "So if God isn't a woman –"

"I never said she wasn't."

I raised a brow. "So if God is only *part* woman —" I paused, throwing a hand up for confirmation. Azrael gave a consenting nod. "Why did she… it… *they* show up as a woman?"

Azrael didn't answer right away; he furrowed his brow instead. Then when he spoke it was in an unsure way. Which was super weird because I assumed angels knew everything. "Maybe," he said. "It's because that's what the world needs at this particular moment."

"Well, the world is conked out right now." I laughed. "I don't think they've noticed."

"Well, then maybe that's what *you* need."

I scoffed. "I don't need another woman in my life judging me." Then I put a finger to my lip, possibly trying to stop other stupid things from slipping through. I thought about putting a finger to his lip to stop whatever stupid thing *he* would say next.

"Oh, has she been?" He offered a coy smile.

I thought about it. "Well, she did send me to hell." And the more I thought about it, the more sure I felt. I grew agitated. "That's exactly what she did. That's the ultimate judgement."

Azrael blinked placidly. Then he finally said. "Well, you did steal her book." He raised both eyebrows, wrinkling his forehead. "And then you reduced her to a cloud of basic molecules."

I shrank into my own body, my face hot. I felt like an ignorant child. Selfish. I nodded, allowing the ball of angst in my gut to unravel. "Touche," I said. "That one was probably on me."

"Probably?"

I decided I would ignore his questioning and get back to the topic at hand. "So, the demons tricked us into trapping a part of God on Earth," I said, determined to just start from the beginning again.

Azrael leaned inwards. Yes," he said. "All that could fit on the planet without completely destroying it, mind you."

"I'd say it's pretty destroyed," I said. "Things are crazy down there."

The cherubs, who had slowly fluttered back from their hiding places, began to fly over us in a synchronized dance. Azrael watched them amusedly for a moment, then sighed. "It could be worse," he said. "Much worse." Then he leaned on an elbow and smirked. "You know," he said. "Shax and Danel didn't expect the experiment to work as well as it did. They never intended for hell to be affected, too."

"That's karma for you," I said.

"Indeed," Azrael agreed. He gave a small chuckle.

I pursed my lips. "You said you didn't know about any of this," I said grumpily. "I could've saved my breath."

"Oh, no," said Azrael innocently. "I never said that. I only said that I'd prefer *you* fill me in."

I glared at him, but he only smiled serenely back. "Okay," I said. "If you know everything, can you tell me why the Book of Life can't find the template?"

"Easy one," he said. "Because it's not hidden. It no longer exists."

My mouth fell open. "No longer exists?"

"Yep," said Azrael. He leaned back. "The demons made sure of that, unfortunately. They had a close eye on the experiment, you know. Of course, they knew God's essence would continue to seep into the world after the process began, but they didn't think she would show up fully formed from the beginning. When they saw her, they killed the technicians that were handling the template and stole it." I clapped my hands to my mouth. Azrael continued. "Had God's presence gotten any stronger it would've destroyed Earth altogether – and probably Hell, too."

I rested my elbows on my knees. So, there was no template. Which means they wouldn't be able to undo the experiment. I never would've had to resort to scumbaggery after all. But the guys at the lab would still be looking for answers, and they'd have the demons to deal with, too. "I need to tell them," I said. "Valencio might not figure it out in time. How can I tell him? Can I, like, *haunt* him? Am I a ghost? Can I write a message on his computer or something?" I jumped from the bench. "They need to get this information."

Azrael scrambled to his feet. He raised his voice over my ranting. "No need," he said. I stopped cold. "You can tell him yourself, in plain language."

"What?" I screwed my face up.

"There's no need to haunt anyone," he explained. "It was never your time to die. I was instructed to send you back."

I stared at Azrael for a small and painful eternity. My brain couldn't understand what he'd said. Then it all became clear, and I was more frantic than ever. "Hurry up!" I yelled. "We wasted *hours* talking about nonsense." I was flapping my arms at him, but I had no idea where I was sweeping him off to. "The demons will be back, and when they get there, they'll all be dead for sure!"

Azrael grabbed me by my shoulders, which made my mouth snap shut. "You'll find that only a few moments have passed once you return," he said. His kind eyes summoned a calmness from within me. He raised a brow. "Time does not govern these realms, as it does on Earth."

"Right," I said. I smoothed my shirt and forced my jittery arms by my sides. "I'm ready to go, whenever you are."

Azrael smiled warmly. "Are you sure you don't want to review your life before you go?" he asked.

"Nope." I turned to walk away, then realized I had no idea where I was going. I took a deep breath. "No, thank you," I said calmly. "Okay, now what do I have to do to get back to Earth?"

With a soft hand on my shoulder, he guided me to the silvery staircase. He beckoned downward. "Just start walking," he said. "You'll find your way back."

"Are you kidding me?" I laughed. "Just walk down the stairs and I'll get back to Earth?" I looked down the shadowy path. There were about a trillion steps.

"Of course," said Azrael. He shrugged. "What, you thought they were just decorative?"

I barked a laugh, but then I realized he was serious. I exhaled a sharp breath and, determined not to waste any more time, put my foot on the first step. Then I paused. "Thanks for everything."

His eyes twinkled. "Until next time," he said. And with one last glance at my version of heaven, I turned and started down the stairs.

Chapter Nine: Perturbations, and More Perturbations

Three steps later, I was no longer on the staircase. I had to blink several times, actually, before I realized that I was lying on the ground. Theo was holding my torso, his face smeared with blood. Tears dropped from his eyes. I felt their warmth radiating over my cheeks where they landed. Then, sound began to return to my ears. At first it was a low, annoying hum, deep within my head, then scrambling, then full on screaming. Conner was yelling at Theo, "There's a medical chamber down the hall – move her!" But Theo was shaking his head. "It's too late," he sobbed. Matt was at the back of the room praying vigorously. He began reciting one of his bible verses. I could tell because his voice had gone robotic again. I moved my stiff mouth. "No point," I said to Matt. "She'll probably just send me back to hell."

Theo shot up, letting my head hit the floor. "Ouch," I wheezed. I hoisted myself to a sitting position and rubbed the back of my head.

Theo's lips quivered. Conner's eyes bulged. Matt slid onto his knees across the floor and scooped me into his arms. "It's a Christmas miracle!" he yelled.

I coughed. "What – oh yeah, you're still drunk," I said, nursing my chest. The hole from Danel's fist had completely healed.

Matt shook his head wildly. "No, I'm not," he said. Then he burped and crudely fanned the gas out of my face. "Those demons sobered me right up."

Conner's mouth gaped. "How are you even *alive* right now?" he asked.

I glanced around the room. Shax had destroyed quite a few more things before disappearing. "Where's Valencio?" I asked feebly, craning my neck. He was right behind me, watching wordlessly. "Good we're all here," I said. I stumbled to my feet and took a smooth, tender breath.

The bloody hole in my shirt was letting my boobs peek out. Theo stared intently, but I could tell it was strictly for scientific purposes. I hiked the fabric up as best I could, but wouldn't be too bothered with decency at a time like this. "I was in heaven," I explained. I shook my head. "There was an angel... It wasn't my time." I pulled myself into a nearby chair as all of my previous urgency started to return. "The template is gone," I told them. "The demons destroyed it a long time ago."

I paused suddenly, which caused the others to reach out with their arms, preparing to brace me in case I fell over. I waved away their help, allowing guilt to wash over me. I realized I shouldn't have told them that. There was no need to now, since I had returned. I could've continued to let Valencio spin his wheels looking for that template for a couple more weeks; could've enjoyed not having to actively sabotage their plans. But it was already said. I could only try and find a solution to our next collective problem. "We need to figure out how to protect ourselves, because those demons will be able to return to Earth in about six days, I think. At least that's how often they've been popping in and harassing me. And you know what's gonna happen when they come back."

Valencio steeled his jaw. "We have the Book of Life," he said, thinking out loud. He plopped down into a nearby chair. "And we can secure the box as best we can." His eyes darted, as they often did when he was thinking.

"But can we secure ourselves?" Matt asked in a mostly serious voice. He hiccupped, then burped into his hand. "How do we survive the next visit?"

Theo ran his hand through his locks. Some of them had slicked along the side, pressed together by my blood. He sighed. "I can maybe devise another weapon," he said. "Be ready for them next time."

"Or maybe a trap," said Valencio. "If we could get more information from them, a better understanding of their plan, it could help us find a solution."

I nodded my agreement. "And that'll buy us more time to carry out that solution!" Then a thought struck me. "But how do we trap demons that can pop in and out of reality at a moment's notice?"

Valencio considered this for a while, saying nothing.

Theo began to think in earnest, his body almost quivering with excitement. "If we can understand the mechanism by which they're able to pop in and out of reality," he said, "we can think of a way to counter it. And if we can think of a way to counter it, then we can build a chamber or a field of some sort in which to trap them." He ignored the perplexed look on our faces and rambled straight through to the end of his plan. "We can use the box as bait, to make sure they enter the intended space and then, boom!"

Conner scoffed. "And do all of that in six days?"

"Well, maybe." Theo wasn't deterred at all. He crossed the room, kicking through the debris to get to a small instrument in a drawer. "If I start scanning the room now, I can probably pick up some preliminary data –"

"No," said Conner. "There's no way, man. And besides, what if your trap doesn't work?"

"Then they'll have the box," said Matt. "And they'll kill us all for sure." Then he gasped. "Do the demons know where we live? What if they pick us off one by one?" He grabbed Valencio, clinging tightly to his arm for protection.

I know Matt was just drunk rambling, but he raised some pretty good points. If the demons knew where to find me in hell, and even where to deliver me when we returned, then they were a lot smarter than I had previously given them credit for. I was instantly chilled by the prospect of being picked off one at a time.

"You know," I said. "They seem to know a lot about us. They somehow knew we found out about their plan, in real time." I stopped short, readjusting my understanding. "They obviously don't know where the box is, though, now that I think about it. Could it be some sort of selective spying?"

Theo nodded slowly. "Maybe their ability to eavesdrop is just as limited as their ability to pop in and out of our reality."

And with that, the room quieted. We each in turn surveyed the space, looking over our shoulders or craning our necks to detect any sign of eavesdropping. Of course we didn't find any, but we weren't exactly motivated to go on talking about our next moves.

Conner was the first to speak. And when he did, it was short and coded. He raised an eyebrow at Valencio. "We don't have any other options now," he said. "You might as well brush up on those perturbations."

Valencio ran a hand across his front pocket. His glasses weren't there. He swiveled pointedly in his chair, searching the surrounding debris briefly before giving up, then he clapped his hands to his knees. "We have all been very perturbed by today's events, indeed," he said. He jutted his chin, thinking. "I suppose we shall all work very quickly and quietly on correcting that."

Conner and I eyed one another with unease. Theo nodded meaningfully, a hint of a grin threatening at the corner of his mouth. Matt also nodded, but in a way that let us know he had no idea what was going on. I thought about filling him in, maybe whispering a reminder about Conner's plan to travel back in time and prevent the experiment altogether, but he'd probably just blurt it out loud and ruin the whole thing. Then I realized this may be the perfect opportunity to undermine our efforts, but I wasn't brave enough to set us up for failure just yet.

Valencio nodded, resolved to move forward with the plan. "If we survive it," he said. "We will be one of a very few, and very controversial, renegade teams in history thus far."

And we all fell silent again. Matt wrinkled his nose, understanding now that he had no clue what was going on.

"Alright guys," I finally said. My body was starting to shut down; my arms and legs turning into lead blocks. "I think we should get some rest for now and reorganize ourselves tomorrow."

Valencio rose from his chair. "Agreed," he said.

Matt cut in, his voice lilting. "But how can we sleep with demons after us?" He grabbed himself dramatically.

Conner sighed. He raised an affirming eye at me. "You certain we got six more days?"

I bit my lip. "I'm pretty sure," I said. "And if they do show up, I guess it's best we're not all in the same place at the same time."

Theo nodded. "And then we fight like hell until they disappear."

It's the best we could come up with, but it would suit me for now. I stretched myself out of my chair. Valencio clapped a hand firmly to my shoulder and gave it a squeeze. I offered him a smile, to which he responded, "Rest well." And we all went our separate ways with the agreement that we would meet in the second-floor conference room in the morning to make an execution plan.

▢ ▢ ▢ ▢ ▢ ▢ ▢

I arrived at the lab very early the next morning, which gave me the coffee advantage. I was able to make the pot palatable, unlike Valencio, who thinks the first cup has the right to make you run to the bathroom crying. I would be able to have my routine second cup, and boy would I need it after another sleepless night.

I brought the pot up to the second-floor conference room and helped myself to one of the larger mugs. The room was wide, with twelve chairs rounding the conference table. Despite its size, there were very few things in it – a projector, a console on the far wall and a telephone. I sat on the far end of the room next to the projector, in case we'd be using it. The door hummed, letting Matt in.

"Top of the morning," he said a little too brightly. He sniffed the air. "Smells safe."

I held out a mug for him. "What are you doing here so early?"

"I live here, remember?"

"Oh yeah," I said.

Matt dropped himself in the seat next to me.

We were quiet for a while. I sipped my coffee here and there, but my mind was in a weird and angry and sad, soggy fog; tormented by my new and improved nightmares. This time Azrael showed up in his true form and absorbed the entire planet into one of his thick, fleshy folds. Cherubs laughed at me while I ran for cover, but I think it's safe to say I didn't survive.

Matt was content to sit quietly, too. Then, after a few minutes, a thought occurred to me. I looked at Matt. His robes were crisp and clean. The little silver cross on his collar glinted in the fluorescent lighting. I narrowed my eyes at him. "You're not drunk," I said.

Matt clutched his collar. "Who do you think I am?" he asked in a pitchy, indignant voice. "It's seven o clock in the morning!"

I blinked several times at him.

"What?" he defended. "I'm not drunk *all* the time. Plus, this is an important meeting. I can prioritize."

I held up both hands to placate him. "Okay, okay," I conceded.

After a moment's pause, he leaned in and said, "I'm chilling some champagne, actually, for celebratory mimosas after the meeting."

I laughed. Matt laughed, too.

It was short-lived, though. My giggles were wicked into the pit in my stomach, dissipating as they went. Then we went back to sipping our coffee in silence. And since I knew I was being weird, I redoubled my efforts to talk to him.

"So, how's life at the lab?" I asked. "Do you plan on partying forever or what?"

"Nah," he said. "Not forever." Matt raised his cup and took another sip. Then he stretched back in his seat. "My life was shattered, you know? I'm just picking up the pieces." He stuck out his lips for a thoughtful moment, then said, "And putting them back together in a slightly different order. I guess I'm making a new picture. Until then I'll live a little." His eyes pointed at a spot on the ceiling, but I knew his mind was far beyond the walls of the lab.

"And what does your picture look like right now?"

"Well," said Matt. He leaned forward and drummed his fingers on the table. "Creation is far too complex for us to act like we understand it all. It's an open picture."

I nodded my understanding. "And what about after we send God back?" I asked. "What does the picture look like then? Will you go back to the church?"

Matt's eyes bulged a little as he thought about it. "I don't know," he said. "There's so much good to do there. I've been able to help so many people, regardless of who God is. God's identity isn't the point of it all. Doing good. Helping others. Bringing peace into the world. Those things matter."

I offered him a small smile. "And living a little in the meantime matters, too."

Matt smiled back, then he sighed. "It does get a little boring around here, though." He looked around the plain room, which actually helped him make his point. "I should think about finding some games to play."

"Oh," I jumped. Then I shoved my hands in the back pocket of my jeans. "You can use my phone," I said. "I carry it out of habit, but I don't really have any use for it since no service or internet." I found the folder where I store all my games and slid the phone over to Matt.

He squinted at the thing. "Solitaire… Candy Crush… Fishdom…" He scrolled through the options.

"You won't be able to download anything new, but those should be alright for now."

Matt's eyes widened, glinting in the light of the screen. "These look awesome," he said, scrolling through the folder.

I realized that I may have just created a monster. He would probably become a screen goblin, just like so many of the students I spotted in the hallways during passing periods. They hid between lockers or plunked down on benches or scuttled off to some of the few less-trafficked bathroom locations for privacy – doomed to infini-scrolling and obsessive-compulsive selfie-snapping. I grimaced. I wasn't sure if Matt was used to a cell phone. Maybe the pull of it would be too strong for him.

"You have played games on a phone before, right? I asked.

Matt paused his scrolling. "At our parish, we're highly discouraged from engaging in such earthly distractions," he said.

I rolled the wheels of my chair sharply, turning to fully face him. "What? So, what about email? Are you allowed to use that? Oh, that means no social media, right?" I put my cup to my lips for another sip.

Matt straightened out the arms of his robes cooly. "Me and the bros have been known to chat with the ladies on the Twitter after youth service on Friday nights."

I had to cover my mouth to keep my coffee from spraying over the table. I choked it down. "Okay, first – youth service on a Friday night? Are they trying to make you a forty-year-old virgin? And second – nobody calls it *the* Twitter." I cackled. "And just so you're in the know, it's called X now."

Matt's voice was suddenly low and breathy and gross. "Oh," he said smoothly. "It's called X? I think I'd like to check that out."

I stared at him for probably a solid minute, my eyes willing him to cut it out. "Matt, you *are* a forty-year-old virgin, aren't you?"

"I'm thirty-one, thank you," he said, reeling in his horndog voice. Then he gave me a look that said, *of course I'm a virgin, why would you even ask?*

I decided I wouldn't continue down this dangerous and, frankly, sad road, so I clarified. "It's the same old Twitter," I said. "They just slapped a new name on it."

"Oh," said Matt. "Well, I'm sure I'd enjoy it all the same."

Glad to have that behind us, I went back to my cup of coffee. It had gotten considerably cooler, so I was able to take a larger gulp. Matt went back to exploring the games on the phone.

The quiet allowed me to once again become aware of the pit in my stomach. I sighed in frustration. And before I could help it, I blurted out. "I need help, Matt."

"Okay, shoot."

For a minute I considered dropping the whole thing. But I knew it would be too late after the mimosas and we were hardly ever naturally alone together. I took a deep breath, thinking about what I might say. Then a thought occurred to me. "You're still offering priest services, right?"

Matt put the phone on the table. "Of course," he said. His voice was suddenly firm, very sure. It was comforting. "Anything we talk about here is confidential."

"Okay," I said, almost in a whisper. I licked my lips. I wasn't sure of exactly what I wanted. I definitely wouldn't tell him I was planning on sabotaging our plans. Though that was causing much of my angst, it wasn't why my insides were all knotted into a tangled mess. And before I could agree on how best to sum up my problem to Matt, my mouth blurted, "When I was fourteen, my mom told me I was going to hell." I was shocked to hear it come out of my mouth, but also relieved. It was something I thought about almost every day, but never quite had the nerve to admit to anyone else. It felt dangerous, saying it out loud. I watched Matt intently, daring him to make fun of it.

He gave a small nod. "I'm sorry to hear that," he said. "Would you like to tell me more about it?"

I shook my head, regretting having said anything. Matt nodded again, his face unreadable. But there was no point in withdrawing now, I figured. That would just be weird. I forced myself to go on. "My mom saw a part of me that I wasn't ready for her to see – that I didn't really understand myself. She didn't understand me…" My voice crumbled to a thin whisper. I smoothed my hands over the cool tabletop, willing myself to continue. "She only judged me. And she's been judging me ever since."

Matt's eyes were soft. I could see the brown flecks in the green of them as he stared into my own. I allowed him to look at me for a brief while. To *see* me.

"Well," he said, raising both eyebrows. His forehead wrinkled. "It looks like you've already gone to hell." He placed a hand over one of mine. It was warmed by his coffee cup. He leaned in and whispered. "And you rose from the ashes…" A smile tugged at the corners of my mouth against my will. He finished triumphantly. "… like a phoenix!"

I chortled. The laugh bubbled up from my gut, filling the pit that had made its home there. "Like a phoenix," I echoed softly. He gave my hand a little squeeze. I gave his a squeeze in return, then dabbed the corners of my burning eyes.

"So, hell's not that bad," he said. "What else?"

"Well, I don't know if you noticed, Matt, but I like girls."

Matt nodded, drawing in a contrived breath and looking me once over. "I don't know if *you* noticed, Alex, but I like booze."

I laughed again. Matt waved a hand, stifling his own laughter. "In all seriousness," he said. "You were killed, and you went to heaven. Shouldn't that tell you something?" He weaved his fingers together and rested them on the table in front of him.

I allowed myself to draw in a low gasp, having never thought about it that way. "Azrael told me the only person judging me was me." I thought about the day I met Matt – the day he realized nothing was quite like he thought it was. "Do you really believe we can do what we want?"

Matt moved his lips, but paused to think some more. "There's gotta be some measure that separates angels and demons, heaven and hell." He bit his lip. "Can we do what we want? I think so. Can you live with yourself and the decisions you've made? That's the question."

I squeezed my lips together, thinking. I literally could live with myself all day long if my mother hadn't made me feel so wrong all these years. What I couldn't stand was having a moment in my life that was so soft and beautiful and alive tainted with such guilt and shame and resistance. Thanks to my mom, that experience would forever bounce around on the inside of my skull, whether I liked it or not. "The question is, how do I live with my mom? How do I live with the decisions *she's* made?"

Matt nodded. "I'm sure your mother wanted to protect you; she did what she felt was right. But she's only human. We fall short. And when we do, God picks up the slack."

I grimaced. "Are you sure about that?" I asked. "I mean, you've been looking at the same God I've been looking at these past few months, right?"

"I'm more sure than I've ever been," he smiled. "I mean, if she can swear and turn buildings into Picassos, then I'm certain we're allowed to simply be ourselves. We're human. We're exploring what it means to be alive, to *live*."

I crossed my arms. "So how is God supposed to be picking up the slack here?" I asked. A lump dropped into my throat. I tried to swallow it down. "When I'm not enough, why isn't she picking up the slack?"

Matt nodded his understanding. Then he simply said, "Grace." I sputtered, rearing to argue, but he continued. "God's grace is what picks up the slack. It erases all of our shortcomings."

My shoulders dropped. "That's the most generic thing I've ever heard."

Matt silenced me with a finger. "You can't deny grace, Alex. It's already yours. It's already in you." He looked me in the eyes. This time I was annoyed by the softness of his. "It's your job to extend that grace to your mother," he said. "Forgive her, for she knows not what she's done. And forgive yourself, too, for ever believing you're not enough."

"But look at me," I said. My eyes stung. I felt words spilling out, but I couldn't stop them. The dam was broken. "I moved all the way out here to get away from her and my dad did a shitty job of taking up for me, so I hate him too, and my cat sucks and my job sucks and I don't know if I'm even helping the kids learn anything, really." I sniffled. Thick tears escaped down the sides of my face. "I feel like everything she says is right, even though I want her to be wrong so bad."

Matt rubbed my back. He allowed me to ugly cry until the intensity of my episode simmered back to intermittent sniffling. "You're a lot more than you give yourself credit for," he said. "You *do* a lot more than you understand. What you feel like is nobody else's business – it's just between you and God, because only the two of you know your life's plan. You can't worry about what people think of you."

I could only stare at him through tired eyes.

He wrinkled his forehead again. "Not even your mom. She may re-live that moment – that belief – over and over again, but you don't have to. You don't have to carry that burden around with you anymore."

I shook my head.

Matt sighed, "Look," he said. "You were the one who led the others to the church, to come find me. You were the one to get the Book of Life and to secure that… *Pandora's box*. Will your mom be impressed by that?" He didn't give me time to answer. "No," he said. "But what you've done has been tantamount to our successes so far – in saving her from eternal *slumber*, or whatever this is that's going on. You're more than enough, in my opinion."

"What successes?" I whispered. Then I felt even crappier, knowing that I most certainly wouldn't be going out of my way to help us succeed in doing anything else from here on out. But I couldn't bring myself to think about that at the moment. I did know that our recent successes weren't even really successes, however, so I added, "We can't use the Book of Life for anything useful and there is no template."

"But you're the idea person, remember?" He smiled. "And we haven't lost yet. So do what you're good at and stop worrying about falling short of someone else's ideas of who you're supposed to be."

I don't know what answer I was looking for, but this wasn't it. Or maybe I just didn't want it to be so simple. Was forgiving someone simple? I took an uneven breath and tried to nod. Matt smiled at me. And though the pit in my stomach probably felt heavier from the extra guilt that had snuck its way in there, I managed a small smile for him. I was ready to be finished with the conversation. "You're right," I said, wiping my face with my shirt sleeve. "She's three hundred miles away. I guess I shouldn't let her breathe over my shoulder anymore."

And I wasn't lying. I was fortified in my decision to keep my mother asleep. She wouldn't be able to breathe over my shoulder neither literally nor figuratively. After all, she was the only one judging me here. God wasn't. I would choose God. That can't be a bad thing, right?

Chapter Ten: Multiple Personalities, in Real Time

Theo and Valencio arrived at the conference room soon after, followed by Conner. And what came next was a very painful meeting – by many senses of the word. First, Valencio suggested we all implant ourselves with some sort of brain chip that would allow us to communicate telepathically. It would only take one teeny tiny little shot to the temporal lobe, he said. No thank you. And fun fact about the temporal lobe, by the way – that's the part of your brain that filters out unimportant sounds, like a dog barking up the street or the hum of a ceiling fan or your mom's incessant nagging about you wearing more skirts and maybe trying lipstick for some stupid reason. If anyone's ever accused you of selective hearing, you can blame the temporal lobe for that. But I digress.

We shot the idea down immediately, only to have Theo pull out a glass pad. He drew up an audio console, which projected over the table. Then he adjusted the knobs, and the room was immediately bathed in the most horrific music you could imagine.' It sounded as though a very fussy robot baby was attempting to sing a lullaby.

Matt smacked his hands to his ears. "What the crap?"

I furrowed my brows at Theo, also demanding answers, but he waved away our concerns. He stole a quick glance over his shoulders, then he spoke urgently. "Interference," he said. "It'll be difficult to hear our conversation. Hopefully."

"Smart," said Conner. "At least it's worth a shot."

I nodded reluctantly, conceding to add auditory abuse to my growing list of traumas.

But thankfully I had time to get used to tuning it out. The first part of the meeting was just between Theo and Valencio, who had to brush up on the particulars of opening a tachyonic hyperstream. And not knowing how we could possibly contribute, the rest of us mostly sat idly around the table. I was patient, though, because my mind was working double duty trying to both identify relevant information and use it to somehow undermine our plans. I did learn quite a lot too, like how sin, cos and tan weren't just decorative functions. They could actually be used to achieve real trigonometric results in quantum physics.

But I couldn't fathom how I might use this information to stop their time traveling. Could I simply alter Valencio's calculations? Change a number here and there? Or perhaps, remove a parenthesis? Would a miscalculation simply make the time machine not work? Or would it turn them all into primordial slime? Or maybe trap them in medieval times? I could only imagine Valencio having to wipe his butt with hay and dying from an ingrown toenail. I decided messing around with the calculations wasn't the way to go.

After the appropriate assessments were made and Valencio and Theo divided up the tasks related to preparing the machine, it was our turn.

"We need a volunteer," Theo whispered forcefully through the noise. "Protocol calls for exactly two people on a temporal mission, and Valencio will have to stay here to keep the tachyonic hyperstream stable."

"I thought we were *all* going?" I hissed back.

Matt shook his head. "Oh, I was always sitting out of this one," he said. He crossed his arms and pulled himself down further into his chair stubbornly.

Conner and I eyed one another. "What exactly will we be doing?" he asked Theo. "What does the mission actually look like?"

Theo rubbed a towel from the pocket of his jumper along his forehead. "Let's start there, since we'll have to figure it out eventually." He pulled up a map of the grounds at CERN on the projected screen, then zoomed in on a thicket of trees. "There's a greenspace at the facility. If we do it right, we can use the trees and shrubs there to conceal ourselves when we arrive."

"Good," said Conner. "We'll take 'em by surprise."

"And then do what?" I asked. "Are we going to fight them? Steal the template so they can't go through with it?" I don't know why I bothered asking. I was supposed to be figuring out how to stop the whole going back in time thing in the first place.

Matt shook his head. "No, that would be dumb."

I scowled at him, then shrugged. Then Theo was looking at me as if I'd say something more, so I said, "I guess if we took that approach, we'd be fighting the scientists *and* the demons. Matt's right."

"Yes, let's assume they'd be there, too," said Theo.

I struggled to keep my helpful mouth shut. It was already open and helping again. "No assumptions," I said. "Azrael told me they would be watching the experiment closely. They'll definitely be there."

I clenched my fists and let out a frustrated grunt, which prompted the others to glance at me with concern. I didn't particularly notice, though, because I was secretly having an internal battle. It was hard to change my programming, having spent so many of my days fixated on sending God back to wherever it is she came from. And I had good information, but blabbing was unhelpful to my new plan. I probably did need to continue participating, though, so as not to rouse suspicion. I would participate in the problem-solving, I decided. When my opportunity to sabotage the plans arose, I would act then. I nodded, confirming the agreement with myself. Then I laughed. I don't know how spies kept their sanity. I was, in fact, developing multiple personalities in real time, and the robot lullaby in the background only enhanced the discombobulation.

Theo drummed his fingers on the table, bringing me back to reality. "Instead of fighting, then, we need to collaborate. Why don't we just tell the scientists the truth?"

I scoffed. "That we're time travelers, coming to stop God from ruining Earth?"

"No," said Valencio. He leaned in closely. "You must never reveal that you've traveled through time."

I nodded. "Right, right. Regulations…"

"You mustn't ever reveal you're from future," he said in a serious voice. "You do not have the credentials necessary for this trip. You will neither be able to properly report to the Temporal Task Force, nor receive any help from them. They will most likely lock you away from society for the rest of your natural life." Valencio's eyes narrowed. Then, he sighed. "What you can do instead is present your findings to the scientists on the project." He gestured to Theo. "You have all the evidence to reveal the true nature of the demons' plan. Explain it to them."

"How are we going to do that without Shax murdering us?" I asked. I rubbed my chest where the hole used to be. "They'll still be watching the experiment closely. And I'm willing to bet they'll be more powerful since we'll be traveling to a point in time where God's essence isn't as strong on Earth."

I traced a line in the wood of the table with my finger, preparing to retire my brain, having contributed more than enough participation in the conversation. Then I realized it had grown quiet. Well, besides the robotic symphony in the background. I looked up, thinking something happened, but everyone was looking at me. "What?" I shrugged.

"You're the idea person," said Conner. "What's your idea?"

Matt gave me an encouraging nod and what I'd say was a decently reassuring wink, but by the look on Conner's face, it gave a different impression to the others.

I allowed my eyes to bulge as my brain scrambled for something reasonable to say. Valencio watched me from behind curious eyes, which felt like an oxymoron to me. He literally just finished talking about programming a time travel machine, but was looking to me for what to do next.

Nonetheless, I did my best to oblige. And I'll tell you this for free – there's a great deal of pressure once you're dubbed the 'idea person.' Especially since at the moment I had exactly none. But still, I strained my brain, knowing that the meeting would have to end at some point, and then I would carry on with my sabotagery.

We left the conference room hours later, frayed and flustered, but mostly happy. As it stood, I would (allegedly) be traveling with Theo within the five-day deadline we gave ourselves, and we would (again, allegedly) be carrying out a very meticulously planned mission. I stressed several times during the meeting that Theo should do as he originally planned and devise a trap for the demons – as a contingency plan – and to pursue that project with just as much rigor, if possible. I did understand that preventing us from going back in time would put us at the mercy of our demon friends, but I trusted Theo's weird gusto for making weapons. My plan was set in motion. And I had five days to find a way to carry it out.

□ □ □ □ □ □ □

The following days were hard pressed. Mainly for Valencio, who was the only one of us educated enough on temporal physics to program the tachyonic displacement drive (he forbade us from calling it a time machine because he said the term, 'lacked couth and precision'). And if I had to put us in order by stress level after that, Theo would be number two since he would have to pilot the thing, having no training on it whatsoever. But what he did have, according to Valencio, was a good intuition for the dynamics of complex machinery. Conner would be a hard third, having paced a visible groove in the tile around his uncle's medical pod. He had become more agitated by the day since Shax and Danel's visit to the lab. Matt continued to enjoy his worldly pleasures, but he wasn't hitting the bottle as hard as he used to. He spent his time mostly gambling against AI on an app he found on one of the lab's desktops.

I don't know where I fit on the list. I was certainly nervous at the prospect of betraying my friends. But the more I thought about it, the more it beat hurling myself through time and space in an unsanctioned trip to the past. Or, at least, that's what I kept telling myself in order to quell the guilt. I felt like I was wearing a big red sticker on my forehead that read: warning, traitor. Nobody seemed to suspect me, though, when I asked to double-check their data reports or convert their spreadsheets to digital formatting. I left no stone unturned when looking for opportunities to halt the mission. I even took the Book of Life for a spin, asking it questions like, *how do you make a report to the time police?* or *How to safely prevent time travel.* I learned rather quickly that the Book of Life wasn't necessarily the celestial Google I was hoping for.

My opportunity came on the fourth day, though, when we were all summoned by Theo. He gathered us by yelling down the fourth-floor hallway until Matt, Conner and I were all present and accounted for. Then he got down to business, pulling up the fussy robot lullaby on a glass pad he was holding.

"Okay," he said. "Valencio and I are just about finished prepping the machine, but we have a couple asks." Conner and I nodded. Matt raised an eyebrow in a noncommittal way. Theo went on, roving his finger down a long to-do list on his glass pad. Many of the items were marked 'complete,' so he had to scan carefully to find the ones that weren't yet. "First up – there are three functional satellites over the D.C. area. We'll need to perform a routine diagnostic on the power source in the displacement drive this evening and we don't need those satellites detecting the field it'll generate, especially if any form of the Temporal Task Force is active right now." Theo looked at me, then Conner, then Matt. I wanted to butt in and tell him that they were, in fact, not functional. But that might raise suspicion on my part. "We'll need someone to manually jam the signal," he said. "Since our automated systems are down."

"What does that look like?" asked Conner. "What would we have to do?"

"You'd just tap the button on the console we've set up in the comm room on the first floor."

"Oh, I got that," said Conner. He nodded reassuringly at me and Matt, and I couldn't tell if he was volunteering because he wanted to pull his own weight or if it was an apology for being so grumpy lately.

"Got you down," said Theo. He skimmed through his notes again, then backtracked. "Oh, I should've clarified – you'll have to push the button in three-minute increments for a two-hour span of time. Maybe even less, if nothing anomalous comes up."

Conner's shoulders dropped, his face pinched with mild annoyance. "Is that all?" he asked suspiciously.

Theo double checked his notes. "Yep, that's it – just push the button every three minutes for two hours." He smiled at Conner. "I'll meet you on the first floor at seven tonight."

This gave Conner permission to walk away. But not before saying, "Ain't nothin easy about science, is there?" He rolled his eyes grumpily. "We gotta make pushing a button extra."

It didn't put a damper on Theo's spirits though. Me and Matt laughed amongst ourselves while he skimmed through his list again. "Here we go," he said, his finger hovering over an unchecked item on the list. "We'll be running low on a few materials after the diagnostic," he said. "There's a storehouse downtown where some of the major laboratories in the region source our raw and rare materials from. We'll need a runner to collect one such material." He looked at me and Matt with a warning in his eyes. "We're approaching our deadline and Valencio and I are locked in for the next thirty six hours straight. It's super important that someone retrieve this chemical element and *nothing* more from that storehouse, and bring it straight back here."

I took a quivering breath, intrigued. "What is it?" I asked. "What's the chemical we need to collect?"

"We need three standard vials of urilium," said Theo. "Nothing more, nothing less."

I laughed at his oversight. "Don't you mean *uranium*?" I corrected. I was feeling quite smug about it, too, but Theo reminded me of my own scientific inferiority faster than I could blink.

"You won't find this element on the periodic table," he said firmly. "It won't be publicly recognized any time soon – not since its only useful application is for powering a tachyonic hyperstream."

The air was sucked out of my lungs suddenly. It was my moment. I had been looking for my opportunity to halt the mission, and I had just found it. "It's the fuel source for the hyperstream?"

"Well, I guess it's qualified as a catalyst," he said. "But yeah."

"I'll do it," I said, nearly pushing Matt to the floor with my elbow. Which was unnecessary, I know, because he was in no way showing any signs of volunteering. He looked downright relieved when I did, as a matter of fact. I straightened myself out and smiled at Theo, hoping he couldn't hear my heart beating wildly against the inside of my chest. I felt queasy and dirty and scummy. But I was going to go through with it. I would pick up the urilium and simply never return to the lab.

⧠ ⧠ ⧠ ⧠ ⧠ ⧠ ⧠

I followed the directions to the storehouse on the south side of town exactly as Theo gave them. But I ended up in the driveway of a dilapidated barn out in the middle of Nowhere, TX instead of a high-tech, super advanced facility. I hiked up my spandex and tied my flannel around my waist, letting my shoulders catch a breeze in my halter top. The afternoon sun was low, but in Texas that meant nothing. The sun had a way of punishing anyone who had the nerve to think cold mornings meant cold days.

I glanced up and down the gravel road, but there was literally nothing to look at but open fields. Of course there was the occasional oddity, like a herd of longhorns in the distance flapping ridiculous and non-aerodynamic wings to hover just above a small cattle run. Like, why would they stay there if they had wings? There was also a huge eagle with a snake in its mouth, but that one could've been real.

Anyway, I assessed my situation as long as I could before deciding I'd move ahead with the directions. I took the keys out of my ignition and approached the door around the side of the barnyard. To my relief, a panel folded out of the wall, just as Theo said. I wouldn't have noticed it, had it not been for the soft hum that I had grown used to.

I searched the smooth siding and found the little console near a sleek mail slot. I shoved my hand in my pocket and pulled out the glass pad Theo gave me. This one was smaller than the ones I'd seen him and Valencio handle before, and a lot thinner, too. It served as a key. I pressed four fingers against it to wake it up, and found the password I would use. It was sixteen digits long and had to be typed all in one go — a hesitation longer than a second would cause the thing to reset, forcing me to try again. I'm not sure why I even had to type in the passcode manually, but I assumed it was because I wasn't officially meant to be here; maybe my eyeball wasn't registered in the database and was unfit for scanning.

I began the sequence of numbers, hovering my glass pad just above the console. I allowed my eyes to ping pong between the two as I pressed against the silent pad, but I hadn't quite mastered the strategy. The pad dinged at me. I took too long. I wondered if it would lock me out after so many attempts.

I began again, this time determined to memorize the numbers in groups of four, like a debit card. This strategy worked better, but not well enough. I accidentally switched the last two numbers at the end. It dinged at me again. My arm was growing tired from steadying the glass pad and my brain was filling with rage. I wanted to shake the thing. But I knew it wouldn't help, so I took a deep breath, steadied my hand, and committed to one last attempt before flying off the handle.

And, thankfully, I was granted access. The siding folded away to reveal a very narrow pathway into the building, with a steep slope of stairs leading downward. The air inside was cool and smelled very sterile – a stark difference against the dry earthy smell of the fields. I let the door fold in behind me, then made my way down the stairs.

I called into the small, clean room. "Anybody here?"

No response. I continued cautiously to the other side. There would be another console that I'd have to operate, according to Theo. I found it behind a picture frame of a dog chasing a giant, floating geosmin molecule and punched in a shorter number. This directed the entire wall to fold in on itself, revealing an incredibly large storehouse. I allowed a gasp to escape me as my eyes drank in the rows upon rows of vials and boxes and refrigerated units. It was like a scientific grocery store. A cool tungsten light illuminated the shelves as

I walked up the aisle. I wanted to touch everything – humanoid robots, terrariums housing suspiciously alien-looking organisms, and various pyrophores. But I forced myself to ignore these distractions and make a bee line for aisle 62A. Mainly because I felt like I was getting dangerously close to finding something really traumatizing, like body parts in jars or cloned dinosaur meat.

I found the aisle quickly and skimmed the row of small, rectangular storage lockers. My hand hovered over the one labeled *urilium*. The light within the unit illuminated through the glass window, revealing six small vials filled with a chunky silver liquid encased in a thick gunmetal box.

I pressed the glass pad against a flat protrusion above the handle, which made a small screen project from the unit. It asked me to confirm my lab credentials. Thankfully, the required information was already populated into the form, so I only had to press the small green button that said *proceed*.

The door hissed as it popped open, and I could almost see a fine mist billowing from the compartment as the case of vials ejected from the unit. I stared at the thing and, for a while, my brain completely stopped working. I almost didn't understand what I was doing. But I had come this far. I reminded myself that this was the power source, without which God would remain on Earth, securing my freedom from so many ails. This was my moment of truth.

Before I could think myself out of it, I scooped up all six vials, casing and all, then swiped a lid from the shelf below. I sealed it, and found that there was a neat little handle along one side for easy carrying. I shut the door and scampered out of the storeroom as quickly as I could, carefully retracing my steps and ensuring the barnyard door sealed behind me.

Then I raced breathlessly to my car. My whole body was jittering with adrenaline. By the way, I do have a fun fact about adrenaline – this is a hormone that engages the sympathetic nervous system, which is responsible for your body's fight-freeze-flee response in fearful situations. At the moment, I was fleeing quite aggressively from the scene of my crime. And as a matter of fact, I was so terrified I was practically pooping myself. But I digress.

I made it safely to my car, as if there was a real threat of anybody chasing me. I had to remind myself that I was technically on an approved mission from an accredited laboratory. But that didn't stop me from checking my rear view mirror and locking my doors. I tucked the small metal case into the backseat of my car a threw my spare jacket over it. Why? I don't know. I know that wouldn't really deter somebody from finding it if they were really determined to get it from me.

My last challenge was only to dodge the natural (well, unnatural) anomalies in the road on the way back from the south side of town. There were new sights to behold here, and with the relief of having what I came for, I was somehow able to actually *see* them. There was a completely fabricated football stadium along the highway that I wouldn't have even doubted until I heard a rumble of cheers coming from it. I slowed substantially only to see that it was empty. There was also a giant owl perched on top of the Frost Bank Tower and, further up the road, a flying dragon that I suspected was following me. It was beautiful but in an unearthly way – both terrifying and regal with deep red and watchful eyes. It snapped at something in the air I couldn't see, showing thin, razor-sharp spikes that looked more like baleen than teeth. Each scale of the beast's skin pulsed, like glowing embers. It twisted in the air, folding in on itself playfully. It might've been interested in me, but I wasn't gonna stop my car to play fetch.

Before I knew it, I got home to a very agitated cat. Milus fussed for five minutes straight after I shuffled myself through the door. I could barely put up a decent fight as he scratched at my ankles and hissed at me. Under normal circumstances I would've enjoyed this level of passion from him, but I was too distracted. I pulled his bag of dry food from the pantry. He helped by clawing at my fingers as I opened the lid, as if that would make me move faster. I poured more food than I meant to into his bowl. It spilled along the floor.

As Milus ate his fill I watched on, but I wasn't thinking about the little critter at all. My mind was probing my most recent life choices. I wasn't necessarily in the criminal zone yet. Nobody at the lab suspected my wrongdoing. But they soon would. And when they did, would they go searching? When they showed up at the storehouse and found all the urilium gone, would they track me down? I bet they could easily find my address. I would have to keep moving, I decided. Because they needed to not find me. They needed to not find me so they could understand how important it was to enact the contingency plan – they would need to prepare to use whatever weapon Theo's brilliant mind had spit out.

I gave myself an abrupt shake, which caused Milus to scoot violently from his bowl, his claws click-clacking against the tile as he went.

"Sorry, boy," I said sweetly to the fat feline. He allowed me to scoop him up from his perch on the arm of the couch. I noticed his favorite feathered lure on the floor. I grabbed it and committed to enjoying an apologetic moment of playtime with him.

Then, when he had had enough of my presence, he slunk through my arms and waited by the door. It was time to go. For good.

Chapter Eleven:
The
Army of Questionable
Meatsource

I left Milus in the foyer just long enough to rip through the apartment, gathering anything I thought we'd need in one of my larger duffels from my bedroom closet. I stuffed in a few clothes, my hygiene bag, Milus' food, and a thin purple leash that I never felt evil enough to use on him. A small chirping sound from within my bedroom stopped me. I crossed the apartment and found the walkie talkie on my chest of drawers. My hand hovered over it for a silent moment. It made this noise sometimes, and I never quite figured out why. I supposed someone on another walkie talkie pressed their button to speak but then changed their minds. A green light from its charger blinked happily into the room. I decided I would take the thing with me, just in case I had a real emergency. I threw it in my bag, charger and all.

Milus and I were in my car in no time. But he didn't go quietly. After peeing on Mrs. Miller's nasturtiums, he was only batting around the dirt, perhaps to find some insects to bully, so I pounced on him and shuffled to our destination. He spit and hissed the entire time, and gave me a good scratch when

I dumped him into the passenger's seat. I guess I deserved it; first I was stealing and now I was kidnapping Milus from his only known home.

I swiped a couple candy wrappers from the backseat and shoved them into the handbag that lives under the seat, then did a brief scan for more junk that may lay hidden among the tan fabric and carpeting. I wouldn't want to add sloth to my growing list of sins.

When I was satisfied with the condition of my backseat, I positioned the duffle on the floor just behind the passenger's seat. My eye caught the corner of the small metal box poking out from underneath my spare jacket. I unzipped the bag and tucked the urilium neatly inside for good measure.

By the time I pulled out of the parking lot, I still hadn't thought about a reasonable place to hide. It only made me bitter to realize I wasn't well-versed in the city of Austin, even though I've lived here for almost three years. My job made sure of that. With long evenings and most of my weekends dedicated to catching up on paperwork and learning new curriculum, I was basically a shut-in. I did know a couple bars, the lake, and that weird ass Dungeons and Dragons themed coffee shop I accidentally ended up at but it was low key awesome.

None of those places would do. I would have to leave town. But where would I go? Home was hundreds of miles away. Was I prepared to make that drive? I glanced in the rearview mirror long enough to see that Milus had jumped over and resorted to pacing the backseat and throwing threatening glances my way. His tail flicked menacingly. "I know, boy," I said. "But we're criminals. We have to thug it out from now on." I couldn't help but give myself a much-needed chuckle. Jeremiah Stone from fourth period often reminded me that I'd have my Black Card taken away if I didn't use cool phrases from time to time. I guess I just renewed my membership. And thug it out, we would. Which just meant we were gonna have to find a way to persevere through our next set of challenges.

I hadn't quite committed to leaving town just yet, but I realized I was moving myself toward Lady Bird Lake – my happy place. I allowed myself to take us the full stretch. Maybe I'd let Milus see where I spent my time when I wasn't with him, or at the lab nowadays I suppose. There, I would muster up the energy to tackle the four-and-a-half-hour drive ahead of me.

I decided it would be best to park in a different place than I usually did, just in case anyone had been keeping tabs on my hangouts. Not that I thought they would, but maybe Conner might be able to extrapolate where I could be based on our previous conversations about the lake. I've bragged several times that I parked by the kayak rental shack just to waltz by the long line with my personalized Lifetime Lotus and get right into the water.

This time I parked at the opposite shore. The lot here was newly paved, but it was surrounded by thick, unkempt flora – perfect for hiding my car. I rifled through my duffle for Milus' leash and, after a moment's pause, grabbed the box of urilium. I should probably keep the stolen goods on my person from here on out, I decided. But before I could get out of the car I hesitated. My fingers moved on their own, unclasping the lid from the box. I opened it, and was greeted by the six small vials. They gleamed at me accusingly, the liquidy chunks globbing along in a way that made me feel very judged.

Milus saved me from an impending bout of self-loathing by scratching the back of the driver's seat. This prompted me to yell as loud as I could for no reason.

"Cut it out!"

Milus was taken aback. As stiff as a statue, he watched me from behind alarmed eyes.

This gave me an opportunity to survey the damage he'd caused, and thankfully, it was minimal. I composed myself with a deep breath and snapped the box shut. Then I took advantage of his newly found calmness and clipped the leash onto his collar. And boy was that a mistake.

As if on cue, Milus' brain left the building. He rolled around the backseat, screaming in a high-pitched way that I'd never heard before. I thought maybe being in the car and having the leash were too many new things at once, so I maneuvered him through to the front seat by tugging on the leash a bit. He carried on with his screaming, and I was convinced he was moments away from evolving the necessary vocal cords to properly curse me out. I tugged one last time and got him out of the car. Maybe if I could get him to the grass, I thought, he'd be distracted by all the new smells there. I tugged him along, but he just continued twisting his body. Eventually he started hopping along in a way that was both ridiculous and impressive; he gave off the appearance of a possessed Twinkie. If anyone were watching, surely they'd think I somehow found a way to tame one of the stray imaginings.

I finally gave up. I walked my fingers down the leash until they came to the clasp at Milus' collar. I dodged a bite attempt and three swipes before I could unhook the thing. And when I did, he streaked into the thicket with the spirit and ferocity of his jaguar cousins.

"Hey!" I yelled after him. "Come back!"

I knew there was no point in yelling. The grass parted violently along the path he was running, as if it couldn't get out of his way fast enough. I locked the car and grasped the urilium tight against my chest before running in after him.

My tennis shoes beat against the uneven ground as I followed the path. Sticky weed clung to my spandex in an attempt to slow me down. I high stepped it, which particularly helped as I passed through a small forest of bull nettle. Milus disappeared into a grove of trees. I knew the lake would be on the other side. He had to stop; there was no way he'd want to get wet. I clutched the box tighter to my chest, hoping that shaking the urilium wouldn't cause some sort of explosive reaction, or worse, and I followed him in.

Once inside the grove, I stopped. I couldn't trace Milus' movements anymore. I relied on my hearing. There was shuffling in several bushes, and something was scampering up a tree.

"Here, Milus," I called out uncertainly.

Several more movements, but none that indicated Milus would be surrendering. I swatted a mosquito from my damp skin, then grumpily put my flannel on. The sun was low on the horizon, making it harder for me to see through the shade of the trees.

I yelled. "Milus, you come back here, you stupid cat!"

Minute shuffling.

"I know you can hear me, stop being such a turd!"

Harder shuffling. I zeroed in; it was just to the left of me. I was there in three strides. I pulled back some leafy foliage and shoved my head through.

"Got you!"

And I realized quickly that I was talking to a pair of knobby old knees.

"I don't think that cat'll be coming if you keep on insultin' it."

The knees belong to a very weathered looking woman. Her top part was very round, poured into a red and white striped bathing suit, and skinny legs held the stump of her up in a miraculous feat of physics. Short black hair bobbed around her face and she wore a wide grin. Many of her teeth were not present for the occasion, but she looked very warm and caring.

I straightened myself out as quickly as I could. "Oh," was all I could say as my brain recalibrated. Then I said, "I was just looking for my cat." Which was obvious, but I couldn't think of anything else to say.

The old lady nodded, her eyes studying me as if she were concerned for my mental well-being.

I shook my head. "Sorry," I said. I tucked the box into my left armpit and shifted my weight onto my right leg. "I just wasn't expecting to run into anyone." Not that I should have been terribly disturbed by this. I knew other people were awake and, I don't know, *existing.* I saw them sometimes driving along the roads, or having bonfires at a public park – and now that I think of it, it's a wonder that nobody's burned the city down – but I've always kept to my myself, and my friends at the lab of course. I grimaced at the thought of them.

The woman examined me for a few more seconds, then said, "You're less frantic than they usually come."

I wasn't sure of how to respond.

She cackled. "Well, I'm guessing you're just as confused as 'em, though." She turned and limped out of the trees, gesturing for me to follow. "Come on over to my camp," she said. "That cat o' yours gotta show up sometime."

I was hesitant to follow the woman. After all, I didn't owe her anything. I could easily just go back the way I came and be rid of her. I glanced over my shoulder. Still no sign of Milus. I decided there's be no harm in hanging out with her while I waited.

The woman didn't have to limp far. Her 'camp' was just a few yards away. It consisted of a fold-out lawn chair, a cooler, a portable charcoal grill and random clothing items littering the spaces in between. The perimeter was marked by possibly billions of empty cans of peaches, and it was all protected by a make-shift awning stretched among four small trees.

"My name's Agatha," she said over her shoulder.

It was very fitting. She looked about as old as an Agatha. "I'm Alexandria," I said. "You can call me Alex."

The old woman kicked aside a pair of jeans and grumbled for me to pardon her mess. Then she produced another fold-out chair and beckoned for me to have a seat. I dropped the box into the thing and lowered myself into it next, realizing it was a little sticky. Then I glanced around the encampment once more and allowed myself to fully regret my current judgement.

Agatha set herself down in her own chair. "You make sense of any of it, yet?" she asked, pointing at the sky with her eyes.

And I realized what she meant by, 'just as confused.' I wanted to correct her, and tell her that I, in fact, knew exactly what was going on. But I didn't necessarily want to discuss the finer details about how I knew it was God since the very first day, and that all of this could be fixed. I didn't want to get into any of it, because I certainly didn't want to accidentally blurt out that I was actively sabotaging the progress of a pretty well-laid plan to bring the world back to normal.

"No clue," I said, eyeing the woman. I followed her gaze, but her eyes were really just darting at random places in the sky.

The woman narrowed her eyes at some unspecified place near a cumulonimbus cloud. "It's the aliens," she said. "They come to create chaos… destabilize the planet." She shifted her eyes toward me, raising both eyebrows, then tapped the side of her nose knowingly. "Next thing you know they'll be comin' down to offer us salvation from this mess."

"Oh," I said. "Well…" I pulled my spandex further down my ankles in hopes of covering them, but it wouldn't matter anyway. The fabric was so thin, I might as well had been naked; the mosquitoes were having their way with me. I breathed in a sigh. There was a sweet scent of peaches in the air, mixed with the damp earthiness of the water. I scanned the surrounding greenery for Milus, but there was no sign of him.

Agatha suddenly jumped, then began to wriggle her way out of her seat. "Oh, where are my manners," she said. "I didn't realize it was this late." She shuffled through a few cans and kicked another pile of clothing further down the bank before she found what she was looking for – a half a bag of charcoal.

"Yep," she said, dumping the coals into the small grill. Then she grunted as she mashed them into formation. "But I tell you what – I'm not agreein' to nothin' they offer."

"Well, it seems like you've been getting along nicely enough," I agreed. "I mean, now you can camp out at the lake every day, right?"

Agatha stood up, a match in her mouth and another pressed up against a small match box in her hand, and looked around the camp site as though she only just realized where she was. "Oh, Darlin'," she laughed. "This has always been my address." She gestured with her chin to a rectangular piece of cardboard that was plunked down in the grass near the perimeter. It read 4716 Lakeway Drive.

"Oh," I said. Many things made sense now.

"Been livin' the good life for years now," Agatha went on. The fire she was attempting to summon made a reluctant appearance, flickering feebly in the pit. She fanned it a bit, then lowered herself back into her chair. "It don't matter to me society crumbled," she said. "Been tryin' to tell my daughters we don't need all this... *fancy* stuff – with the online banking and the twelve different types of shampoos and whatnot." The light from the growing flames illuminated her face, but it still seemed that a shadow had crossed it. She was suddenly embittered. It appeared she'd had this conversation with herself many times before. Her eyes darted toward me. "Can you believe they stopped talkin' to me?"

I wasn't sure if she wanted an answer or sympathy. At this point, I wasn't even sure if I was an active participant in this conversation, because she just kept on going. "Sarah Jean – that's my oldest – went and convinced the other two I needed to go to one of those looney bins," she said. Her voice started to quiver, which prompted me to crane my neck as far as it would go to scan those bushes for my damned cat. Agatha didn't seem to mind, though. "I'm their mother," she groused. "How could they do that to me?"

Agatha paused again, her silence deep enough to snap me back around. When my eyes met hers, I almost didn't recognize them from before – sad and dark and tired.

"I'm so sorry," I breathed. I wanted to reach out and touch her shoulder, maybe hug her. I wasn't sure if it's what she wanted, or if it would even help. For a few moments stuck in time I watched her sadness, and I sat with it. And I didn't know what else to say, so I asked, "Where are your daughters now; do you know? Maybe now that things are –" I waved my hand at the sky and allowed my voice to trail off. In the distance I spotted the giant owl perched atop the Frost Bank Tower flapping its wings into a comfortable position.

"Nah," Agatha said bitterly. "They're all out." She brought her hand across her neck in a swift slicing motion. "The cryogenesis took 'em."

I stammered, attempting to fight the urge to clarify that cryogenesis was entirely the wrong word for what she was referring to. It wasn't important enough in the moment, I decided. I simply nodded. "I see." I cleared my throat. "Well, maybe there'll be a time when you all can reconcile your –"

"No bother," Agatha said, batting the air. She blew a raspberry. "They're asleep, and it's better that way." She produced a pack of hot dogs from the grass near her chair and pulled out two of them. She offered one up to me and I crawled out of my chair to meet her halfway. "We don't fight like we used to now," she said.

"I see," I said. And there was an odd tugging at the base of my stomach.

Agatha went on. "Yeah, they can stay like that 'til Jesus comes to fight the aliens." She bit into the hot dog cold, and chewed contentedly. Then she stretched back into her chair.

I settled into my own chair, but I wasn't thinking about any of this insanity. My brain was probing at a thought that I couldn't quite flesh out, much like no matter how hard you run your tongue across a tooth, you can't quite feel the cavity there along the surface. I resorted to focusing on tearing my hot dog into little bits, but I wasn't going to eat it. I dropped the pieces around my chair in hopes that Milus would soon get hungry and follow the scent of free food back to me.

Agatha went on and on all evening, telling me stories of her youth and pointing out some of the lesser known sounds coming from the wildlife around the lake. She swore there was a growing population of chachalacas living in the trees, but those birds weren't really known to be this far north in Texas. I argued with her on this, saying that San Antonio was as far as they'd been, but she had a good point that Austin's green parakeet population was also an anomaly – a result of a couple of blowhards who imported a few and then set them out into the wild to reproduce. We enjoyed the debate, and even attempted to sneak through the trees and find one, or at the very least isolate a solid bird call, but with all the other animals and insects chorusing in, the evidence was inconclusive.

By the late evening I had scooched myself closer to the fire, thrown broken up bits of hot dog into the grass nearby, and fallen asleep in my chair. And I think I could go without saying that rest didn't come easy. I slapped at mosquitos frequently and repositioned myself about a billion times since the box had all but carved a hole in my back. Agatha, on the other hand, slept like a champion, smartly drawing up a pile of clothing around her legs at the first sign of trouble and then conking out for the rest of the night.

The morning came eventually, and by then I was a lumpy, cranky and frizzy-haired mess. The first light of the sun pierced over the horizon and straight into my eyeballs. I groaned a gristly protest, hoping for another few minutes of sleep, but the facts of my reality snapped into my brain.

I shot out of my seat, forcing my eyes to recognize the details of my surroundings. They panned the smoldering ashes in the pit, the littered peach cans on the perimeter, Agatha splashing around in the muddy soup that was near the bank of the lake. More cumulonimbus clouds had tiptoed in from the west, sneaking up on the rising sun. The air was thick with the promise of rain. I do have a fun fact about the rain, by the way. The smell of rain is always strong-est after a long dry spell, and the word used to describe the smell of rain is petrichor.

But I digress. I pulled the box from its living quarters in my kidney and scanned for Milus. The bits of hot dog still surrounded me; I was a castle, being guarded on all sides by an army of questionable meatsource. This was my reality; the culminating result of all my recent decisions.

My heart started to race, my stomach tight. My cat still hadn't returned, not even to swipe my food. I might have truly lost him.

I shimmied out of my seat, clutching the handle on the box of urilium. Then I considered for a moment I could have accidentally acquired time traveling capabilities in my kidneys, but I couldn't worry about any proximity effects at the moment. I scooped up a couple pieces of the hot dog in hopes to continue to try and lure Milus. Some of them were being commandeered by a battalion of ants, but I shook them off easily enough.

"Mornin', Darlin!" Agatha gave me a toothy smile from the water. She wore the same red and white striped bathing suit from the night before, but this morning she had a red handkerchief tied smartly around her neck.

I waved at her, which was the best I could do with the lump that was currently forming in my throat. I started for the bushes, but something paused me. I wanted my cat back, but I didn't want to storm off from the old woman without a proper goodbye. She deserved a polite parting, at least, after being such a welcoming host.

"Come on in," she called, beckoning me into the water. "Get yourself cleaned up."

I couldn't be sure that 'cleaning up' was what she was doing. She scooped up hands full of murky water and splashed them happily onto her face. I humbled myself, thinking about Mycobacterium vaccae. Maybe this old woman's secret to a more… *relaxed* lifestyle was a daily serotonin boost straight to the face. I forced myself to follow her lead and take five minutes out of my morning to wash up. I untied my tennis shoes and threw them off.

"I don't have a bathing suit," I said, allowing my bare feet to slap against the mud on my way down.

"Skivvies'll do you just fine," said Agatha. "We're both girls here, aren't we?"

I pulled off my spandex, stale and smokey from the night's fire, and threw them over a low hanging tree branch. I stacked my flannel and halter on top, so as not to get them further soiled by the moist fungal life of the tree. Then I took an unsure step into the coolness of the lake and was immediately relieved, having only realized how clammy my skin had felt from being stuffed into my moist clothing all night. My mosquito bites were quickly disarmed, and much of my angst had gone as well. I splashed some of the clearer water up against my skin, allowing my brain to slow down. I knew I needed to find my cat. I needed to leave town. I needed to do it fast, and in an orderly fashion.

Agatha went on talking to me, recounting her dreams and then offering me a can of peaches and her (highly recommended) Little Debbies. I politely agreed to take some for the road and finished my cleaning up. By the time I was dressed, I had a decent plan.

I would return to my car to see if Milus was waiting for me there, and if he wasn't, I'd lay my hot dog lure around the car and give him three hours. That would give me time to rest a bit more before rotating on to another hangout. I wouldn't leave town without the dumb cat. I would just check in periodically. He was too spoiled to tough it much longer in the wild. He'd come back on his own.

When I got to my car, I was disappointed to find Milus wasn't there. But I wasn't disheartened. I splintered the bits of hot dog into smaller pieces with my fingers and threw them at various lengths around the perimeter of the parking lot. I carefully tucked the box and Milus' leash back into my duffle and turned on the car. The clock read 7:24 AM. I grimaced. It was already an hour and a half past our scheduled departure. I wondered how much Theo and the gang hated me right now. I closed my eyes and said a little prayer, hoping they'd be turning their attention toward using Theo's weapon on the demons by now. Then, with no point in allowing the guilt to settle in – I had made my choice – I pushed away everything in my mind except resting and finding Milus. I rolled down the back window, just wide enough for him to climb in, reclined my seat, and forced my eyes shut.

It didn't take long before I was swimming in and out of consciousness, and my dreams seemed to be pretty telling of my mental state. There was coldness, even as I was blinded by a surge of light. I could have been dying perhaps. Loud thumping came from the left side, but no matter how hard I tried, I couldn't move my body toward the source of the sound. Then there was the gurgling of a robotic voice fizzling in and out. A softness rested against my face, attempting to save me from the freezing chill. A firm force moved my fingers, bringing me back to life. I finally snapped out of my catatonic state and realized several things were going on at once.

"Milus!" I hugged my cat, but he only struggled against me. I quickly rolled the window up, trapping him in the car for good. He slunk into the passenger's seat and batted at my hand impatiently. I realized he had been licking the hot dog residue from my fingers.

While moving around in the front, he must've brushed up against the air conditioning controls, because the cold air was blowing straight into my face. I reached up and turned the dial all the way down and as soon as I did, I heard a voice.

It was low and muzzled, and then there was a staticky pause. Then a chirp. I reached behind me and dug the walkie talkie out from my duffle. The voice came again. It was Theo.

"We're really running out of options," he said. My heart jumped. Was he talking to me? I dropped the thing as if it were a ticking time bomb. It bounced off my knees on the way to the floor between my legs. My brain was suddenly numb.

Conner's voice came in next, his voice laden with distress. "Man, let's just… let's just bring it back to square one," he said. "Just get back to the lab. Matt's freakin' out."

My eyes suddenly burned as thick tears pooled up in them. I couldn't go back now even if I wanted to. I had caused everyone so much anguish. Of course, I knew not returning with the urilium would let them down – would devastate them – but there was a coward in me that would rather not had witnessed it. I picked up the walkie talkie, which was difficult because it felt like my hand was made of ice – too numb to properly wrap my fingers around it. I put it to my lips. Then I shook myself.

"What would I even say?" I asked Milus. "If I say anything, I'd pretty much have to go back, right?"

Milus watched me from the passenger's seat through smooth, calm eyes. His tail flicked back and forth lazily.

"You're right," I said. "Best to just ignore it."

I turned the volume dial down on the walkie-talkie then stuffed it back in the duffle. Then I strapped my seat belt on and steadied my hands on the steering wheel. I glanced at the clock. It read 10:51 AM. It was almost four hours past our scheduled launch. And it was time for me and Milus to leave town.

I pulled out of the parking lot and wound my way down a narrow byway in order to get to the main road leading to the highway. The sun pierced sharply through a break in the clouds but before I could properly put my visor up, they had swallowed its rays back down. Then the sky cracked as a bolt of lightning ripped through it and rain spilled out – heavy and loud and miserable.

Chapter Twelve: Thick As Thieves

I fumbled behind the steering wheel before successfully turning on the windshield wipers. Milus practically screamed as I swerved to avoid a bus in the road.

"Oh, shush." I cut my eyes at him long enough to see that he had dug his claws into the fabric of the passenger's seat. "You know, if you didn't run away we wouldn't even be out here," I said. "These are the consequences of your actions."

Milus complained with a series of low-pitched yowls, his ears plastered to the sides of his fuzzy head.

"Oh, no sir," I lectured. But I didn't take my eyes off the road, since the rain was coming down in thick sheets. I barely dared to blink. "You don't have the right to be mad. Or sad. Or anything else except happy," I said.

More yowling.

"Stop talking while I'm talking," I argued. "That's not going to make this situation any better. Now, buck up and accept what you've done."

My eyes were suddenly burning, but not because I had been staring at the road blinklessly. I navigated around what might've been a mini-petting zoo that had been imagined up along the access road. Then I drove on for three full minutes before saying anything more to Milus. Another side-eye told me he had relaxed considerably. His ears had come up and he had tucked his legs neatly under him in a sitting position.

"I shouldn't have yelled at you like that," I whispered. I cleared my throat. "It's my fault we're out here. These are the consequences of *my* actions, not yours."

Milus accepted my apology with dignity, offering me a short meow. Then I was allowed to pat him on the head.

We drove on in silence, each mile slowly won as I battled the rain. It seemed the further from home I got, the harder the storm. But I was determined to leave town. Or at least make good headway, because I couldn't stay in Austin while my friends collapsed into hopelessness.

Just when I hit a good driving groove, and considered taking the onramp to the highway, my car dinged at me. A light on the dashboard told me I would have to stop for gas.

I've gotten used to getting gas since the world went crazy. It was an easy task, going behind the counter at a gas station and hitting the necessary buttons on the cash register. I stayed on the access road, scanning for the next convenience store.

I found a 7-Eleven and pulled in. As I circled around the gas pump, I caught a glimpse of someone rummaging around in the building. I thought about driving to the next station. Stealing gas right in front of someone would be a little awkward for me. But then I was curious. Agatha didn't turn out to be so bad in the end, after all. I parked my car at pump seven, but I didn't go in right away. I wasn't sure what I wanted from this person. I guess I was curious about their experiences, and what their explanation for all of this could be. I mean, it couldn't get wilder than aliens, right?

The rain lulled to a tolerable smattering of heavy drops. I grabbed my handbag and sprinted into the storefront before it could start up again. Then I realized too late that I recognized the person inside. My first instinct was to turn and run, but the chime on the door prompted God to whip around and spot me.

She smiled brightly. "Hey there!" she said. Then she waved dramatically as if I weren't only ten feet away. She wiped cheese crumbs from the bag of chips she had been eating on the skirt of her dress and strode over.

I glanced over my shoulder, still considering making a run for it. I decided against it. "Hello." I attempted a smile.

"You ever had these?" asked God. She extended the blue bag for me to see. It was mostly crinkled in the clutches of her orange fingers, but I could see *cheese blast* written along the bottom. They advertised that one right.

I frowned at her. So much for 'thou shall not steal.' This did count as stealing, right? I'm sure it did. And by the looks of the scraps lying around – candy wrappers, crushed juice boxes, various tubs of ice cream, and weirdly, toothpaste tubes – there was plenty thievery afoot.

But maybe that's why she didn't care I stole her book. Was petty theft on the table when it came to God? I figured I'd say nothing about it and just assume we were cool. As a matter of fact, did this make us thick as thieves? Sure, why not, I decided. And that eased my guilt ever so slightly as I thought about my most recent smash and grab at the storehouse.

Instead, I settled with simply saying, "Those'll mess up your stomach."

She grabbed a chip from the bag. "My stomach's been great," she said, then popped it in her mouth.

I watched her peruse the aisle. She picked up a wrapped chocolate cake and turned in her hand, leaving grease all over the packaging. She put it in a pocket along the side of her dress and continued down the row. I wanted to get my gas and go, to leave town as quickly as possible, and I didn't have time for extra hang ups or trips to hell or anything like that. But I was too curious. "What are you doing?" I asked her.

She frowned, chewing on a mouth full of gummy candies. "What does it look like?" she said. "I'm eating."

I screwed my face up. "But all of that junk is gonna make you sick."

God wiped the crumbs from her face. "Nonsense," she said. Her eyes popped open. She beckoned me to one of the shelves. "Look at these," she said, holding up a candy bar. "These are the best."

I scoffed. "*Please*," I said. I opened my bag and unzipped my secret pouch. "I get these from my neighbor," I said, pulling out a bar. "They're so good they'll make you cry."

Before I could pass the candy over, God snatched it from my hand. She held it up to the light, then unwrapped it. It was like watching a kid open a Christmas present.

She took a small bite. "Oh yeah," she nodded her approval. Then she took another bite, chewing slowly to savor the rich flavors. She smelled the bar, then folded the wrapper neatly back over it and placed it in her pocket. "I'm taking this one with me," she said. Then she moved on to the refrigerated section.

I cracked a smile, but it quickly faded. She knew nothing about the template, or the demons' plot. And though it was clear we wanted her to leave, she didn't know there was a plan in place that was so close to being carried out, and that instead of betraying her, I had betrayed my friends. She was naïve to it all – naïve to all the decisions that I'd been forced to make. I watched for a while longer, and the longer I watched, the more I noticed how uncomfortable I was getting. Something familiar was edging its way up from my gut; something that I couldn't push back down. Maybe it was curiosity. Maybe if I asked more questions, the answers would soothe me.

"God," I started. She handed me a sparkling water, her face puckered with displeasure. I took it and placed it next to a stack of canned goods on a shelf. "Why do you like it here?" I asked. "Besides the food."

She didn't answer right away. She put a hand to her face, gently tapping on her bottom lip. Then she burped – a loud, rumbling belch from her diaphragm. We laughed. Then she simply said, "I've been bored."

I didn't understand. I tilted my head.

"I didn't realize it until I showed up," she explained. She paused briefly, then continued. "I know everything. I *am* everything. But here… I can be surprised." She picked up a bottle of tomato juice and began unscrewing the top. "For example, I have no idea what this tastes like," she said, holding it up. Then she tipped it to her mouth and immediately spit it over the floor. She dabbed her mouth with the hem of her dress. "See," she choked. "That was surprisingly disgusting." She put the cap back on it and placed it back in the refrigerator. Then she shook her whole body as if it would help remove the taste from her mouth.

"I guess bad surprises are better than no surprises," I said.

"Bad, good…" God shrugged. "Either way you learn something." She opened a pineapple soda and sniffed it. Her eyes lit up. She took a cautious sip, then a gulp. "These are really good, too," she said. Then she handed me one with a beaming smile. She took another swig of her own. Then her voice sombered. "And you guys are only here for a beautiful, sparkling fractal of time." She sighed, and for a moment went quiet. Then a grin crept across her face, her eyes flashed. "Mortality," she said. "What a rush it must be!" Then, having glimpsed the cereal boxes in the row behind me, continued her exploration.

I figured at the rate it was going now, I'd be able to enjoy a lot more of my own mortality. With no job and no familial obligations, I really was free to do what I wanted all day. And just like that, I had begun trying to convince myself that everything was going well. But then why was I feeling so inconsolably empty? The pain in my gut felt a lot like hunger, but I didn't think food was going to satisfy it. I picked up a can of Campbell's split pea and ham, then placed it gently back on the shelf.

"God?"

She looked up from a box of Fruity Pebbles in her hands.

For a while I just stared at her, hoping my neurons would start firing off properly. But before a full thought could be produced by my brain I said, "Is it wrong that I don't ever want to talk to my mom again?"

"It's your call," she said, struggling to pull apart the plastic packaging inside the box. "The world is your oyster and all that, right? You can do what you want."

"Yeah, I get that. But how do I know if I'm making the right choice."

God finally got the packaging open but, unfortunately, most of the cereal made its way to the floor in a colorful sprinkling, raining down over our shoes like confetti. She used a boot to scoop some of it into a pile, but after realizing the futility of it she stopped. Then she sighed and looked up at me. "You know the answer to that," she said. Her eyes locked into mine as if she was reading my soul. I tore away, choosing to look at my shoes instead. "The right choice would feel good," she said. Her voice was soft, but I felt like she was scolding me. "It'll feel clean. It won't hurt anybody." She lifted my chin with her index finger, forcing me to look at her. "Most of all, it'll feed your soul."

I scoffed. "I had two options, and I chose to feed my soul. Somehow, it's not working, though."

"Oh?"

"I could leave town," I said. "I'd be betraying my friends, but I'd live in paradise."

"Or?"

"Or I could be a good friend. But that would mean I have to go back to being a bad daughter with a miserable life."

God scooped a few of the straggling pebbles from the bottom of the bag and popped them in her mouth. She rolled them around on her tongue for a thoughtful moment before swallowing them. Then she simply said, "You'll figure it out."

I threw my hands in the air. "But I need you to tell me what to do," I said impatiently.

"Why?"

"Cause you're God!"

She put a hand on her hip, then slapped the cereal box back on the shelf. "Don't you dump your responsibilities on me," she said. "Then it'll be my fault if things don't go the way you thought they should've gone."

I sputtered at her. Mainly I was trying to suck back in the attitude that may have leaked into the atmosphere. I certainly didn't want to be sent on that detour. "Couldn't you just tell me what *you'd* do?"

"Nope." She squeezed her lips together. Then she said, "The decision has to be yours."

"Why?"

"Because then there might as well not even be a *you*. There'd be only me." She threw a few more pebbles in her mouth and let them roll around in there. Then she side-eyed me before moving on to the next box. "Now go and do what you want."

I watched her examine a box of shredded wheat. I hoped so badly she'd open it next and let the little pencil shavings inside dry out her mouth.

I sighed. "This is all so stupid," I grumped. "I shouldn't even be in this situation. I'm not even doing anything wrong. *You're* the one who whacked out the planet in the first place. It's not my job to fix it!"

Thwack!

Before I knew what was going on, God smacked me on the top of the head with the shredded wheat. I grabbed my head with both hands, though it didn't actually hurt. "You hit me!"

"I should've hit you harder," she said, returning the box to its place on the shelf. She squeezed her lips together and glared at me. Stray flecks of light floated lazily from her bang. "Stop making excuses and start making choices."

I wanted to complain. To moan and groan and roll around on the floor. I huffed an insolent breath. Then I drew in a calmer one, determined to find a way to get rid of the incredible heaviness in my gut. But the longer I stood there, the more I realized how childish I really was. The thoughts I'd considered before seemed to take on new meaning. They unraveled from my brain like ribbon falling off a spool. Of course, we can do what we want – Matt was right about that. I chose to betray my friends, and it didn't feel good. I wouldn't be able to live with the consequences of my actions at all. It was just that simple.

And with a quivering movement in my stomach – the black, mucky pit had awakened and begun to move and twist inside me – I thought about my other option. If Agatha deserved another chance to hash it out with her daughters, it meant I should try and work it out with my own mother, too. The thought of talking to her voluntarily, to actively dive into our problems; clearing the air for good, terrified me. The festered pit in my stomach seemed to agree it was the best thing to do. It fluttered, confirming the idea.

"I guess what I should do is pretty obvious, then," I breathed.

God raised her eyebrows, but said nothing.

I checked my watch. We were five and a half hours past launch. "I better go."

She smiled, giving me a small nod before turning her attention back to the shelves. I thanked her and zipped behind the counter to give myself access to the gas pump. Then from the door, I paused long enough to wave goodbye to God, who had become interested in the first aid kits along the wall. She uncapped a bottle of peroxide.

"Don't drink anything on that shelf," I warned. "None of it's food." Then I crossed the parking lot to pump number seven.

The clouds had stopped their tirade and were slowly peeling back. The sun had begun forcing its way through the thinning billows, illuminating them in a remarkable display. Birds and other flying things returned to the skies, bringing with them a cacophony of playful noise. I filled my tank, uselessly urging the pump to pump faster, then I got in my car and turned the key in the ignition.

But I couldn't leave the lot just yet.

I got back out of the car, swinging my door harder than I meant to; it hit the pole that I guess stops you from running into the pump. But I didn't care. My feet raced back toward the store, though I had no idea what I might say once I got there. The bell chimed again, but God didn't look up.

"Hey," I said to her. "If you ever found yourself back up in… *heaven*, I suppose… maybe you wouldn't have to wait on a science experiment to visit Earth." God's forehead creased. I waved my hands to help me make my point. "You could just sneak down, you know, every once in a while. Just for a little bit – for some fun."

God gave me a thumbs up, but she may have been too distracted by a bag of sour candies to care. Her mouth drew up into a perfect circle as she squeezed the corners of her eyes.

When I got back in the car, Milus was pacing the back seat. He yowled at me indignantly.

"Sorry, boy." I offered an apologetic smile. "It's gonna get worse from here." Then I accelerated out of the parking lot and pointed my car toward the lab.

Chapter Thirteen: Something, Something, Something, Black Holes

I arrived at the lab a day late, and only six hours past our scheduled launch. Though the drive was long, it seemed like only minutes as my brain chewed on the many unanswered questions that were rolling around in my mind. God must've known she helped me decide to undo the experiment and get rid of her. Was she not afraid of her own demise? Or, since everything was part of a divine plan of hers, did she simply understand that we were always meant to send her back? I was so deep in thought that I didn't have time to prepare myself to face my friends. I realized this as I pulled into the gravelly parking lot. My face and neck grew uncomfortably hot, and my heart pounded against my chest. Milus' animal instincts must've allowed him to pick up on the vibe, because he had also grown quite irritable. His tail flickered and he slicked his ears back against his head.

I parked the car and wrangled the box of urilium from the duffle. Then I patted him gently. "One more strange visit and then I'll never make you leave the house again," I promised. Then I scooped him up and forced my legs to take us to the door.

My hand hovered over the space where the pad would fold out of the wall, but I didn't dare press it. I licked my lips and, noticing how heavy Milus really was, hiked the cat up further along my side. Then, without warning, the door folded out with a hiss and Matt came spilling into my arms.

"Oh, thank you *Jesus!*" he yelled, wrapping his arms around me and the cat. Milus clawed me on the way out from between us and skittered off into the woods. "Oh, please tell me you have the urilium – please, please, *please!*"

"Damn it, not again." I started for the woods but took a hard stop. I realized it would be pointless to find him, since we'd be going back in time. None of this will have technically happened if we were successful. And if we weren't successful, then I'd probably be dead or something and it still wouldn't matter. I allowed Matt to cling to me for another moment, then struggled with him when I realized he wasn't letting go. "Wait – Matt, are you drunk?"

Theo ran out from the vestibule next. He shouted over his shoulder for Conner and jogged up to peel Matt off me. Then he held me at arm's length, getting a good look at me.

"He's drunk, isn' he?" I asked Theo.

"*No,*" Matt's wild eyes bulged.

Theo ushered the two of us into the lab. "He ran into God last night."

Matt reeled around, squirming out of Theo's grasp. "You know how she hates me!"

"Stop being dramatic," said Theo. "She spared you this time."

Matt swung his arms dramatically in the air. "She spared me *this* time." Then he added. "But you know who won't? That's right – the demons!" He pulled his sleeve back dramatically and checked his watch. "And only negative five hours until they get here," he announced.

Theo pinched the bridge of his nose, but didn't say more. Valencio was jogging up the hall to meet us, and suddenly everyone had grown quiet. My skin prickled. I wanted to shrink myself into the tiniest space possible – to hide from everyone's gaze. There's a fun fact about black holes that comes to mind, but now wouldn't be an appropriate time to share it. I fought the urge to be little. I straightened my back, standing tall. I didn't have the right to shy away from my own shame.

Valencio was the first to speak. "I trust there's a very good reason you've been unreachable," he said softly. He watched me through tired eyes. I wondered if he knew the truth.

"I was… lost," I said, working hard to keep my lip from trembling. "I got really, really lost." I was squirming so badly it felt like my skin would melt right off and crawl away. I forced myself to smile. "But I'm back now." I offered him the box. He folded it under his arm.

And it seemed to be enough, because without wasting another second, he ordered everyone to get to their positions. With a newly ignited buzz of excitement, we scrambled down the hall. We ran into Conner on the staircase and swept him along with us. He shuffled down the staircase, sputtering all the while, until we reached the second floor. Then we all split in different directions.

I knew I would need to visit the Protective Equipment Division before we ran into Danel and Shax again. My hand automatically rubbed where the hole should've been in my chest as I strode down the staircase leading to the third floor. I was on a mission to find some sort of impenetrable tee shirt or something.

Soon after, I joined Conner and Matt in the vestibule at the end of the hall on the fifth floor. For the great majority of the laboratory's staff, this was the farthermost end of the facility. But Valencio – and now Theo and the rest of us – knew that the vestibule marked the entrance to a concealed passageway, which led to the warehouse that stored the tachyonic displacement drive.

"Nice sweater," said Conner. His voice jittered just a bit. He pressed his lips together as he looked at me, and I was grateful he didn't ask for an explanation for my absence, even though I was certain he was thinking about it.

I glanced down at my turtleneck and slacks, determined not to give him an opening. "All bulletproof," I bragged. And I really was happy to have been successful in my hunting. "Plus, I have to look like a scientist," I added. "Smart people dress like this, right?"

He scanned my outfit. "Right down to the tennis shoes with the slacks," he said.

Matt lifted his robes. "Tennis shoes are the way to go," he said, showing off a black and silver pair. He had calmed considerably in the last twenty minutes, but I could still see his hands shaking as he held out the garment.

I nodded my agreement, but couldn't say anything more because Valencio was rushing up to the vestibule to join us. "Sorry to have you wait," he said. "Now we just need…" he counted heads. Then he noticed Theo jogging to catch up with us. "Ah, yes – "

"Just finished triple-checking my calculations," Theo breathed, waving his glass pad.

Valencio punched in a code on a small keypad along the back wall, then he jutted his chin out, allowing the device to scan his eyes. A door opened along the wall, revealing an unexpected sight. The passageway was dark, tight, and cavernous. Valencio took a cautious step down, bracing himself on the smooth part of the door. We all glanced at one another. I laughed. "Did the budget run out when they got down here?"

Conner grinned. "Maybe they spent it all on the time machine," he said.

Valencio rolled his eyes.

"I'd say so," said Theo. "It's impressive alright." And he followed Valencio into the damp tunnel. Conner and I followed, then Matt. He yelled to us whether he should close the door behind himself, but before anyone could answer it snapped itself shut.

We practically had to jog in order to keep up with Valencio, but it didn't take long before the tunnel opened up into a spacious cave. At the center, glass consoles were placed on each side of a white hexagonal pad on the ground. The device sharply contrasted against the raw simplicity of the cavern.

Valencio didn't waste any time. He accessed each panel one by one, powering them up, then doled out his orders methodically. "Phase one," he announced. "Begin initiating the pre–launch sequence."

Theo walked over to another console and began pressing knobs and buttons. "Condensing controls to panels one and two," he said. Then he circled to the next panel and did the same thing. My mouth began to dry. I licked my lips. Conner squeezed my shoulder, but I didn't look at him. I focused on keeping my breathing even.

Valencio toggled between two consoles, rotating the knobs and putting in codes from a handheld glass pad. "All systems accessible from panels one and two," he reported.

Theo joined him. He double checked everything Valencio had done, then pressed something that cast a holographic set of controls and data above the console. "All systems functioning nominally," he reported.

Valencio exhaled a sharp breath. Then he said, "Phase two – generating the tachyonic hyperstream."

I didn't know all of the phases, but I did know that the tachyonic hyperstream would be what we would use to do the time traveling. It was happening so fast that my head started spinning. I found a chunk of fallen earth along the wall and sat on it. Matt joined me.

"Hey," Matt said. His voice lilted. He looked as though he wanted to say something more.

"What's up?"

Matt bit his lip, thinking. Then he said, "When we get rid of God, do you mind coming to visit me at the church?"

"Are you really going back?" I raised my eyebrows dubiously.

He shrugged. "I don't know. I imagine if the experiment never happens, I'll never know what I know now."

"And what makes you think I'll know?"

"Well," Matt sputtered. "You're the one going back in time. I would imagine you'd be immune when everything… shifts."

I considered his logic, and when I couldn't find any argument for or against it, I said, "If I retain all my memories, I'll come visit you." Then I scrunched up my face. "And why exactly am I visiting you if you won't remember me?"

Matt drew in a slow and steady breath. "I guess I want you to just try and remind me to live a little."

It seemed like a tall order. I couldn't imagine a sequence of words that would convince Matt – a previously devout and honorary forty-year-old virgin, to loosen up and 'live a little.' But I decided to take on the challenge. "Okay," I said. "I'll give it a shot."

Matt grinned, then slapped his hands to his knees. Theo and Valencio continued their sequence. "Stabilizing present quasiparticles," Theo announced.

Valencio nodded. He monitored a series of gauges for a moment. "Quasiparticles are stable," he reported. Then he announced, "Generating access point within the temporal entanglement continuum."

And with that, the hexagonal pad started to spark and fizzle as if being electrified. The hairs on my arms stood on end. Matt and Conner looked at their own arms, too. Theo turned a knob slowly. "Adjusting the phase intensity," he reported. The pad began to buzz smoothly and evenly.

"Phase is at a nominal degree," said Valencio. "Erecting the drive." He typed in a series of commands. Thin, metallic rods rose from the corners of the pad, then folded outwards several times to create a geometric dome of some sort. The honeycomb pattern made me think of a beehive. Along one part of it, the rods flattened to create a small panel. A red–orange glow illuminated the new structure from within. "Isolating exit coordinates," he said. A moment later Theo confirmed, "Exit coordinates are identified."

It took a minute for me to realize the process had been completed. Theo had to walk over to where I was in order to collect me.

"Don't tell me you're afraid," he said, scooping me up by my arm.

I tried to put a smile on my face, but I didn't lie. "You bet," I said.

Theo let out a hollow laugh. "You've been to both heaven and hell," he said. "The past'll be nothing for you."

I stopped just short of the console to look at him. "Are… are you nervous, too? Cause we can't both be nervous. Somebody's gotta be in charge here."

Theo waved away my concerns. "I'm cautious," he said. "There's really nothing to be *worried* about." But I could still see the shadow of a frown on his face.

Valencio interjected. "The hyperstream is safe," he assured me. "And you have a solid plan. You won't fail."

I nodded, forcing another smile. "You're right," I said. "No sense in backing down now."

Valencio extended an arm, inviting us to enter the structure. "When you're ready," he said.

Theo grabbed my hand, squeezing it tightly. When we approached the pad, the metal rods folded in order to allow us in. I stepped onto the pad, into the warmth of the red–orange glow. I could hear Conner and Matt wishing us luck, but before I could look over my shoulder, I was fighting gravity. My eyes rolled, and my body felt like it was a thousand pounds for about five seconds. Then everything lost meaning.

My brain tried to understand what was happening. I could feel Theo's hand still in mine – that much I understood – but it took a while to recall what trees and the sky and sunlight were. When I came to, I realized we were in a heavily wooded area.

Theo let my hand go. "Woah." He grabbed his head. "I haven't felt like that since college."

I wanted to be amused, but something caught my attention. Or the lack of something, I should say. I turned frantically in a circle. "How are we getting back?" I asked. "The stream, or the drive thing… it's not here!" I started to sprint, thinking maybe we were separated from it – that it was just somewhere else in the woods – but I suddenly hit an invisible force. I fell to the ground. All I could do was grab my face with both hands as Theo laughed at me.

"I should've warned you about that," he wheezed. I peeked over my hands. I could see the thin metal rods flickering along the siding where I ran into it. Theo ran his hand across it, making it flicker even more. "Best to not do that again," he said. "I don't think that impact should've caused any harm, but this *is* a delicate piece of technology."

"So, is it invisible?" I looked down at my hands. "Are *we* invisible?" Then I realized my mind was moving a thousand miles an hour. "Don't answer that," I said. I closed my eyes and took a deep breath. I needed to be more methodical. That helped Theo and Valencio stay in step with one another, and I didn't want to be a bad partner. When I felt calm, I opened my eyes again. "We're here," I said. "Next step – let's confirm that we're at the correct time and space."

"Right," said Theo. He ran a hand along the invisible interior of the dome, leaving a flickering trail, until he found the panel and started typing. Then he paused.

"Is something wrong?" I asked, fighting down an unreasonable panic.

He put a finger up. "The computer's just taking a little longer than expected," he said. This prompted me to allow the panic to fully mature. My chest squeezed so tightly I was sure I'd have a heart attack on the spot. I didn't have to warn Theo of my impending funeral, though. A smile crossed his face. "We are at the correct facility – exactly nineteen years, seventy–two days, and six and a half hours in the past."

I clutched my chest, allowing relief to wash over me. It was the day of the demon's initial proposal. And we were going to expose them. Without dying in the process. Hopefully.

He continued typing. "Running preservation protocol number three," he said. I tilted my head. "That means I'm ensuring the tachyonic signature is dampened, and that the dome's beacon can only be received by us – oh!" He jumped, then patted his pockets. Then he shoved his hand in his left pocket with a groan of relief and pulled out two watches. He threw one at me. "They won't tell you the time, but they'll lead us back to the dome if we get lost." I put mine on. Theo continued on the panel. "Lowering the stabilizing field," he said. Then he beaconed for me to try leaving again. I walked cautiously toward the edge of the dome until it began to flicker again, and the rods folded away to allow me through.

It was much warmer outside of the dome. I shielded my eyes to take in the lush greenery, then I looked back. Theo seemed to appear from nowhere as he stepped out behind me. I looked around, making sure nobody else had seen, but we were alone.

"According to our maps," Theo said. "The main facility is southeast of here." He looked at the sun, then followed its trajectory with his arms. Then he said, "We need to go this way."

I stared at him for a moment before following. "You know," I said, jogging to catch up. "Your nerdiness never fails to amaze me."

A corner of his mouth quirked up. "Thanks, I think."

We were able to get into CERN's main building with no problem. We just pretended to be with a group of tourists who happened to be going in at the same time, then we broke away as soon as the tour guide turned her back.

Theo scanned the various off-shooting passageways as we ambled through the main lobby. I tried my best to look aloof, as if I'd belonged. It wasn't terribly hard. After all, I *was* a scientist. Science teachers count as scientists, right? I should probably know that.

We were nearing the hallway that would lead us to the courtyard just outside the conference room where we needed to be when I noticed something strange. A man went out of his way to glare at me. Further down, a group of people cut their eyes our way. They seemed concerned, but not enough to stop what they were doing and approach us.

I slowed. Theo matched my pace. "Do you notice something weird?" I asked.

"Yeah," said Theo. "We're attracting attention for some reason."

I glanced up the lobby, then back down. Something was drawing attention to us. Another minute's scan of the hall made me realize it was a *lack* of something. I stopped walking, forcing him to double back. "Everybody down this hall is wearing badges," I whispered. "Or at least a lab coat."

I felt like such an idiot. Because I actually thought about this possibility when we were in the initial meeting, planning the details of the mission. Of course we needed to sneak in with a group of tourists, because we didn't have the credentials to get in on our own. I didn't bother bringing it to anyone's attention that once we were inside, we might run into identity issues, because I never actually intended on being here in the first place.

Theo let out a small groan. "How could I have missed that?" He huddled in closer to me, hiding our fronts. Perhaps if someone weren't paying attention, they could assume we were wearing badges.

"You?" I hissed. Though I wasn't nearly as shocked as he was, I did understand we were, as they say, in a pickle. "How could *Valencio* miss it? He works here!"

Theo shushed me. "We were bound to forget something," he said cooly. "The most important thing is we find a way to continue with the mission. We can adapt."

But the gravity of the oversight – no, the price of my betrayal – was about to bring the whole mission crumbling down. My hand shot straight to my support curls on the left side of my head. But before I could twist the locks in my fingers properly, Theo lowered my hand. "Take a deep breath," he said. He inhaled slowly. I followed. Then we exhaled. "We made it here," he said. "That was the hard part."

"One of the hard parts," I interjected. "But still, you're right."

Theo scanned the hall, clearly thinking of a solution. I racked my brain, too. The seconds turned to minutes as we mumbled to ourselves. Then I had it.

"Okay," I said. "We'll need to find a way to blend in, right?"

"Right," said Theo.

I nodded. "Then I think we need to go to the lounge, if there is one." Theo's forehead creased. "Trust me, I have an idea."

Chapter Fourteen:
I Totally Tricked
Those Nerds

Finding the lounge would have been easy if we'd just asked someone, but Theo insisted it would raise even more suspicion. Luckily, though, we were able to eavesdrop on a couple of scientists on their way to the cafeteria for lunch. We followed them there.

"Yeah, this'll do," I said. My eyes swept the massive cafeteria. A low hum of hustle and bustle permeated the place. I didn't know exactly what I was looking for, but I knew I would recognize it when I spotted it. After a minute or two I found it, then beckoned for Theo to follow me.

We wound our way through the tables toward a group of younger people with purple lab coats. Many of them smartly draped their coats over the back of their chairs so as to not get them dirty while eating. I noticed an unaccompanied clipboard along the way and scooped it up. It contained a few unimportant–looking printouts and a sticky note that read 'call Amery at three.'

"Hello," I said louder than I meant to, but I was glad my voice didn't shake. The chatter died down. I looked at the clip board. "Are you the group from the Smithsonian?" I asked.

One of the young men from the group spoke up. "No, we're in the summer student program," he said rather rudely. He rolled his eyes dramatically and then looked at a girl across the table who seemed unimpressed.

"Oh," I said. I rifled through the pages on the clipboard. "Oh yeah, you guys are really late," I said. "The schedule changed today because they just discovered a star is going supernova."

Theo choked on his spit. Then he coughed, his eyes bulging at me. I second guessed myself, but at least one of the students bought it. A young woman with thick glasses and a high ponytail stood up. She slammed her hands on the table, making everyone jump. "We'll be able to witness Betelgeuse going supernova?"

Everyone broke into excited chatter.

I sighed in relief. "Yes," I said. I raised my voice again. "And they recommend you go immediately to the hotel up the street in order to catch the shuttle. It'll take you to the observatory to watch it." I looked at my watch, which didn't tell me the time. But I didn't need to know what time it was. "You've got forty-two minutes before the shuttle leaves," I said.

In a flash, everyone shot out of their seats. They grabbed up their trays and shuffled out of the door in a chaotic and discombobulated mess. Theo turned to me, eyes still bulging. "What was the point of that?" he asked.

I gestured at the purple lab coats left behind. "We have our disguises."

Theo smacked his lips, grabbing two of them. "And they'll be back in forty-two minutes when they realize there's no shuttle – or sooner, better yet, because you didn't even give them the name of a hotel!"

"Eh." I shrugged. "Those nerds can't do anything about it." But I did consider I could've just set us up for failure. "They'll probably just chalk it up to a prank," I said, maybe more to myself than to Theo. But he didn't bother retorting. We slunk from the cafeteria unnoticed and slipped on the coats.

Once we were down the hall, I didn't think twice about it. Theo allowed me to sit on a bench while he searched for our targets – a guy named Jaques Dupuis, and a woman called Amalia Muller. These were the two candidates most likely to take our claim seriously and the least likely to report us to the Temporal Task Force, if it came to it. This allowed me to keep a lookout for our demon friends. And it didn't take long for me to spot them.

Shax and Danel strode confidently through the front doors, along with a third person. She was just as beautiful as the demons, with short blond ringlets around her dainty face. None of them had lab coats. Instead, they wore lanyards with generic visitors' badges on them. I tracked them, keeping the jitters welling up in my chest from reaching my hands. I rubbed the place in my chest that had long healed. I was so intent on not losing track of them I didn't notice Theo had snuck into the seat next to me.

"I don't think they were very receptive," he whispered in my ear. I jumped, but Theo barely noticed. "Jaques refused to take my files, but he let me present my findings." He bit his lip, allowing his eyes to sweep toward a tall woman in a lab coat. Her blond hair was in a very neat braid. She brushed it behind her as she lowered herself into one of the chairs along the lobby. "Amalia asked a few too many questions."

"She was suspicious?"

"More like annoyed." He cocked his head. "It's her job to know who has access to the preliminary data. She thinks someone on the team was sharing information."

"Did you tell her you were doing the third-party verification or whatever?"

"Exactly as Valencio said." He smoothed his hands over his lab coat. "I don't think I was very convincing, though."

I shifted in my seat. My eyes swept the lobby and I found the demons again, huddled together in quiet conversation near the front. "So we move on to the next step, right?"

"Yep." Theo sighed. He scanned the lobby and spotted a large bronze clock. "Thirty-two minutes until the proposal in conference room 7–E."

"Shax and Danel are already here." I gestured toward them with my eyes. "There's a third demon, too."

Theo nodded. "Shouldn't interfere with our plans," he said. "Let's just focus on being in position when the meeting starts."

"And if neither of them speak up," I raised my eyebrows. "Are you ready to present the findings to an entire room of scientists?"

Theo shook his head and nodded at the same time, which just made his head twirl in a small and chaotic circle for a brief moment. I understood him completely.

I laughed. "Let's just focus on getting into the room."

"We'll have to time it perfectly," he said. "Sneak in with the girth of the crowd."

"That part should be easy," I said. "The way my school is run – nobody ever knows what's going on. I'm willing to bet every organization is just as clueless. If we just walk in like we're supposed to be there, nobody'll give a crap."

"I don't know," Theo said. He scratched his head. I noticed his curls were flatter than usual today. I concluded that either he'd rubbed his hands through it one too many times, or time travel just isn't good for hair. I ran a hand through my own locks without thinking. Suddenly someone dropped into the seat next to me. I glanced over to find that it was Shax. I instantly shrunk into my seat, but quickly realized he wouldn't have recognized me because this was *his* past too.

"Did I startle you?" he said. His voice was deep and rich. It made me want to scratch him in the eye.

I straightened up. "Oh no," I said, forcing a smile. I glanced down the row of seats. Danel and the other demon were eyeing one another in an amused way. "I'm… uh… just a little jumpy since it's my first year here." I pointed at the emblem on my coat. It read, 'Summer Institute.'

Shax leaned in closer than he needed to. "I would be delighted to show you around the beautiful city, if you haven't had a chance yet," he said. He glanced over my shoulder. "Unless your friend here…"

I glanced at Theo, too, turning my head completely in order to hide the look of disgust on my face. I didn't want to give the demons any reason to suspect us, so I made sure that

I was wearing a decent smile when I turned back around. "No," I said. "Seeing the city would be lovely."

"Great," said Shax. He checked his watch. "I have a very important meeting in a few minutes," he said. "After that, why don't we meet for lunch… I could really eat."

I smiled, but I knew just how dangerous he was. "I bet you could," I said. Then I realized an opportunity. My eyes popped open. "You're not talking about the proposal in room 7–E, are you?" I glanced at Theo. His eyes flashed.

"Yes," said Shax. He gestured at Danel and the other demon. "We're to give a presentation today."

"Great!" I clapped my hands together. "We're in that same meeting. Once it's over, we can run right out."

Shax tortured me with ten more minutes of his flirty mumbo jumbo before we all made our way to conference room 7–E. On the way, Theo tugged my coat, pulling me behind. "Why would you tell him you'd leave with him afterward?" he whispered.

"I never said I'd *leave* with him," I whispered back. "I said we'd be running out of there, and I meant that." I gestured at the demons. "They're not gonna let us skip off into the sunset after this, now are they?"

Theo conceded with a nod.

The conference room wasn't what I imagined it would be. It was the size of my classroom, but instead of desks or tables, there were rows of seats facing a podium, much like an auditorium. It was rather cramped. Especially since about fifteen people were already seated. With a swift nod at Theo, I walked in confidently. He followed.

I chose a row and shuffled down. Then I noticed from my periphery that someone got up from their seat and was shuffling down behind us. I looked straight ahead, crossing my legs.

"Excuse me," they said.

I recognized the voice. My eyes shot up. It was a much younger, but still very smart-looking Valencio. I smiled. "Hi," I said. "How can I help you?"

Valencio shook his head in confusion. "Are you sure you're in the right place?"

"Yes," I said. "Conference room 7–E. We're here for the proposal."

"But you're students," said Valencio.

Theo interjected. "We've actually done some research on the preliminary data that was sent over," he said. "It was extra work, since we're on the accelerated track."

Valencio nodded as if he understood, but his forehead was still bunched up as he walked off. He took his seat, then opened his laptop and logged himself in. I held my hand low, between the seats. Theo clapped me a silent low five.

We waited longer than I anticipated for the meeting to start, though. I kept looking at my watch, but then remembering it didn't tell the time. Everyone else was growing restless as well. Some people got up and stretched. Others checked their own watches. The demons paced the front of the room. I wasn't sure what we were waiting for, until someone jogged in. He was a very tall man with a strong jaw and a full head of white hair. "Sorry," he said breathlessly. "We had a little emergency…" He shook Danel's hand, then

Shax's, then the new demon's. He laughed, giving a small bow to the room. "There was a report of inverted tachyons emitted on the grounds," he explained to the scientists. "But turns out it was nothing!"

Several people laughed. But the room fell silent as soon as he sat, which was the cue for the meeting to start. I realized we had been waiting on this man – the director. He seemed at ease, sinking comfortably in his chair, but I was the exact opposite.

I whispered to Theo. "Do you think they found the time machine?"

He leaned in close. "It doesn't seem likely," he said. "But one thing's for sure – they'll keep investigating the source of those tachyons, so as soon as our part's over we'll sneak out."

I nodded, allowing my eyes to find our two targets. Amalia was seated two rows in front of us and Jaques had taken a seat at the very back.

The new demon pulled up a slide deck on a holographic projector then introduced herself as Balencia. She began by explaining the purpose of their research, spinning it as a way to end all wars, bring an era of peace and all that crap. Then Shax walked through all the scientific specifics of the experiment – including how they would use the template, and how preliminary experiments had been successful. It was all very confusing to me, but Theo seemed to follow. Every time I glanced at him, his eyes were wide in awe. Every once in a while, he would mumble, *yes*, or, *that explains it.*

Then it was time for Danel to speak. After she addressed some of the major ethical concerns, she invited the scientists to ask questions.

I perked in my seat. Several of the scientists had raised their hands. Amalia wasn't one of them. She glanced nervously over her shoulder instead and remained firmly quiet. Jaques had his hand raised. Theo and I eyed each other hopefully as Danel answered each question in turn.

By the time she called on Jaques, my palms were considerably sweaty. I nodded at Theo, encouraging him. He would have to jump in and help Jaques if needed.

His eyes darted toward us for a fraction of a second. But to our dismay, the man didn't bother addressing any of our findings. "You seem to have made incredible gains," he said. "How quickly do intend on carrying out this project. Weeks? Months?"

I rolled my eyes. Theo sank into his seat.

Danel laughed. "Eager, aren't we?" Her chocolate eyes twinkled. Had I not known she was a demon, I'd be completely fooled by her feigned wholesomeness. She shuffled through the slide deck to a timeline graphic. "If we follow the recommended pacing, I predict the project could be completed within the year." The room buzzed with quiet mumblings as teams discussed among themselves. Danel cleared her throat. "I'll take the next question," she said.

Theo didn't waste any time. His hand shot in the air. "Hi," he said before anyone called on him. "If you'll go back to slide sixty–four, I've got a question about the inert emissions Balencia mentioned."

Balencia hesitated before moving to the slide. "Yes," she said. "As a reminder, these particles will be a naturally occurring byproduct of the magnetization process —"

"That appears to be untrue," said Theo. Some of the scientists toward the front turned around to look at him. "I'm speaking particularly about the pentaquarks," he continued. "First of all, the antiquark in that grouping is being shrouded by the four quarks."

Balencia nodded. "It's a tight group of particles," she said offhandedly. "That doesn't seem to have any bearing on the outcome of the experiment."

She moved on to the next slide, but Theo persisted. "I've done a preliminary particle characterization," he said.

"As did we," said Balencia. "You're looking at the results right here." She flipped back to slide sixty–four. "We have identified all present elements of the inert emissions."

Theo gestured at the holographic image. "If you cared to zoom in on the image and remove quarks two and three, we can get a closer look at the antiquark," he said. Balencia glanced cooly at the director, who nodded. She obliged, zooming in on the image half–heartedly. Then she swiped her hand over it to remove the two particles.

"Ah, there it is," said Theo. "The antiquark appears to be technological – some sort of chip, the construct of which is consistent with materials capable of housing an artificially intelligent program." He looked smugly at Valencio, who was craning his neck in order to gawk at him. "That would seem to make it an *unnatural* occurrence."

Balencia's eyes narrowed. She looked at Danel. The scientists began muttering in unison. Danel spoke up. "That's an outrageous claim," she said. "Especially since embedding technology inside of a quark would be scientifically impossible."

Theo retorted. "It's not impossible if you already have the knowledge and ability to break quarks into smaller components," he said. "That should be the true scientific discovery here. I'd be more impressed with it if I weren't so wary of what you may be trying to hide in that particle."

A middle–aged woman turned in her seat. "It seems unlikely that's the case," she said. "What evidence could you possibly produce for your argument?"

Shax scowled. If he was going to be eating humans today, I was willing to bet Theo just moved to first on the list. "Director," he said sharply. "We've traveled a long way… too far to be derailed by conspiracy theories."

The director licked his lips. Then he waved his hand briskly. "All concerns should be explored," he said. He turned an eyebrow up at Theo. "Have you brought your particle characterization data with you today?"

Theo stood up. "I did," he said, producing a small chip from his pocket. "You can also enhance a programmable particle imager to increase the sampling efficiency on morphological parameters with a simple algorithm," he said. "Anyone can do it."

A man who was sitting two rows behind us stood as well. "My characterizations never turned up anything of the sort," he said. His eyes flashed at Theo for a fraction of a second before he smiled at the director. "We mustn't allow ourselves to be thrown into a frenzy by a couple of students," he said. "Let's focus on *real* concerns, like how we might select a template for the project."

Theo interjected. "You're diverting from the actual problem," he said. He turned to the director. "Do I have your permission to present my findings?"

The director raised his chin, interested. But a young woman gently tugged at his coat from the row behind him. She whispered something in his ear. I narrowed my eyes to try and read her lips, but a lock of brilliantly orange hair fell over the side of her face. The director's forehead crinkled. "You two," he said, nodding at Theo and me. "You're enrolled in the Summer Institute, is that correct?"

Theo thrummed his fingers on the back of the chair in front of him. "Yes," he said uncertainly. Then he quickly added, "Mr. Director, sir."

The director cut an uncertain glance at the woman, then me, then his eyes finally fell back on Theo. "Who's your lead instructor?" he asked.

"Oh, of course," Theo said. His voice flittered just a bit. "And what do you mean by 'lead,' sir?" I eyed Theo violently, but I knew it wouldn't help. I, myself, didn't have a helpful clue as to what to say here. Theo continued struggling for words. "There are so many that we interact with, you know. It's... such a... *robust* program."

There was low murmuring in the room. The orange-haired woman leaned back in her seat. She swept the hair from her face and flashed me a satisfied grin. There was a tugging at my stomach. I couldn't place it at first, but then I realized what it was. Could this woman also be a demon? She was certainly beautiful enough to pass for one, with her perfectly sculpted face and, frankly, very perky boobs. I glanced at the man who asked about the template. He sat cooly, unaffected by the frenzy unfolding among the scientists. Was he also in on it? I eyed Theo. He seemed to have the same idea. He flashed me a warning with his eyes.

Unfortunately, I didn't heed it. We were beat. The director was on to us, and it appeared the demons had infiltrated CERN far more than we anticipated. We could only stonewall for so long.

I shot out of my chair, holding both hands up to quiet the room, but nobody was paying attention. "Shhh…" I said. Still nothing. I yelled, "Everybody, shut up!" The room quickly quieted. I took a deep breath and apologized to Theo with my eyes. "There were inverted tachyons reported on the grounds not too long ago, right?" The director confirmed with a silent nod. A look of understanding crossed Danel's face. Her eyes bulged. I spoke faster. "That was because of us. We've come from nineteen years in the future, where this experiment was successfully carried out. Ninety-three percent of humanity is in a permanent coma and the planet is wrecked. This project is meant to bring chaos to the planet, and it's meant to drive us further away from God."

Theo shook his head, but it was too late. I continued. "God has no interest in making our lives a paradise, anyway," I said. My lips forced their way into a tight grin as I thought about my recent run in with her at the gas station. A sudden surge started in my gut and worked its way up, escaping from me in a laugh. "That's not God's job. That's *our* job. Each of us has the power to find the magic in the mundane, to appreciate the good *and* the bad – and learn from it, too." I accidentally locked eyes with the director. It was terribly uncomfortable, but I didn't dare look away. "And we have the power to change course when we realize the decisions we've made weren't what was best for us."

I removed my lab coat and gestured for Theo to do the same. I looked at the scientists, each one in turn. "You're our witnesses today," I said, moving from my row of seats into the aisle. Shax mirrored my movements, following me. I knew we were blocked in, but I had to finish what I started. "These guys won't stop until they carry out their plan, so we're requesting that you report this experiment to the Ethics Review Committee, and have it permanently banned."

Balencia's nostrils flared. She clapped her hands together with such force the sound echoed off the walls. At this, the door slammed shut and locked with a crisp thud. "Kill them all," she said, then disappeared in a flash.

For a moment there was a thick silence in the room, then several people moved cautiously from their seats. Danel grabbed a leather bag and stuffed their files into it, then disappeared as well. Shax held up his hands to the ceiling and brought them down on either side of him, sending streaks of flames into the room. They charred a path along the walls, catching on the ornamental square patches of fabric that lined the conference room. It took no time at all before the carpet was emitting a thick smoke. Then, with one last malicious glare around the room, he was gone.

There was immediate chaos as everyone raced toward the door. But of course, it didn't open. The scientists screamed desperately. My mind raced for a solution. At least Shax had gone, I reasoned. We could stand a chance against fire, but not him. And as a matter of fact, I think I preferred the risk of being burned alive over going on whatever weird and horrible date he had planned. Maybe I was just being optimistic.

I fanned the smoke from my face and looked for Theo. And this may not be an appropriate time, but I do have a fun fact about burning, while we're at it – teeth don't get burned in fire. Or at least, they don't turn to ash. It's because they're made of calcium phosphate. Even in crematoriums, they have to grind the teeth down into a fine powder before adding it to the rest of the ash.

But I digress. I was able to find Theo quickly. He was crouching over Valencio's computer, typing vigorously. "What are you doing?" I yelled.

He bit his lip in concentration before answering, "I'm adding the subroutines into the scanning algorithms that'll make the A.I. components recognizable," he said.

I shook my head, then glanced around the burning room. Terrified, everyone squeezed as tightly around the door as they could. I coughed. "I don't think that'll matter," I said. "This… this might be the end for us."

"Nonsense," Theo yelled over the screaming. "Help will come." The flames were only feet away from him. I found some papers on the ground and began to fan them, but that only made it worse. I threw the papers into the fire. That didn't help either. Then the fire alarm sounded. Theo looked up. "Even if they don't come in time," he coughed. Then he closed the laptop and held it close to his chest. "Valencio's entire department has access to the algorithm now."

I contemplated joining the desperate scientists in pounding at the locked door, but then it suddenly opened. Bodies spilled out of the room, piling onto one another before disseminating in all directions. I turned to grab Theo, but he had already moved. He was helping Valencio to put out a flame that had reached the director's pant leg.

"Let's *go*," I urged, grabbing his arm.

He shoved the laptop into Valencio's chest. "I left everything you'll need here," he said. He pushed Valencio toward the door. Valencio coughed, confusion painting his face for a moment. Then he nodded.

Before we could get to the door, people started rushing in. At first glance, I thought they were paramedics or the fire department, because they were grabbing people and scanning them with small, handheld devices. But a glance at their sleek looking uniforms told me that they were here for other reasons.

Theo pulled me into a crouching position. "That's the Temporal Task Force," he said, gesturing to the nearest officer. Then he dragged me through the chaos at the door. Once outside of the conference room, we slipped through a throng of older women who were helping a man peel off his lab coat.

One of the women locked eyes with me, and without hesitation, she yelled over her shoulder. "There they are!" She whipped around to find the nearest officer. And though she didn't need to, because the officer was already sprinting down the hall at full speed, she continued. "Both of them are right over here, sir!"

Theo cursed.

I sneered at the woman for as long as I could, which was only a fraction of a second. I thought about reminding her that snitches get stitches, too, but there wasn't enough time.

"Run!" Theo yelled.

He didn't even have to tell me once. I had already chosen a direction and bolted. Unfortunately, though, it was the wrong direction. Theo ran back toward the lobby, which would make more sense, since that was the easiest way to exit the building. I ran further into the building.

I realized my mistake as soon as I made it, but it was too late to backtrack. The officer was right behind me.

Chapter Fifteen: Do You Enjoy Being A Pervert?

I turned corners as fast as I could, hoping to lose him. Or to get back to the main lobby, whichever came first. And as the seconds passed, I was certainly grateful for one thing – I chose a great pair of shoes for this mission; the grip was phenomenal.

But as good as the shoes were, I only had so many corners to turn. Thankfully, though, it seemed as though I lost my pursuer. I stopped along a narrow passage between a water cooler and a fake plant. It seemed I was only going further into the building – opposite of what I intended. I checked my watch, and quickly realized I didn't even know how to use it. There were several buttons, none of which were labeled. I pressed one, then another, then another until a tiny holographic map projected just in front of me.

"Take me to the time machine," I whispered frantically. Nothing happened. "Um, take me back to the dome." Still, nothing. I glanced up and down the hallway. It was still clear. I smoothed my hair back, pulling strings of it out of my face.

Then I tried the map again. I zoomed in with my fingers, then roved around. It was a topographic map, which was frustrating. I could barely make out the major landmarks on the facility grounds. It wouldn't help me navigate the building.

But it did tell me what direction I needed to go. I was currently facing south, and I needed to head northwest in order to get to the grove where the dome was concealed.

I smoothed my sweater down and combed my hair over my shoulders with my fingers. Then I strode back the way I came. If I could blend in with the crowd, I thought, then maybe I could walk out unnoticed.

When I came to the end of the hall, I ducked my head slightly. A group of men were coming out of the bathrooms, talking excitedly about their weekend plans. I checked my watch again and turned left, then right. I could see a foyer up ahead, bustling with a stream of passersby. I walked a little more quickly to get there. I nodded politely to a woman who paused to allow me through, and she gave a brisk smile. Then she let out a clipped gasp, clapping her hands to her face, and I immediately knew why.

An officer was ambushing me. He grabbed me from behind, cupping my mouth with a firm hand, and ripped me backward into an obscure passage.

"Don't struggle," he whispered in my ear. But in a really pervy way. He was all breathless and gross. I paused. Just long enough to make sure he was in fact the time police – or whatever these people were individually called – and not some weird kidnapper. Imagine time travelling to the past only to get kidnapped in broad daylight. That would be such a twist.

A moment's glance told me he was an older man, with tired brown eyes. He wore a sleek uniform. It was, in fact, the time cop.

I continued struggling, but it didn't stop him from producing a small device from his utility belt and holding it to my face. I thought it was a gun, but quickly realized he was scanning me. He read the gauges on the device and put it back in his belt. "I *have* to bring you in," he said. He yanked my arms behind my back and cuffed them. "Don't make it worse than it already is."

His voice sounded apologetic enough. I wondered if he would let me go if I put on a damsel in distress act. Maybe flirt with him a bit.

Blech.

I tried.

There was no way that would work. So I did what I usually do when I've been caught in a precarious situation: I started asking stupid questions. "What are you gonna do to me?" I asked. "Where's my friend? Did you find him, too?" The officer ignored me. That just made me try harder as he pulled me along the passageway. I struggled wildly. "Do you always follow orders? I'm trying to save the world here." I grew more belligerent with each step. "And stop grabbing me so tight. Do you enjoy being a pervert?"

The officer gave me a firm jostle, stopping me in my tracks. "You are ignoring temporal protocol, refusing to comply, and resisting arrest," he said. "Should I add harassment to the list?"

I pursed my lips together and seethed at him. "That's not harassment —"

"It's harassment." He eyed me threateningly. I started thrashing my limbs again. "And you're still resisting arrest."

I huffed and let my body go limp. It was useless anyway. He'd dragged me a considerable way down the hall so far. I wasn't resisting as well as I had hoped.

He continued. "You'll dig yourself into a hole with this behavior," he said. "Cooperation is your only friend right now. Are you gonna keep fighting me?"

I shook my head slowly, indicating that I would cooperate, but my mind was already reaching for an escape plan. I scanned my surroundings as he escorted me down the passageway. We were moving nearly parallel to the foyer. I wouldn't be able to escape his grip on my upper arm, and even if I did, I would be limited by my cuffed hands.

He pushed me through a set of doors and down some stone steps. It wasn't the same way we came, but the wooded area in the distance looked quite familiar. I shuffled down the steps and was swept to the left – toward an unmarked car. I scanned the area, hoping to find a way to escape. There were trees dotting the pavement. A garbage pail. Further down, a shovel and a shallow hole where someone was planning on planting a tree.

I slowed my feet, trying to stall. The officer pulled me gently along. "Uh, what's gonna happen to me next," I said.

"You'll be able to make the proper reports – " he said. "Authentication. Provide your permits – the standard protocol that comes with a licensed jump. This could've been avoided if you'd reported straight to the Temporal Department when you arrived."

I stopped in my tracks and looked at him. He was surprisingly old–looking, with a smattering of white hairs sprinkled throughout his otherwise pitch-black beard. Of course, I didn't have authorization. But I couldn't admit it to him. I would be incriminating myself, right?

"Oh," I said. I tried to keep my voice relaxed. "I left all my documents in my, um…" I didn't want to call it a time machine. That would probably give it away that I wasn't even qualified to be time traveling. "…at the location of my arrival," I said. Then I had a bold idea. "I actually arrived not too far from here," I said. "If you could just swing me by, I could grab my permits."

The officer drew his face up in a way that told me he wasn't buying it. "There's no way I'm allowing you to –"

There was suddenly a hollow thud, then I was yanked to the ground. The shovel that I'd seen only moments ago dropped beside me with a clatter. I rolled over the man and struggled to get to my feet again, which was nearly impossible with my hands cuffed behind me. But I didn't have to struggle for long. Valencio was shoving a key in the cuffs with shaking hands.

"You killed him," I blurted. I checked to see if the man was breathing, but Valencio interrupted.

"I don't need to tell you we must hurry," he said breathlessly. He grabbed the officer under the arms and began dragging him into the nearby shrubs.

"What are you doing?" I hissed, following him up the lawn. My eyes darted. A group of people were entering an adjacent building in the distance, but they didn't seem to notice.

He dropped the man in a bush with a quick apology and turned to me. "You've risked your livelihood by coming here today," he said, wiping sweat from his brow with a sleeve. "You have effectively saved all of *our* livelihoods by doing so, but temporal regulations will not see it that way. I can at least help you get back home." Then he beckoned for me to follow him into the thicket.

I hesitated. "You're going to be in a lot of trouble if they catch you,"

"Well, let's not wait around for that," he said. Then he pulled me along a narrow trail into the trees.

I checked my watch. "This way," I said. And we sprinted through the greenspace toward the dome. I was impressed by how quickly he moved. Then I remembered he was almost twenty years younger than the man I knew. A few minutes later we slowed to a trot, but I could hear car tires screeching in the distance. "You should probably go," I said to Valencio. "I'm close enough. You need to get away before they see you."

Valencio nodded. But before we could part ways, four officers sidled through the trees and into the clearing. They were only thirty yards away, but they were facing the wrong direction. I hoped we could make a quiet descent back into the bushes, but they all turned around at once. We were caught.

Without another thought, my arms snapped behind me as I threw myself backward into Valencio. He risked himself to get me this far. I could only return the favor. "Get off me!" I yelled. He was confused. I grabbed him firmly by the wrists, encouraging him to play along. He understood. He quickly clasped my forearms, and I was able to struggle earnestly.

"You mustn't turn yourself in," he whispered urgently. The officers were approaching quickly.

I twisted around, breaking his grip. "I don't intend to," I breathed. "I'm so sorry." And I kicked him as hard as I could in the crotch. His eyes bulged. He fell to the ground. Then, with an apology on my face, I ran.

One of the officers shouted something. I looked over my shoulder just long enough to see that two of them were helping Valencio up and the other two were right behind me. I yelled over my shoulder, for good measure. "I told you I'd get away from you, just like I did the last guy!"

I was winded from my previous run, but the path began to look familiar. I knew I was close. I only hoped to not run straight into the dome and knock myself out.

I squinted into the distance at a strange sight. Theo was poking his head out of the dome. It appeared to float in midair. Something whizzed by my ear and landed in a tree with a crack. Then another, and another. I was able to glimpse one of them. They were some sort of projectile taser. I glanced back. The officers could see Theo, too, and they were about to outpace me. "Start it up," I yelled. I was winded and my legs seemed to stop working. I wouldn't allow him to get caught because of me, though. It was my fault for running the wrong way in the first place. "You have to go, now!" Theo's face was confused, but I know he understood. He disappeared into the field of the dome. The honeycomb grid sparked as the machine powered up.

Defeated, I slowed to a pitiful shuffle and prepared for the officers to secure me. But they were taking an awful long time doing so. I turned to see that they were no longer chasing me. Instead, they were crouching at the perimeter of the clearing, extending black rods and erecting them into the ground. I made a break for the dome.

The structure unfolded to let me in. "I thought they had me," I breathed.

Theo barely looked up from the console. He typed fervently. "We're not out of the woods yet," he said. He glanced over his shoulder at the officers. They moved swiftly and in unison to erect another rod. "One more emitter and they'll have us trapped. They're trying to collapse our field."

"Okay." I clapped my hands together. I searched the dome for something productive to do to help us escape, but my brain was scrambled. "What are we... what do I…?"

"I'm finishing the pre–launch sequence," said Theo. "We need more time."

"Okay." I scanned the panel from over his shoulder. "Is there, like, a weapons array I could use or something?"

Theo paused long enough to contort his face. "*What?*"

"You know," I said. I was trying to hint that maybe I could shoot them, but I would never say it out loud. And it was strictly in order to complete our mission to save the world. I wouldn't find any pleasure in it whatsoever.

"First of all," said Theo. He continued adjusting a delicate dial. "This is a time machine, not a warship. What kind of movies have you been watching?"

My arms shot in the air. "Well, I don't know what to do," I yelled unhelpfully.

"Second," said Theo. "We can't hurt these people!"

"Says who?" I demanded. And I genuinely wanted to know if he was just being generally polite or if it was one of the time travel regulations or something. I bet it was, because technically if I killed them, I'd be erasing all of their descendants. That would probably be one of the first rules in the time travel handbook, now that I think about it.

Theo shoved past me to access a panel. "We don't have time to mess this up," he said. "Give me a minute."

I understood. I was slowing us down. In an effort to actually be helpful, I turned my attention to the officers just outside the dome. The last rod was erected and a pale amber light was emitting from them. There was no way I could help except to report it. "Looks like they've turned on… whatever that – "

Gravity changed at that moment. At the same time, the amber light grew brighter; its richness threatening to swallow us. I wondered if we could be torn into pieces from being pulled in two different directions at once. I opened my mouth to ask Theo, but all of my words lost meaning. My eyes were rolling again.

Chapter Sixteen:
I Absolutely Blame
That Dumb Experiment

My body reeled as gravity righted itself. Lightning raged in my hands and feet, which had gone numb in the transit and were in the process of reviving themselves. I braced myself against a wall, and noticed it was plastered with all sorts of papers – handmade infographics, announcements, reminders, and a weirdly placed inspirational cat poster. I whipped around to find that I was at Rockwell Middle school.

I was almost too afraid to believe it. A current of students parted around me and crashed down the hall in a screaming, laughing, and cursing river of chaos. I laughed out loud. A tear escaped the corner of my eye. I wiped it on a sleeve and noticed I had been clutching my favorite travel mug. I hesitated, then put it to my nose. It was coffee. I sipped it, then spit it back into the cup. It was *cold* coffee.

I was suddenly shoved from behind. I turned to see a couple of kids from Mr. Yates' video game club. "So sorry, Miss," said one of the boys. He gave me an exaggerated bow.

"No," I laughed. "It's totally okay." A smile stretched the skin on my cheeks so wide it started protesting. But I didn't care. "Everything's perfect," I said.

The boy smiled back at me, raising one side of his lip just a bit. Then he said, "Does that mean you want some of this?"

Ew. I should've remembered not to look straight into a hormonal teen's eyes. It confuses their brains. I turned a half circle and walked pointedly up the hall.

The kid yelled after me, "Miss, I'm already fifteen, though!" But I didn't bother responding. I was trying to remember how to get to my classroom. It seemed like a small eternity since I had last been there.

Right around the next corner my team lead, Mr. Downy, waved me down. "Ms. Torey!" he yelled. Jittery as ever, he fumbled through a pocket with one hand and hiked up a stack of papers in the other. "Don't forget your online training modules are due Friday, and grades are due Thursday," he said. Then he found what he was looking for. He handed me a sticky note from his right pocket. It was scribbled on with names from front to back. "And these are the students you need to get to a passing grade before then." And before I could even respond, he scrambled up the hall.

"Thanks," I called out into the chaos.

Then I found a familiar flight of stairs and navigated to my classroom. I closed the door behind me and leaned against it. This would give me a few moments to laugh, or cry, in privacy. I didn't know what my body would do. For the time being I could only nurse the excitement and disbelief that had tangled into a knot and was sitting in my chest.

I whimpered, allowing more tears to spill over my cheeks. I made it back. And I had so many questions. Where did Theo end up? Was he snapped back to the lab, doing whatever random task that was assigned to him today? Did he also remember everything that had gone on? And what about Matt and Valencio? With a sudden thought, I was sour. Why the hell did I end up at work? It was supposed to be my summer break.

I sighed.

Through the window across the room, I could see the city. Skyscrapers reached into the pale winter sky. The sun reflected off of many of them, but somehow it wasn't quite as dazzling now that it was void of the fantastical creatures that once roamed there.

I moved to my desk, running a hand across the thing. It was old and rickety, with a few chips along the edges. Some kid carved their initials into one of the corners. I noticed my bulletin board. A few of the letters that spelled *February* had fallen off, and someone had ripped the corner of my newsletter. I smoothed it out, looking for a stapler to fix it, but a sudden flat feeling in my stomach made me stop short. There was really no point in stapling it back. It would, no doubt, be torn again by some other careless kid.

I rifled through the documents on my desk next, and was rewarded with the information I was seeking. It was eight months after the experiment took place. Why would I arrive at this point in time? Is this where we would naturally be, timewise, if the experiment hadn't taken place at all. Had it taken us eight months to undo the experiment?

A bell in the hallway made me jump. Then the door swung open and a timid looking girl in an oversized hoodie made a beeline to her desk. Another student sighed loudly at the door and stormed in. He scowled at me as he plopped into his desk. Then a raucous group of them began jumping into the room, one at a time, each slapping the top of the door frame.

Having realized I had no idea what I was supposed to be teaching, I rifled through the disheveled stacks of papers on my desk. A familiar urgency pressed in my chest. If I didn't engage my students quickly enough, they would derail the whole lesson and I'd lose the class period to fart jokes, love connections and general misbehavior. The room began to buzz with chatter as more students filed in. A voice barked up the hall, but I was intent to ignore it until it got closer. A girl with a round and angry face stomped in and pulled her hood over her head. Mr. Sepeda, the assistant principal, stormed in after her.

His face was firm as he stared her down. "I have faith that you'll still be in this classroom when the dismissal bell rings, young lady," he said.

She grunted and shrugged her shoulders.

Then Mr. Sepeda noticed me. "Ah, Ms. Torey," he said.

I was hoping he'd notice I was busy and come back later. I crouched to continue searching the perimeter of my desk, desperately hoping the lesson plan had merely fallen off. But he continued.

"Speaking of attendance," he said. "I'll need you to correct your fifth period attendance for last Tuesday before the end of the day today."

"I'll try," I said offhandedly. Then I looked under the desk.

"It's not optional," Mr. Sepeda pressed. "You *must* get that done today."

I sighed. "I have a class to teach," I said, gesturing toward my students. One of them was already leaning over his neighbor's desk, ready to rip one. "I have three more classes then dismissal duty. And after that I have online trainings, then grades. Can't you ask one of the clerks in the front office to make the correction?"

Mr. Sepeda shook his head. "We could, but that wouldn't teach you to be accountable for your responsibilities." He raised his eyebrows. "I'm sorry, but we can't just do what we want."

My mouth shot open, but I stopped short. The three students who were hovering at the pencil sharpener near my desk froze, and I could tell they were listening for what I'd say next. I sighed. Then I tried to find something appropriate to say to Mr. Sepeda. I could tell him I'd been duped; lured by the promise of fulfillment. My eyes fell on each of my students – their faces a light at the end of a dark tunnel. Somewhere in that tunnel – along the twisting, shifting, snaking passageways – a forced detour guided me to endless checkboxes and compliance for the sake of compliance. Was I even able to reach their light? Having been away from my classroom all this time, I was able to clearly see it now. Teaching had become an unnecessarily uphill battle that I was surely losing.

Then an unexpected thrill bubbled up from the pit of my stomach. It reached my brain in a seedling of a thought. My neurons fired off like firecrackers at the new year.

I spotted the blue folder I had been looking for in my rolling chair. "As a matter of fact," I said. "We *can* do what we want." I pressed the folder into Mr. Sepeda's hands.

"What's this?" He opened it.

"It's my lesson plan," I said. "You'll need it to teach my classes for the rest of the day." Then I made my way toward the door, giving my class a solemn salute. They mostly clapped. The angry girl nodded her approval and put two fingers up in a peace sign.

Mr. Sepeda sputtered. "You can't just walk out like this," he said. "Where are you going?"

I was already in the hallway. "I'm gonna go visit a priest on Tenth Street and Brazos," I said over my shoulder. "Maybe eat some junk food at a gas station… I don't know, sit on a bench… I quit!"

I heard his voice in the hallway, but I knew he wouldn't leave the class unattended. I walked faster in order to get out of earshot. He yelled something about my contract, but I didn't bother listening. I shuffled down the stairs and found the double doors that led to the parking lot; to the unknown.

And with a jittering hand, I pushed through them. The afternoon sun blinded me in the most beautiful way. I breathed in the crisp city air. The sound of traffic found my ears. And with the sun warm against my skin, I walked away.

¤ ¤ ¤ ¤ ¤ ¤ ¤

And so in the end, here I am with no job. And it *is* because of that dumb experiment. But maybe it wasn't all that dumb after all.

God sent me to hell – a passionless, dead, and hollow world; a mockery of the thing that makes us human – and a demon sent me to heaven. I can firmly say the cherubs are *not* recommended, but Azrael was cool. And he actually taught me something, too. He made me realize how much my own expectations could shape my reality. I can create any experience I want. And something tells me I don't have to die in order to do that.

And I learned something else, too – and maybe this was the whole point of God's divine plan and all that. I had been running from myself, and from my own problems, and that's always a recipe for disaster. Because your problems always find a way to sneak up on you and force you to make some pretty shady decisions. Dealing with your crap head-on might be the best solution – that is, if you want to avoid strange ass dreams and spending the night at the lake with a lovely woman named Agatha.

And dealing with your problems shouldn't be just to avoid the bad stuff, either. Because God was right – we're only here for a beautiful, sparkling fractal of time. Maybe we shouldn't spend it running. Maybe we should spend it making the right choices – especially the ones that are hard, because those are the ones that make you feel the most alive. And maybe we should spend it doing what we love, with the people we love.

So, I guess if I'm gonna make the most of this lifetime, I better have a chat with my mom. And I better find a job that I actually like – one that makes me excited to be alive. And I better figure it out fast because rent will be due soon. After all, I still have that beautiful apartment I can't afford and Milus, who I'm sure still hates me.

What will I do now? Not sure, really. I know I want to help people – *actually* help people – without the constraints of bureaucracy. Maybe I'll sign up to be an intern at Valencio's lab. Or maybe I can become a priest like Matt.

Or maybe I'll be something totally different. Maybe I could start a business. I bet I'd be great as some sort of kayak therapist.

Do those exist?

I should probably know that.

From the Author

I want to extend my many thanks to you, dear reader, for giving my book a try. As they say, I hope it was as good for you as it was for me. Is that inappropriate to say? Probably, but it's already there in black and white, so I guess we'll both have to deal with the consequences of my actions. But I digress.

The book wouldn't have been possible without help from a couple of awesome people, so I guess this is a great place to shout them out. There's a smart, funny and diligent librarian by the name of Stacey Smith who helped to send my book baby off to editing. Thank you, Stacey! I also want to thank Henry Jaeger, who knows so much about everything in the teaching world I'm surprised he doesn't have a spare head in which to keep all his brains. Is that weird to say? Probably. But moving on – thank you Henry for contributing to round one of beta reading. There's also Jess S., Alenzia M., and Nikki B., who were my beta readers. They helped with the slashing and burning, so my story could rise from the ashes like a phoenix. Nikki also served as my editor, so she gets double credit. Thanks, ladies!

Of course, my toddler and teen helped, too. And by 'helped,' I mean they allowed me to take frequent breaks in order to cook, race hot wheels, count the clouds, chase our very patient chickens around the backyard and, on occasion, watch something outrageous on *the TikTok*. And that's what's really important in life, right?

That isn't nearly everyone I should be thanking. For instance, my husband was a key player in this whole thing.

Sometimes when you're married to an author you have to understand an entirely different (and often made up on the spot) set of rules. Like when your author spouse is rummaging through an untidy mound of scribbled upon papers, you don't speak or even offer to help, because that's crazy and how could you possibly expect me to stop what I'm doing to explain the particulars of the paper I'm looking for? Or when you're at a restaurant, or perhaps the bowling alley, when they suddenly and ferociously begin dictating into the notes app on their phone. At those times you pause what you were saying and then resume again as if nothing ever happened once they're finished with their dictation frenzy and their phone is safely tucked back into their pocket. Or when they're crying in front of their manuscript late on a Friday night. In those moments the best course of action is to offer more hot coffee and zero eye contact. My husband's an expert at all of these things.

And there are many other people who I've met along the way, who have some degree of influence on the writing of this story – like the staff at the Starbucks on the corner of 290 and Lexington in Manor, Texas. They've also done a great job of delivering the coffee hot and pretending I'm not in the corner repeatedly acting out weird body movements and facial expressions in order to *feel* what my characters are feeling and describe it. They understand my process.

And my circle of friends, who have had the unfortunate task of listening to me go on and on about the story for the last three years. Thank you all! And if there are any others that I forgot to mention, just know that it's not you, it's me. My brain is just about shot after having birthed a book baby of this size. Does pregnancy brain count if you've only given birth to a book? I think yes is a fair answer.

But anyways, dear reader, if you found that you've enjoyed Alex's adventure, I want to encourage you to tell a friend or two. Word of mouth is an indie author's best friend! And if you're feeling extra generous, a review on your favorite platform goes a long way, too. Please visit my website for more information about me, my books and any other shenanigans I might be involved in!

Best,

Sasha DeVore

www.ingramcontent.com/pod-product-compliance
Lightning Source LLC
Chambersburg PA
CBHW032243310726

48973CB00008B/2263